SAVAGE FIRES

CASSIE EDWARDS

LEISURE BOOKS   NEW YORK CITY

A LEISURE BOOK®

July 1999

Published by

Dorchester Publishing Co., Inc.
276 Fifth Avenue
New York, NY 10001

If you purchased this book without a cover you should be aware
that this book is stolen property. It was reported as "unsold and
destroyed" to the publisher and neither the author nor the publisher
has received any payment for this "stripped book."

Copyright © 1999 by Cassie Edwards

Cover Art by John Ennis

All rights reserved. No part of this book may be reproduced or
transmitted in any form or by any electronic or mechanical means,
including photocopying, recording or by any information storage
and retrieval system, without the written permission of the
Publisher, except where permitted by law.

ISBN 0-8439-4551-6

The name "Leisure Books" and the stylized "L" with design are
trademarks of Dorchester Publishing Co., Inc.

Printed in the United States of America.

Michiana Health &
Rehabilitation

UNTAMED KISS

"Your name, Wolf. Was that given to you after your time of fasting and vision quest?" Jo asked softly, again thinking about what she had thought were white wolves running through the forest close to where she and Wolf were riding. She could not help feeling there was some connection between those wolves and Wolf.

"Yes, I earned the name Wolf and carry it with me proudly," he said. Then when he saw her shiver, he scooted nearer to her, swept an arm around her shoulders and drew her close.

His heart beat like a thousand drums within his chest when her eyes moved up and she gazed intently into his. He recognized sexual hunger when he saw it, and his own hunger, which had not been fed for so long, caused his lips to go to hers, trembling and hot.

Taken, heart and soul, by the kiss, Jo slid her arms around Wolf's neck and pressed her breasts against his chest. The mere touching of their bodies sent a spiraling pleasure throughout her.

Other *Leisure* and *Love Spell* books by
Cassie Edwards:

TOUCH THE WILD WIND
ROSES AFTER RAIN
WHEN PASSION CALLS
EDEN'S PROMISE
ISLAND RAPTURE
SECRETS OF MY HEART

The *Savage* Series:
SAVAGE JOY
SAVAGE WONDER
SAVAGE HEAT
SAVAGE DANCE
SAVAGE TEARS
SAVAGE LONGINGS
SAVAGE DREAM
SAVAGE BLISS
SAVAGE WHISPERS
SAVAGE SHADOWS
SAVAGE SPLENDOR
SAVAGE EDEN
SAVAGE SURRENDER
SAVAGE PASSIONS
SAVAGE SECRETS
SAVAGE PRIDE
SAVAGE SPIRIT
SAVAGE EMBERS
SAVAGE ILLUSION
SAVAGE SUNRISE
SAVAGE MISTS
SAVAGE PROMISE
SAVAGE PERSUASION

With much love I dedicate *Savage Fires*
to my son Charles F. Edwards,
and his sweet wife, Kathleen,
and with much pride I also dedicate this book
to my adorable grandson, David Scott Edwards.

Love,
Mom *and* Grandma

PROUD PEOPLE

They were always proud people, backs straight, heads held high, they always kept their respect and their pride. Without it, they'd rather die. They cherished their families, their lives, and the land, always giving back, with a helping hand. They fought for their women, their children and their lives. They were always brave, even as some lived and some died. In the end . . . their land was taken, along with their pride. Their eyes lost their light; with it went their will to survive. Beaten and betrayed, time and time again, by the white men they tried to befriend. They signed the treaties, with hopes for peace, wanting the battles to finally cease. But the soldiers kept coming, more and more, every time, taking what they wanted, and leaving nothing behind. They took the animals, the land and with it, their souls. It was a hard journey that eventually took its toll. The Native Americans of all the tribes, even till today, have survived. They continue on, with their heads held high.

To the proud people; let your spirits soar high. Your ancestors are with you, from far in the sky. They fought for what was theirs, and for this, they did die. But the American Indian will always survive!

Billie McBrearty, Poet

SAVAGE FIRES

Prologue

Lone Branch, Michigan—1891

The room was filled with foreboding dark shadows. The moon made scarce light as it shone through the panes of the small bedroom's lone window. Suddenly there was a smell of sulphur as a match burst into flame. A squat little man smiled as the flame reflected in the lenses of his gold-framed eyeglasses.

Laughing maniacally, the man held out one of his wife's white, lacy dresser scarves while with his other hand he brought the flame of the match to the tail end of the scarf.

His eyes gleaming, his heart pounding, the man watched the flame lap hungrily at the scarf like a rolling scarlet wave.

After dropping the match, he watched it

11

turn into charred, curled ash on the wooden floor, and then he focused his attention on the scarf again.

Laughing throatily, he fanned his free hand slowly back and forth over the flames, then shuddered with intense gratification as he held his hand into the flame and allowed its heat to burn into his palm.

When he heard footsteps approaching outside the room, the man's heart skipped a beat. He hurriedly dropped the scarf to the floor and stamped out the fire with the heel of his shoe. His wife had never discovered this lurid side to his character. All she cared to know about him was that he was a skilled attorney and brought in enough money for her to mingle with the most affluent people of Detroit. Tonight she was going to the opera. He had told her that he couldn't accompany her. He had a case to prepare for.

Going to the window, the man watched his wife leave their two-storied brick home and get into a carriage. He watched the horse and carriage until it turned off into another street.

Then he stepped away from the window and struck another match and watched its flame. He chuckled, for his night was not going to be spent studying boring law books. He had other plans.

The thought of setting fire to someone's barn gave him a thrill his wife's body could never provide.

"Tonight . . . tonight . . ." he whispered, a stream of drool rolling from one corner of his thin lips.

Chapter One

There was a fresh crispness in the air. The leaves of autumn, with their myriad colors, waved gently in the breeze over the *Mi-zhe-gam*, Grand River, as a procession of canoes swept noiselessly through the clear, blue water. Chief Wolf, of the Grand River *Sinago*, the Black Squirrel Band of the *Addowa* or Ottawa Nation, rode in the lead canoe.

His long, raven-black hair hung down his back to his waist, and Wolf's noble face reflected his pride in the successful fishing venture today. It was *chi-bin-dah-ah-naud*, a big catch!

Autumn and spring were the Ottawa's main fishing seasons. It was now mid-September. In preparation for *bi-boon*, winter, the canoes were piled high with rainbow trout.

13

But because of a difference of opinion between themselves and the white community about the Ottawa's fishing rights, the Ottawa warriors' spears and nets had been left hidden in a swamp once the fishing was done.

As his muscled arms rhythmically drew the paddle through the water, Wolf became lost in thought about Bart Gowins, the sheriff of Lone Branch, who had warned the Ottawa about over-fishing with their nets in the Michigan rivers.

Under Wolf's lead, his people had ignored the sheriff's warning. Many fish were needed to sustain the Ottawa through the long winter that lay ahead of them. And his people were protected by treaties. Because of such treaties, the Ottawa had even ignored orders to purchase a fishing license.

Ae, yes, Wolf felt proud, for he had thus far eluded being dominated by *chee-mo-ko-man*, whites. Living on a reservation was not as demeaning as he had first thought it would be when he was a small brave and his people signed treaties to live within assigned boundaries.

He laughed to himself when he thought about how the Ottawa now had the advantage over many *chee-mo-ko-man*, white men. The Ottawa had precious lumber within the boundaries of their reservation, lumber that whites wanted . . . land and trees that whites had lost when they signed it away by the terms of the treaty.

Nonetheless, the white lumberjacks moved

closer and closer to the Ottawa's land each day with their large saws.

To thwart the lumberjacks' plan to overstep their boundaries, armed Ottawa warriors were placed in strategic places on the outskirts of the reservation, where they waited and watched for the lumberjacks to trespass on land that was not theirs. If the *chee-mo-ko-man* were allowed to clear the Ottawa land of trees, there would be no lumber for the Ottawa people, nor would there be the animals that made their homes among the trees.

Both the animals of the forest and the fish of the river were vitally important to the Ottawa. If the Ottawa were not allowed to catch as many fish as were needed to keep their people fed, if the wild life fled the land, then one day soon there would be no Ottawa people.

Ae, yes, in Wolf's twenty-five years of life he had witnessed much greed and scheming against his people. As a young boy, he had silently watched how his chieftain father dealt cleverly with the greedy *chee-mo-ko-man*. Wolf had been proud to see how the strength and character of his father led him to often outwit white men.

But things had changed when Wolf's father's body betrayed him. A joint ailment had downed him several years ago, the pain clouding his mind too much for him to fulfill the responsibilities of a chief.

The elders had met in council and had quickly named Wolf chief.

Nush-ska-wee-zee, strong and capable, Wolf

felt honored to have been deemed worthy of such a title as chief and had proudly accepted the leadership of his people.

Since that first day of taking over the duties of chief, Wolf had never wavered in his determination to keep his people well fed, clothed, and safe.

And Wolf worked well under pressure. It made him awaken each day with determination and pride. It made him proud to be called *Ogema* by his people, the name given to all respected Ottawa leaders.

"Wolf, what do you think of the outbreak of fires in the town of Lone Branch?"

The voice of one of Wolf's most trusted warrior's broke through Wolf's deep thoughts. He turned his eyes to his left where Red Hawk sat beside him, sharing the same canoe.

"The fires? I believe they have been started by one who sets fires solely for the pleasure of watching the flames," Wolf said, in his mind's eye recalling the reflection of fire in the sky even last night. He had known even then that someone had set another illegal fire in the small town of Lone Branch.

"I will never understand how anyone can get satisfaction by setting fires and watching things burn," Red Hawk said, his face as young and noble as Wolf's.

They were even dressed in the same fashion. They had put away their breechclouts long ago and now wore buckskin trousers and shirts.

Their feet were clad in comfortable moccasins made by the women of their village, who took pride in their skill at making the footwear and sewing fancy beadwork onto them. Wolf's mother had personally made her son's moccasins.

"Who can understand the minds of most *chee-mo-ko-man*?" Wolf said. "For we both know it is a white man who is doing the burning. The red man has too much pride to destroy needlessly."

"It is good to know that Sheriff Gowins has someone of his own kind tormenting his people," Red Hawk said, laughing sarcastically. "At least while he is searching for the evil doer he is distracted from thinking up ways to torment our people."

"Do not be fooled into believing that Sheriff Gowins ever forgets about the Ottawa," Wolf said harshly. "Although he has troubles in his own community to deal with, he will never relent against our people. He will not rest until he destroys us," Red Hawk uttered, his voice tight. "I am surprised he has not come and accused us of setting the fires."

"If he thought he had even one shred of proof, he would," Wolf said, his eyes narrowing when he thought that he saw movement among the trees along the riverbank.

His shoulders relaxed again when he saw a doe leap out of the thicket, followed by a fat buck.

"I hope the corrupt sheriff does not invent

ways to make us appear guilty," Red Hawk then grumbled.

"My concern is that this evil fire person might bring his fires to the Ottawa reservation," Wolf said, wincing at the very thought of how quickly his people's homes could burn. They were constructed of logs and the roofs were made of bark.

He knew that the evil man would even get pleasure in burning the tall totems that stood protectively at the entrance to the village.

As Wolf's canoe rounded a bend in the river and he caught sight of his village and the matching totem poles that sat opposite each other on the riverbank, he gazed proudly at the carved figures on the poles. They included bears, henhawks, sparrowhawks, wolves, eagles, and beavers. There were wolf tracks carved into the base of each.

As a child, Wolf had watched those totems being carved and then erected. In fact, they seemed to be a symbol of his childhood, for it was seeing the totems and the power they represented that had made him first dream of being a chief like his father.

Proud of their catch today, anxious to share it with everyone in the village, the Ottawa warriors paddled with renewed vigor in the direction of the sandy beach where people were gathering to greet them.

"*Hai-ay!*" Wolf shouted. His people waved and gave an answering shout.

After the canoes were beached, Wolf held up

a fat rainbow trout for them all to see. "My people, it is a *chi-bin-dah-ah-naud*!" he shouted. "It was a good day on the river! Our bellies will be warmed by fish when *bi-boon* arrives and snows are blowing against our windows!"

"*Oneegishin*! *Oneegishin*! It is good!" some of his people cried in their excitement. "*Oneegishin*!"

Absorbed in their merriment, his people laughed and began to unload the fish from the canoes; no one noticed they were no longer alone. Suddenly many white men on horseback came out of hiding from the dense trees that grew along the river. Their rifles were aimed at Wolf and his warriors.

Wolf's jaw tightened angrily when he stared at Sheriff Gowins, whose firearm was leveled at Wolf's chest. Wolf hated the very sight of this short, paunchy, whisker-faced *chee-mo-ko-man*, whose eyes were only slits beneath thick, black eyebrows.

Ever since Gowins had been appointed sheriff two years before, he had been a thorn in the sides of the Ottawa, leaving a deeper wound each time he came among them.

Wolf's gaze swept quickly over the sheriff. Unlike Wolf's people, who took much pride in their appearance, this man, who reeked of perspiration, was dressed in frayed denim trousers and a soiled shirt. The sheriff's badge shone back at Wolf from where it was pinned on his leather vest. He wore a sweat-stained ten-gallon hat, and sported worn leather boots on his feet, the scuffed-up toes secure in his horse's stirrups.

"Chief, I see by the look in your eyes you don't welcome a visit by us whites," Sheriff Gowins said, laughing throatily as his eyes locked with Wolf's. He laughed into the wind. "As for your sentries? Thanks to the butt ends of our rifles, they are takin' a nap."

"*Ani-mosh*," Wolf growled out. He used the word "dog" to address the corrupt chief since "dog" was the worst way a man could address another man. "If you have badly injured our sentries, you will pay."

"Yeah, sure, and just what do you think you'll do about it?" Sheriff Gowins said, leaning his face down closer to Wolf's. "You're outnumbered by whites and you know it."

Knowing that words were wasted on this evil man, Wolf said nothing else to him. He just waited to find out the true reason the sheriff had trespassed on Indian land today.

Then when he saw the sheriff glancing down at the canoes that were overflowing with fish, Wolf felt terrible anger fill him. He suspected he now knew why the sheriff had come with so many armed men.

The *chi-bin-dah-ah-naud*, the big fish catch!

Surely the sheriff and his men had watched from a hiding place and had seen the Ottawa catch the fish. No doubt they had purposely stayed hidden until the canoes were filled to the brim and brought home so they could come among Wolf's people to embarrass him when the sheriff ordered him to hand over the fish-catch to his deputies.

If that was the sheriff's purpose, Wolf knew he had no power to stop him. When deadly firearms were aimed at a man, he was rendered helpless.

But only for the moment, Wolf reminded himself.

"Alright, enough of this small talk," Sheriff Gowins said, shoving his hat back from his brow with a forefinger. "I see you went against the law again and caught rainbow trout without a license. And I watched you catching them in illegal nets. I guess you know what the penalty is for that, don't you? You must appear at the courthouse in Lone Branch to pay a fine for both fishing with nets, and for not having a license to fish."

Still Wolf said nothing. He had expected the sheriff to do something like this one day. But had hoped that he was wrong, and that his people would be left alone to live their lives, as the whites were left alone to live theirs the way they wanted.

But he knew now that he had been wrong to think this evil, power-hungry man could stay away and leave the Ottawa in peace. He should have known that the sheriff was just waiting for the Ottawa to take their autumn harvest of fish. Everyone knew that many fish were needed to sustain the people through the long, cold months of winter. Whites had their cattle that they raised behind barbed wire. The red man was at the mercy of nature for his nourishment.

"Men, those of you who were assigned to take the fish, do it! Fill those bags we brought with us!" Sheriff Gowins shouted, his eyes dancing as he stared into Wolf's. "You others keep your firearms trained on the Injuns. If anyone so much as moves, plug 'em." He laughed throatily. "Hurry up. We've got women waitin' for us with their skillets. Seems we'll be the ones having the feast tonight, not the Ottawa!"

Wolf's insides grew cold, and his heart ached when he heard the gasp of his people behind him. But he could do nothing to save this autumn's fish harvest. He and his people were helpless under the threat of so many firearms aimed at them.

His heart pounding, Wolf watched his people's precious catch being carried away as the sheriff and his men rode off with the fish. Wolf's insides tightened when the sheriff's cruel laughter carried in the wind back to the Ottawa.

His brow furrowed, his eyes narrowed, Wolf turned and looked slowly from man to man, woman to woman, and child to child, his anger felt more deeply when he saw the looks of puzzlement in the eyes of the children. Today they had seen their chief bested by white men! Today they had seen how *chee-mo-ko-man* could still take from the red man!

Today's lesson would remain in those young minds throughout their lives!

Then Wolf remembered something else . . . some*one*. His injured sentries. He turned to Red Hawk. "Take several men and bring in our injured sentries," he said, his hands tight fists at his sides. "Take them to their lodges, then meet me at the council house."

Chapter Two

An angry determination etched on their tight faces, the warriors sat on blankets in the council house, attentive to their chief as they looked to him for guidance.

"My warriors, you know that the first rule of the Ottawa society is respect for the individual," Wolf said, as he sat in the middle of the half circle of men, his back to the council-house lodge fire. "No one person determines the fate of another. Each person is respected because of his or her individual powers and achievements. Decisions which affect the entire group are arrived at by mutual consent. Ottawa leaders do not command. They represent. So today, my warriors, speak your mind. I am here to listen. By mutual agreement, we shall come to a decision about what happened today."

"I say pay the fine," Red Hawk mumbled. "It is only fourteen white man dollars. If we do not pay it, more trouble will come to our people. I felt our people's sadness today. I felt their defeat. I want to do nothing more to add to those feelings."

"*Mee-goo-ga-yay-ay-nayn-da-man*, I think the same way. I also do not want our people to feel defeated," Wolf said flatly. "But I believe we should fight paying the fine and prove our right to catch as much fish as we need in the Grand River and all other Michigan rivers. We were shamed today by whites. We must never allow that to happen again, especially in the presence of our young ones. Do you wish for them to grow up giving in to the *chee-mo-ko-man* every time a demand is made of them?"

"Today it was done by the force of firearms," one of the warriors said. "Perhaps we should reciprocate and go into Lone Branch with our weapons and surprise the whites."

"What Sheriff Gowins said about the whites outnumbering the Ottawa is too true," Wolf said, his voice drawn. "So we must fight them in ways that do not include firearms."

"And how can that be done?" Red Hawk said, sighing. "Fire power rules, does it not?"

"There are ways," Wolf said, his jaw tightening. "I hope you all agree that we must *not* pay the fine. It is time for us to stand up for our rights or never again will we have a say in the matter of fishing or hunting. Because of the greedy white people, the Ottawa have lost too much already."

"Then tell us, *chee-o-gee-mah*, chief, what can be done without force of arms?" another warrior said.

Wolf rose and stood over them. He folded his arms across his powerful chest as he looked from one to the other. "As you know, there is an Indian Claims Commission created solely to deal with Indian rights," he explained.

"*Ae*, yes, we know that," Red Hawk said, daring to interrupt his chief. "But the Indian lawyers there are in short supply. In the past, the Ottawa tribe has had to turn with decidedly mixed results to non-Indian legal counsel."

"As we will this time," Wolf said. "I will go to my friend Fast Horse. You all know him and trust him. He is of the St. Croix band of Chippewa. Although he is now a Methodist minister who lives away from his people's village, he will still guide us well in this problem at hand. He knows white people who are lawyers, who are smart and have ways to win battles in the white man's court. He knows lawyers who are willing to work for the rights of the red man."

Wolf went quiet and all heads turned when Sleeping Bear, Wolf's ailing father, was carried by two warriors into the council house. Sleeping Bear's skin was drawn taut over his bones and his long hair was thinning and gray. He wore the traditional breechclout of his youth and a bear claw necklace.

Wolf was always deeply saddened to see

how his father had been weakened by the disease that caused large, painful knots on his joints. The pain had disabled him so much that he could no longer walk; he was carried everywhere.

Wolf went to his father and helped him down onto soft blankets and pelts beside the slow-burning fire.

The warriors turned on their pallets of blankets and faced Sleeping Bear and Wolf as Wolf knelt down beside his father and told him the council's plan.

"*Nin-gwis*, son, *mee-goo-ga-ysy-ay-nayn-da-man*, I think the same way. Your plan is a wise one," Sleeping Bear said in his deep, authoritative voice. "If we do not prove our rights once and for all with the white eyes, then I see no good future for our younger generations. The fight will be no more in their hearts. They will go around with heads hanging and with an emptiness in their hearts. I say fight now, or never more."

Feeling so much for his father, and always trusting his judgment in everything, Wolf leaned over and gave his father a warm hug. "*Ho, ho*," he said, in his people's way of voicing approval.

Then he moved to his feet again when someone else entered; all eyes followed the woman as she sat down beside Sleeping Bear. It was Blue Moth, Wolf's mother, a woman whose hair still held its richness of dark color at the age of fifty, and whose body was still as petite as it had been when she was a young girl newly married to a proud chief. She reached her arms out for her son and hugged him, then settled in beside her husband and listened to Wolf as he explained the plan to her.

"And what was your *gee-bah-bah's* response to such a plan?" Blue Moth asked in her soft, lilting voice, her eyes smiling into her son's as she spoke.

"Father agrees to it," Wolf said. "And what is your opinion, Mother? You know that I always value your words."

Blue Moth's eyes momentarily wavered, then she took Wolf's hand and held it. "My *nin-gwis*, I usually agree with your father's decisions, *and* yours, but this time I cannot," she said, swallowing hard. "My son, I am afraid of what you wish to do. I am afraid that if you proceed with it, *everything* will be taken from our people all at once, not in bits and pieces as it is now taken."

"*Gee-mah-mah*, Mother, if we sit by and allow the white people to do as they did today, over and over again, and we do nothing about it, yes, everything *will* be taken from our people," he said, careful not to show her any disrespect by disagreeing with her. "This way, by doing what our council has decided upon, at least we are fighting for our rights instead of just standing by, allowing the whites to make fools of us time and time again."

"Then do as your heart guides you, my son," Blue Moth said. She kissed the palm of Wolf's hand, then scooted closer to her husband and placed a gentle hand on his bony, malformed knee.

"I shall leave now for Lone Branch," Wolf announced. "I will meet with Fast Horse. I will return home, my warriors, and we shall meet in council again tomorrow. It is then that I will relay to you news of my meeting with Fast Horse."

He gave his father and mother a long, silent gaze, their eyes speaking volumes that need not be said aloud, their love and respect for him always there. He bent and kissed his mother's brow, and then his father's. Moments later he was mounted on his black stallion Midnight, riding through the forest on his way to Lone Branch.

Suddenly six white wolves rushed from behind a thick stand of bushes and began following Wolf's galloping horse.

Laughing, Wolf gazed over his shoulder at the wolves. Then he drew a tight rein and stopped his horse.

"My friends, *nee-may-nan-dum-wah-bum-eh-na-wa*, I am glad to see you," Wolf said, sliding from his saddle to the ground.

He knelt and drew one wolf and then another into his arms, cuddling them and lovingly running his hands through their thick, white fur.

He chuckled as first one and then another licked his face and hands.

When one of them became more boisterous and rough in his play than the others, knocking Wolf to the ground on his back, then pouncing on Wolf playfully, Wolf laughed and allowed it.

But realizing the danger of someone coming along and seeing him with the wolves, Wolf sat up and drew the most playful wolf into his arms. He held him still as the others lay down before him, their bluish-gray eyes watching him.

"You must stay hidden better than this, my friends," Wolf said softly. "You cannot allow the white hunters to see you." Although Wolf's own people tanned skins for their own use, the white hunters were seeking the pelts of the rare white wolves. White pelts were the most valuable of all, and rare.

"Run quickly back to your den," Wolf said, shoving the one wolf from his lap. "All of you. Go. *Wee-wee-be-tahn*, hurry. Stay hidden and only come out at night when your instincts tell you that it is safe."

He hugged each of them, then watched them leap away into the dark shadows of the forest.

Then, smiling, Wolf rode again in the direction of Lone Branch.

In his mind's eye he recalled a day many long years ago when he was but a small brave out alone in the forest. He was using his new, small bow to practice shooting at small creatures such as crickets and grasshoppers.

That day he had fallen into a hole in the ground that had been dug for trapping. He had been knocked unconscious.

When he awakened he found himself somewhere else. Wolves had rescued him from the hole and had dragged him to their den.

His ankle had been sprained so badly that he could not walk, and Wolf hadn't been able to leave to find his way back home. The wolves, all snow white, had kept him safe. They had brought food to him. Water was close at hand in a stream. He was kept warm at night as the wolves snuggled around him.

Wolf had stayed with the wolves for several days and nights until his father finally found him.

Since then Wolf had often visited his friends the wolves and their offspring. He had even taken the name "Wolf" for his adult name when his vision quest time had arrived at the age of thirteen winters.

His thoughts were brought back to the present and the issue at hand when he rode into the outskirts of Lone Branch. His friend's church steeple loomed high above the white clapboard houses of the small town.

Wolf and Fast Horse had attended school together in Detroit. There they had learned the alphabet, how to count, how to write their names, and how to recognize various denominations of money.

They had also learned basic reading and writing, and how to speak four languages.

But the language used when speaking to each other was usually Chippewa.

They had become fast friends but had parted ways when their paths had taken different courses. Wolf had returned home to be chief when his father became too disabled to continue.

Fast Horse had gone on to Albion College. And even though Fast Horse became a Christian, and eventually a Methodist minister, he had maintained a strong sense of his Chippewa identity and a bond of friendship with Wolf and his Ottawa people.

Wolf smiled when he saw Fast Horse, who was now called "Father Samuel" by his parishioners. He was at the back of his church. He was a man of gentle heart and spirit, evident today in the way he was spreading bread crumbs for a flock of birds. It always warmed Wolf's heart to be with his friend.

But today, the meeting was to be one of deep seriousness. Wolf hoped that Fast Horse would know someone who could help his Ottawa people in their continuing time of trouble with *chee-mo-ko-man*.

Chapter Three

Her hands resting on her lap, Josephine Taylor Stanton, called Jo by her family and friends, was sitting in her wheelchair in her father's fine, one-story brick home on the outskirts of Lone Branch.

A warm breeze blew through the window beside her, ruffling the lacy sheer curtains as Jo peered outside, watching her father, Addison, pluck the last roses of summer from his huge rose arbor.

Her father's glorious roses were special to him, as was his apple orchard. He had shaped some of his rose bushes in the shape of hedges, while others ran riot over several trellises. Some even vined up apple trees which stood like sentinels on one side of the arbor.

Since Jo had been small, her father's favorite pastime was pruning and caring for his roses.

Seeing her father limp made Jo's breath catch with an ache that she had become familiar with, yet hated. She looked quickly away from him. There was more than his limp that made her heart hurt. Tears splashed from her eyes when she was overwhelmed by vivid memories of her mother walking through the roses with her father, her laughter sweet and soft as her husband teasingly plucked a rose and thrust it into her hair above an ear.

"I'll never hear or see her again," Jo whispered to herself, a sob lodging in her throat. She stared through her tears down at her lifeless legs, cursing the day of the train wreck when so much changed in her family.

Her mother's death had come quickly as she was thrown through the train window when the train derailed.

Her father, who had been thrown to the floor of the train alongside Jo as the train flipped over sideways, had been left with a terrible limp.

And Jo, at age twenty-six, had lost her ability to walk.

Now twenty-seven, Jo ran her long, lean fingers over her lifeless legs. She had to get her mind off things that she had no control over. She placed her hands on the wheels of her chair and quickly wheeled herself from her bedroom and down the long corridor to the family library.

She stopped just inside the library door. Her

gaze moved slowly along row after row of leather-bound books.

Anger grabbed the pit of her stomach when she was reminded of how her disability kept her from doing even the most simple things. The books were too high. She couldn't reach up and choose a book for herself.

But as she had each day since the train wreck, she tried once again to push herself up from the wheelchair to prove to herself that *today* she *could* walk. The doctor had said that her disability was all in her mind, that the trauma of having lost her mother on the day of the train wreck had taken away Jo's will to walk.

Another doctor had said that Jo was somehow blaming herself for her mother's death, and felt that she didn't deserve to live, much less walk.

Jo did blame herself. She had chosen to sit in the aisle seat on the train, forcing her mother or father to sit beside the window.

Her mother had chosen the window seat because she said she loved to watch the countryside float by outside as though *it* were on wheels, not the train.

"Still, I shouldn't have forced the issue by choosing the aisle seat myself," Jo whispered to herself, falling back into the chair when once again she couldn't stand up.

She wheeled herself further into the library and turned and waited for her father when she heard his familiar footsteps coming down the corridor toward the library.

Hating to cause her father pain at the sight of her tears, Jo forced herself to smile when he walked into the room.

When she saw what he was carrying, she was transported to those times when her father would bring bouquets of roses to her mother. Today he had brought Jo the last roses of summer in her mother's favorite crystal vase.

"Aren't these the most beautiful we've ever grown, Jo? For sure, they are prizewinners," Addison said, handing her the vase. "Bury your nose in them. I promise you that you will feel as heady as I."

Fighting back tears and her remembrances of times not so long past, Jo burrowed her nose into one of the thickest roses and inhaled. It was a rose that her father had named his "ballerina" with its dense, arching shape that spread like a ballerina's tutu. Its fine-petaled, soft pink blossoms had a deep pink edge and a white eye, forming large clusters with a musky scent.

Again Jo heard her mother's soft, sweet laughter.

In Jo's mind's eye she saw her mother's blue eyes gleaming with happiness as she danced amidst the beautiful roses, a ballerina pirouetting, the very reason Jo's father had since called this particular rose his "ballerina."

"Jo?"

Her father's voice brought Jo out of her reverie.

She smiled awkwardly up at him as she drew her nose away from the roses.

"Please set them on the table beside the window for me, Father," Jo said, holding the vase out for him. "I shall enjoy them so much while I read."

Limping, he took the vase and placed it on the table, then knelt and placed fresh logs among those that were already smoldering on the grate.

"How are you today, Jo?" he asked, pushing himself up from the floor, his blue eyes wavering as he gazed down at her. He saw that she had taken pains with her appearance today. He hoped that was a sign that she was ready to break out of her shell of isolation and get back to the business of living.

Her golden hair shone from brushing and hung in wavy curls down her back to her waist. She wore a lovely blue dress that Harriet, their maid, had helped her put on.

The dress brought out the blue in Jo's eyes, and Addison tried to ignore the red of her eyes that proved she had been crying. He felt overwhelming sorrow, too, when he got to thinking about his precious wife of twenty-six years.

Addison had decided to go back to work soon to help him get past his mourning. He even had an appointment in Detroit he hadn't told Jo about.

"Would you like to go outside today, Jo?" he said. "Soon it will be too cold for us to take our daily walks."

39

"Walks?" Jo said, trying to keep the sarcasm from her voice. "You walk, Father. I . . . I . . . am pushed."

"Jo . . ."

"Father, what I truly want to do today is just sit by the fire and read a good book," Jo said, interrupting him before he had the chance to start talking about her disability. She had thought enough about it already this morning to last a lifetime; she had no wish to debate her problem with her father.

She gazed up at him and saw sadness in the depths of his eyes. She realized that the wrinkles around his eyes and mouth were there because of the despair he felt over the devastating losses he'd known.

But those age lines didn't take away from his handsomeness. A man with thick, golden hair, a square jaw, straight nose, and long lashes over blue eyes, he still drew women's attention.

And his expensive wool breeches, white starched collar, and shining leather shoes proved that he still cared about his appearance, and that he might be ready to move on with his life. Surely he missed being a banker. He had always arrived home from work with tales of this client or that one on the brink of becoming rich because of his advice.

Yes, surely he would return to work soon. *She* planned to finally resume working tomorrow.

But today was Sunday. She had one more day to ponder the challenges ahead and how she would do things that she had always managed when she had the ability to stand, walk, and run.

"Which book do you want me to get for you?" Addison asked.

"I want a frivolous one, Father, not something serious," Jo said, laughing softly. "Tomorrow, when I resume working, I'll have my nose deep in the more serious books."

Addison chose a book for Jo and handed it to her. "I'm so proud of you, Jo, for resuming work tomorrow," he said, clasping his hands behind him as he gazed down at her. "You know how few women achieve the kind of success you have achieved. And it is rare for women to go to college. I have always admired your spirit. I knew you would not give up what you went to college for."

"I shouldn't have waited this long, Father," Jo said somberly. Then she lifted her chin proudly and smiled up at him. "But I did and now I *am* going back to work. I'll prove to everyone that I might not have muscles in my legs, but my brain is begging to be used, and damn it, Father, I'm going to use it. I won't let my college education be wasted any longer on pitying myself."

"I wouldn't call it pity," Addison said thickly. "You just had to have time to adjust to things."

He went behind her and wheeled her over beside the fire. "Would you mind if I sit in here at my desk as you read?" he asked, stepping around and questioning her with his eyes.

"I've some entries to make in my journal and then I'm going to go out to the orchard and pick apples for our yearly giveaway of apples at the orphanage. I love to see the children's eyes light up when I hand out the ripe apples to them."

"You are such a dear, caring man," Jo murmured, taking his hand and resting her cheek in its palm. "The children adore you."

"Well, I don't know about that," Addison said, chuckling as he slid his hand away from Jo. "But I do adore *them*."

She watched him limp to his huge oak desk and sit down behind it. She tried, but she couldn't get the mention of children off her mind. Her heart ached to believe that she would never have children of her own. She had given up on having children on the day she was crippled.

She wanted to believe the doctors when they continued to tell her that there was no physical reason why she could not walk, and once she got past feeling guilty about things she truly had no control over, she should be able to walk again.

Her newest doctor had tried to encourage her by saying that one day she *would* get past that grief.

She *would* walk again.

Although she liked her new doctor and wanted to trust what he said, she felt that she had been in the wheelchair for too long now ever to believe she could walk away from it.

Her gaze was drawn to a photograph on a table next to her. An anger she could not help feeling raged through her as she gazed at the picture of a man she now despised with all her heart.

Her jaw tight, she laid the book on her lap and picked up the framed photograph of Maximilian Schmidt.

Filled with a silent loathing, she slid the portrait out of the frame and leaned low to place it in the flames of the fire.

"Goodbye, Max, and good riddance," she whispered so that her father couldn't hear her.

She truly felt relieved that Max was out of her life; in truth, she had felt only a momentary twinge of rejection when he had told her that he wouldn't marry her.

More and more, these past years, she had seen him for what he had become . . . a ruthless lumber baron who was now a cold, shrewd, calculating person, who would do anything to get what he wanted.

And that most certainly wasn't Jo. He had abandoned her because he saw her as a helpless person in a wheelchair.

This gave Jo even more reason to get back to work and prove to Max that although she was helpless in some ways, she was still able to do what she did best . . . be an attorney who had never lost a case!

She could hardly wait for her first client since her hiatus to walk into her office!

Chapter Four

Sitting in the small office at the back of the church rectory, accepting a cup of tea from Fast Horse, Wolf did not feel as out of place in these surroundings as he had the first few times he had come to visit Fast Horse. The Bibles and hymnals stacked on a table against the far wall, the sun streaming through the high windows of the room, drew Wolf's eye as Fast Horse sat down in an upholstered chair before the fire.

Fast Horse had earlier explained the meaning of the hymnals to Wolf; he had opened a Bible and pointed out those passages of God's word which had drawn Fast Horse to choose the white man's religion over his own people's way of worshiping. The words had been filled with peace and warmth, but the meaning behind them had confused Wolf.

But he knew that was the difference between himself and his preacher friend. Fast Horse had studied the white man's religion at a special school.

Wolf had not.

Wolf still adhered to his own people's way of thinking about the beginning of time and how life was created.

Just because he did not agree with his friend's viewpoint about such things, that did not weaken the special bond that had formed between them.

"You are in such deep thought, my friend," Fast Horse said, setting his cup of tea aside.

His friend wore a black robe, with his long, dark hair tied back from his face by a thong of leather. Fast Horse leaned closer to Wolf and placed a gentle hand on his shoulder. "You have not come today only to share tea and small talk," he said softly. "Wolf, I can see it in your eyes. I can see it in the way you hold your shoulders rigid and your jaw so tight. Tell me, best friend. Tell me what is troubling you. Perhaps I can lessen your burden in some way."

"My people have been humiliated by *chee-mo-ko-man* again," Wolf said, setting his cup of tea on the table next to Fast Horse's. "They came and took the rainbow trout my warriors and I caught in the Grand River. We were so proud, taking the fish back to our village for our families. Right now, my people should be

46

celebrating the fish harvest. Instead, heads are hanging with shame and anger."

"Sheriff Gowins is responsible?" Fast Horse said, his dark eyes filled with quiet loathing at the thought of the corrupt sheriff.

"*Ae*, he is the one who came and kept his firearm aimed at my chest as he gave orders to seize the fish from my warriors' canoes," Wolf grumbled.

"And what did he claim as his reason for doing this?" Fast Horse asked, sighing heavily as he sat back again in his chair.

Wolf explained what had happened, not leaving anything unsaid.

"I will not pay the fine nor will I purchase a license for fishing the rivers my forefathers have fished before me," Wolf then said, his eyes flashing angrily. "As you and I know, all of the treaties agreed upon by Michigan Indians and whites guaranteed our people the right to hunt, fish, and trap. Sheriff Gowins had no right to come and take from us what I and my warriors legally took from the river."

"*Mee-goo-ga-yay-ay-nayn-da-man*, I think the same way. You are right to be angry, for what you have just said about the treaties is true," Fast Horse said. "Your people and mine are not bound by such things as a license to fish. The treaties have given both the Ottawa and Chippewa the right to catch as many fish as we need to sustain our people through the long winter months when other food is scarce."

Cassie Edwards

"I need someone who knows how to argue this law with whites, to argue it for me and my people," Wolf said. He leaned forward and clasped his hands tightly together before him. "I have come to ask you if you know a reputable attorney who can help my people win their case against the *chee-mo-ko-man*, for surely if we win this time, we will be able to fish in peace forever."

Fast Horse's lips lifted in a slow smile. He nodded. "*Ay-uh*," he said in his Chippewa way of saying "yes." "I know the right person . . . a J. T. Stanton. J. T. is the best attorney in these parts. And J. T. believes in Indians' rights. *Ay-uh*, the Ottawa will win their case if J. T. is there to argue it for them before the white man's judge."

"I trust your judgment," Wolf said, his eyes lighting up with excitement. "When can I meet with this Attorney Stanton?"

"I will arrange a meeting between you and J. T. for tomorrow," Fast Horse said, lifting his teacup. He would enjoy the drink now that he felt things were better inside his friend's heart and mind.

"*Ay-uh*," Fast Horse then quickly added, as he lowered the cup from his mouth. "*Ho-boo-chee-goo-nee-gah-ee-shee-chee-gay*, yes, I will do it for you."

From the beginning of time, Fast Horse's Chippewa tribe and Wolf's Ottawa people had been politically linked by kinships and joint interests. Should one suffer at the hand of the *chee-mo-ko-man*, soon after, the other suffered as well. As far back as any could remember, they had come together to fight for the same causes.

Even though Fast Horse lived separate from his people now, to do the work of the Lord that he was called to do, he went home often to check on things. Whenever he was needed there, his people knew they could depend on him. With him being so educated and learned, they looked up to him, especially the children.

And because of Fast Horse, many of the children planned to further their education and attend college. Their aspirations meant that the future for the Chippewa people was brighter than it would be if the children chose the road that took them toward alcoholism and defeat.

"It is so good that we are still close friends," Wolf said, then took a sip of his tea. He didn't truly like the taste. But to be considerate of his friend, he drank it anyway.

"Nothing could ever break the bond that formed when we were small and wandered in the forest seeing whose new bow could shoot arrows the farthest," Fast Horse said, chuckling. "Our *gee-bah-bahs*, fathers, were always the best of friends."

Fast Horse's eyes lowered. "Until my father's life was taken by someone's arrow," he said, his voice breaking.

"I regret that I have not been able to help you find the one responsible for ambushing your father," Wolf said, setting his cup aside. "We exhausted ourselves looking, yet we never found anything that pointed to the guilty party."

"And how is your *gee-bah-bah* faring these days?" Fast Horse asked, quickly lifting his eyes. He heaved a deep sigh, for he knew the answer before asking the question. He had been at the Ottawa village only a few days ago and saw how Wolf's father's health was failing. And it tore at Fast Horse to see the once powerful man carried about by others because he no longer had the ability to walk on his own.

"My father's good days are far behind him," Wolf said, his voice catching. "I wish I could give him my legs, for I would gladly give them up to see him walking again among my people. But my *gee-bah-bah's* pride is no less now than when he could walk. He is still noble in his bearing and always will be."

"And your *gee-mah-mah*, Blue Moth?"

Wolf laughed softly. "Still herself and wonderful," he said, loving his mother so much. It pained him to know that one day she, too, would be downed by one thing or another that old age inflicted upon one's beloved parents.

"I will come again soon and sit with your mother and father and listen to your father's tales of the past," Fast Horse said softly. "That takes me, also, to my father's past, for their lives were entwined so often."

"*Ae*, as *our* tales will be similar when *we* are old and looking into the past for stories to tell," Wolf said, smiling. "Of course, our paths have gone in different directions, but not before many memories were formed between us that can be shared with our children."

"Yours, not mine," Fast Horse reminded Wolf. "I have given my all to the Lord. The only children of my future are those of my church." He reached over and took one of Wolf's hands. "The children of my future will also be yours. And yours will be mine, if you will share them with me."

"Always," Wolf said, clasping Fast Horse's hand. "Always. What is mine is always yours."

"I am very happy in what I do, Wolf," Fast Horse said thickly as he eased his hand away from his friend's.

"I can tell that you are by the look in your eyes and by the sound of your voice," Wolf said. "And since I know you are happy, I am happy for you."

He rose from the chair, stretched, then gave Fast Horse a warm hug. "Until tomorrow, my friend," he said. "I've got to go now."

"Until tomorrow," Fast Horse said, then stepped away from Wolf and watched him leave the room.

Wolf walked down the long aisle of the church, without pausing to look at the long rows of pews on either side of him. He had never been able to understand how Fast Horse could have chosen the white man's God over the red man's Great Spirit.

But all that Wolf needed to know was that his friend's heart was good, regardless of the religion he practiced.

And Wolf was confident that Fast Horse would come through for him. Whomever he chose to represent the Ottawa would be the best attorney for the job. Wolf could hardly wait until tomorrow to meet this J. T. Stanton.

Fast Horse went to the window and watched Wolf ride away on Midnight, then left the rectory and hitched up his horse and buggy to go and make a call on J. T. Stanton. He hoped that this case would give J. T. a reason to return to work after too long an absence.

Ay-uh, he knew that he could depend on J. T. This case was exactly what she needed to forget the loss of her mother.

He smiled as he thought about how this case might even give J. T. a reason to walk again!

Chapter Five

Wolf walked with Fast Horse into a posh office on the outskirts of Detroit, quickly realizing that his friend had brought him to a successful attorney. It showed in how the office was furnished.

He stopped just inside the room and looked slowly around him, immediately impressed by the largest oak desk he had ever seen, as well as expensive, overstuffed leather chairs positioned in various places around the room.

What impressed him most, though, were the rows of bookcases along the walls, which were filled with many expensive-looking leather-bound books, the likes of which Wolf had never seen before, not even in the schools he'd attended.

Then his attention was captured by a different sight: The sun pouring through the far windows cast a soft glow on a woman coming from an adjoining room. But she was not walking. She was rolling herself into the room in some sort of contraption with wheels, her long, lean hands stopping the wheels when she saw him standing there with Fast Horse.

"Wolf, this is J. T., the attorney I told you about," Fast Horse said, gesturing toward Jo.

Although Jo was used to being stared at since she had been confined to the wheelchair, she could not help blushing under the scrutiny of this handsome Indian. She could tell that he had never seen a wheelchair before. She was sure that he had never seen a woman confined in such a way.

It made her suddenly aware of her helplessness. She wanted now, as never before, to be able to stand up on steady feet and stretch out a hand to make his acquaintance.

She knew this was Wolf, the Ottawa chief who sought her help in fighting for his people's rights. Fast Horse had come to her home yesterday and asked her if she would represent the Ottawa.

Always on the side of the downtrodden, Jo had said a firm "yes" to the offer.

And now that she saw Wolf face to face, she felt drawn to him in a quiet, sort of mystical, way. She was glad that she had agreed to the challenge.

But the way he was backing away from her made her realize that he didn't feel the same way about her. She could see the doubt in his eyes. She knew that he only now understood that J. T. Stanton, Attorney at Law, was a woman confined to a wheelchair.

She started to roll herself closer to him, then stopped as he turned and walked hastily toward the door.

A deep hurt plagued Jo's heart, yet she knew that this would not be the last time the fact that she was disabled might stand in the way of someone wanting her to represent them.

Or was it because she was a woman? Perhaps the wheelchair had nothing to do with Wolf's decision to leave even before formally meeting her and giving her a chance.

Wolf grabbed hold of the doorknob. He was disappointed in Fast Horse. How could his friend think that a woman would be capable of defending Wolf's people, especially one who was only able to get around in a moving chair?

He was reminded of his father, whose own powers had been diminished so much by his inability to walk that he had given up his position as chief.

Although Wolf still saw his father as a vital man, his brain still as active as when he was a young warrior, Wolf knew that under certain conditions his father was not completely the same. He had been right to give up the responsibilities of chief.

As for this woman, now was not the time for him to take chances with his attorney. He had to know that whoever represented his people was fully capable of doing so.

But he was ashamed of himself for being so

rude to the lady. He was never the sort to be rude to anyone.

But now? When so much depended on his good judgment? How could he not doubt Fast Horse's choice of attorney?

Seeing that Wolf still hadn't opened the door to leave, guessing that inside himself he was debating his decision to leave, Jo felt better about things. Surely he was weighing everything in his mind and would realize how wrong he was not to give her a chance.

Surely he knew that Fast Horse wouldn't choose an unskilled attorney for him and his people. Fast Horse was an intelligent, learned man, who knew far more than most white people.

And she knew that Wolf was just as smart. Fast Horse had explained to Jo that Wolf had attended school with him and was an intelligent leader of his people.

She understood Wolf's need for a topnotch attorney. Sheriff Gowins was pressing hard to take the Ottawa's fishing rights away; and the lumberjacks, under Max's orders, were pushing closer and closer to Ottawa land.

Yes, the more she thought about it, the more she understood Wolf's hesitance. She no longer held it against him, or felt hurt by it.

She would prove her worth. Wolf would never be sorry for having stepped through her door today.

She was going to try to keep him from leaving before she had the chance to make him understand that she was the right person, perhaps the only person, to help his people.

"Wolf, I *am* J. T. Stanton," she said, though his back was turned still to her. "But please call me Jo. My friends and family always do."

When he still didn't turn and face her, and she saw his shoulder muscles tightening, Jo continued talking. "I know all about the problems you are having with the whites," she said softly. "I have read all the treaties and understand that for the most part they were worded incorrectly. And most interpreters didn't interpret honestly. I will bring all of this to the court's attention, and even more, if . . . if . . . you will allow me to. I would be happy to represent your people. I assure you, Wolf, that I will win. You will walk away the victor."

She paused, then said, "I saw your reaction to my wheelchair. It is the same as most people who see me. Let me assure you, Wolf, although I am confined to this chair, I still have the ability to enter the courtroom and fight for your rights . . . and win."

Hearing the woman's confident voice, and taking to heart what she said, Wolf turned slowly and gazed down at her.

He found himself in awe of her, a woman with so much conviction, knowledge, and the courage to speak up against people of her own race.

He found himself looking past the wheelchair. It did not take away from the woman's loveliness. He was drawn to her large blue eyes and flowing golden hair and the strength in her character.

He saw her as a woman who had a great knowledge of the law.

He began to believe that she *could* help his people's cause.

Wolf walked over to Jo. "My people would be honored to have you represent them in a court of law," he said thickly, his hand reaching out toward her.

When her hand slid into his, her fingers long and lean against his palm, and she gazed up at him, he was taken, heart and soul, by her. He couldn't get enough of looking at her delicate features, or the long lustrousness of her hair, or the bewitching color of her eyes that seemed to touch his very being.

And when she smiled up at him, obviously glad that he had accepted her as his counsel, he felt like a clumsy boy again who was bewildered by the first knowledge of things such as girls and what their sweet smiles could do to his insides!

He was lost to her, *ah-pah-nay*, forevermore.

From the first moment she had seen Wolf, Jo had fought the instant attraction she had for him. He had come to her for business, not socializing.

And she could never allow herself to forget how she must look sitting in her wheelchair. How could any man look past the wheelchair and see her true self?

But no matter how hard Jo tried to concentrate on the business at hand, she could not

help silently admiring Wolf's noble appearance, his handsomeness, and his gentle way of
speaking. He stood tall over her, his long, jet-
black hair flowing down his back past his
waist.

His face was sculpted and his midnight dark
eyes seemed to penetrate clear into her soul.
Her heart thumped wildly when in his eyes
she now saw an appreciation for the woman
before him.

"I'll be so glad to represent your people," Jo
murmured, aware that their hands were still
twined, their eyes still holding.

Self-consciously, she eased her hand away
and looked quickly at Fast Horse, whose eyes
were dancing with understanding. She knew
that he had seen her reaction to Wolf once the
ice had been broken, and also Wolf's to her.

She knew that Fast Horse understood that
he had brought them together for more than a
court case.

If she had her way about it, she and Wolf
would have a long-lasting relationship!

"The name J. T.," Wolf said as Jo rolled herself away from him and went behind her
desk. "Why do you prefer to sometimes be
called J. T.?"

"I felt compelled to use a less feminine
name so that I might be more readily accepted as a lawyer in a world of mostly male
lawyers," Jo said softly, busying her hands by
stacking papers neatly on top of her desk. She
held the papers steady between her hands and
gazed up at Wolf. "Too often it's hard to be

taken seriously as a lawyer once someone discovers that I am of female gender."

"That was my reaction, also," Wolf said, walking slowly toward the desk. "I apologize for that. I was wrong to make assumptions about you." He cast Fast Horse a quick smile. "Fast Horse has never let me down. I should have known that he would not let me down now when life has again turned sour for my Ottawa people."

Fast Horse, his long, black robe billowing around his legs, went and placed a warm hand on Wolf's shoulder. He turned his friend to face him. "Sometimes things are not as clear as they should be," he said softly. "I ought to have explained to you earlier that J. T. is short for Josephine Taylor Stanton. But I never saw it as necessary. I know Jo. I trust her. I believed you would trust her as quickly."

"Today I was wrong about many things, but my mind is clear now," Wolf said, casting Jo a quick apologetic smile.

Again he was reminded of their handshake. At that instant it was as though their hearts had been fused into one. He would never forget the electricity that had come with their touch. He knew it was meant for them to meet. It was their destiny. This was something positive that had come from the white man's threats.

Wolf walked away from Fast Horse and went to stand at the side of the desk, his eyes once again on the wheelchair. He kneaded his

chin as he studied it. Then when he realized
that his regard was making Jo uncomfortable,
he laughed softly.

"I was studying the chair and the ease with
which you are able to get around in it," he
said. "I wonder about my father, who is crippled by a joint ailment. Could a wheelchair
possibly work for him?"

"I'm sure it would," Jo said, her heart hammering against her ribs over his interest in the
chair.

"Where can I find one to take to my father?"
Wolf asked, bending to a knee and gingerly
touching one wheel of the chair.

"I know where you can purchase one just
like mine, but that won't be necessary," Jo
said, her eyes holding his when he gazed at
her. "I have a spare. If you like, I can come to
your reservation tomorrow and bring it to
your father. Your father can use it for as long
as he wishes."

Enjoying the thought of being with her
again, especially away from the stiffness and
official business of her office, Wolf felt his
heart soar. "I appreciate your kindness," he
said softly. "Yes, do come. And if you wish, I
will come and escort you there."

"I need no escorting," she murmured. "I
know my way there well enough. Before the
train wreck, I enjoyed riding my horse and
rode past the reservation many times. I had
wanted to stop and become acquainted with
your people, but was afraid that would be too

forward of me. I was afraid that I might not be welcome."

"You are welcome anytime. Do come whenever and however you like," Wolf was quick to say.

"Thank you," Jo said, feeling almost bashful beneath his steady, warm, wondering gaze. "I shall come by way of horse and buggy.

"But we must get back to work today," she continued, laughing awkwardly as she grabbed a pen and paper. Her first day back was far more than she had expected it to be. It had proved to be quite challenging, and no one loved challenges more than J. T. Stanton!

She cast Fast Horse a slow smile, knowing that she had him to thank for everything that had happened today.

Then she looked at Wolf, confident that she could right the wrongs done his people. "Now, Wolf, let's discuss your case," she said, her confidence evident in her voice. "I want to know everything about it. I want to do everything I can to prepare. I want the court to be stunned by my representation. I want to show Sheriff Gowins and his cohorts a thing or two."

In her mind's eye she saw Max sitting in the courtroom, stunned by her victory for the Ottawa! She smiled at the thought.

"I'm not sure how much you know about my people or why it is that we are still in Michigan when so many are elsewhere," Wolf said. He sat down in front of the desk, and

Fast Horse settled down beside him in another comfortable leather chair. "My band of Ottawa resisted removal to Nebraska and we were allowed to stay in Michigan. The Treaty of 1855 was the last treaty between the white people and the Ottawa, and it guaranteed us the right to hunt, fish, and trap in ceded land."

"But that wasn't a written treaty, was it?" Jo asked. "Fast Horse said that it was only agreed to verbally."

"That is so. Still a verbal agreement is supposed to be as binding as one written in blood," Wolf growled out. "But now the State of Michigan and its sportsmen's organizations interpret the lack of such a written clause in the treaty to mean that the Indians may no longer hunt or fish without obeying state restrictions."

"And those restrictions cover such things as your buying a fishing license, and your people agreeing not to use nets when you fish," Jo said, kneading her chin thoughtfully. "Isn't that right?"

"The Ottawa maintain that even though the government didn't include a written clause concerning hunting and fishing, these rights should be undisputed," Wolf said. "No matter how the treaties were agreed upon, the whites are still fighting to take from the Ottawa what is rightfully ours."

"I'm going to go back many years in the records, and I guarantee you I will find enough written clauses to protect you against those who are wronging you," Jo said softly. "I *will* win this case for you and your people. You can count on it."

"Too often the government used trickery to negotiate treaties in order to acquire more acreage for white homesteaders," Wolf said. "My ancestors at first trusted the white man no matter how many times they were fooled or cheated. My ancestors did not want to believe that the white man only knew how to cheat and take land, that all the white men knew was how to be crooked. But this is now. I know that it will never be any different. The white men will never stop their greediness, not until everything that is rightfully the Ottawas' is taken by whites."

"And that is why there are courts and attorneys who have knowledge enough to speak in your behalf in the courtrooms," Jo said, wheeling herself from behind her desk. She rolled up next to Wolf. "I need time now to study my law books and to go to the court and search their records. But I will take time away from my studies tomorrow and bring the wheelchair to your father."

"*Ki-ki-jew-adis*, you are very kind. Your kindness is appreciated," Wolf said thickly. "Thank you for everything." He rose from the chair and turned to walk away, then turned and gazed down at Jo again. "At first I did not trust that you were the right person to help my people. I was wrong. I trust you. Totally."

"Thank you," Jo murmured, touched by his

honesty and by the way he spoke so gently to her. "I won't let you down."

Wolf nodded at her, smiled, then left the room with Fast Horse. He felt strangely exhilarated by the meeting, and he knew that the feelings within him were not solely because he was confident that Fast Horse had led him to the right attorney. It was the woman. She had touched him on an emotional level.

After mounting Midnight, Wolf gazed over at his friend, who was riding on his own brown steed. "Why is she in the wheelchair?" he asked. "She said something about a train wreck."

Fast Horse told him about the train wreck and about Jo having lost her mother in the accident.

"I have met often with Jo to comfort her in her time of grieving the loss of her mother," Fast Horse said tightly. "The white doctors say there is no true cause for her inability to walk, that it is caused by her emotional pain at the death of her mother. In time, everyone hopes that she will rise from the chair and walk again."

In his mind's eye, Wolf saw her standing tall and straight and walking toward him, her arms outstretched, beckoning him to her.

The thought warmed his heart, yet he knew that his attraction for her was so strong, he cared not that she moved around only by way of a chair.

He saw the woman, the loveliness, the beauty of her smile.

He could still hear the gentle ring of her laughter.

Tomorrow could not come soon enough for him when she would bring her magical chair to his father!

Chapter Six

Feeling eyes on her, Jo maneuvered her horse and buckboard wagon down the middle of the Ottawa village. Tall trees like giant multicolored umbrellas shaded the many log cabins.

All activity around her had ceased as she had made her first entrance into the village.

The children were even holding their dogs, keeping them from running after the stranger with the strange contraption sitting in the wagon.

Keeping her promise to bring the wheelchair to Wolf's ailing father, Jo had asked her own father to place it in the wagon. He had had many words of caution for Jo. Except for Fast Horse, who to Addison was Father Samuel, her father had not had many dealings with Indians.

Cassie Edwards

Jo had explained to her father how kind and gentle she had found Wolf to be. She reminded her father about how close she and he had become with Fast Horse, and that even though he was Chippewa, there were few differences between the Ottawa and Chippewa tribes. They both worked at keeping peace with the white community. Apart from troublemakers like Sheriff Gowins, most settlers wanted peace, too.

Although some white people talked boldly of their dislike for Indians, they had to admit that no one could have been as peaceful as the Ottawa and their neighbors, the Chippewa.

But then there are Max and his cohorts and Sheriff Gowins, she thought angrily. If they had anything to say about it, the Ottawa and Chippewa would have been gone long ago. They are hell-bent on destroying them.

A wave of relief rushed through Jo when she saw Wolf step from one of the two largest cabins in the village. She surmised that the one next to his, which was also large and well kept, was his parents' lodge.

A thought sprang to her mind that hadn't occurred to her until now. Perhaps he lived with someone in his large cabin.

Perhaps children?

Perhaps a wife?

She had failed to ask Fast Horse if Wolf was married, for nothing even akin to that had entered her mind during her meeting with the minister the day before she was introduced to Wolf.

There had been no true reason for her to wonder about his personal life until she had found herself instantly attracted to him. Her fascination with him had kept her awake most of the night while she thought of seeing him again.

The painful realization that he would again see her inability to walk had prompted her to try to walk last night, only to fall to the floor like a limp gunnysack. Her father had come running to her room when he heard her cry out, more with rage than pain. She knew the foolishness of trying to walk when it was obvious that she still couldn't.

But even though she must appear before him in her wheelchair, she had come today to meet with Wolf as planned. If she could help Wolf's father in this small way, by giving him the ability to move around on his own in the wheelchair, the trip would be worthwhile.

She just prayed that she wouldn't see that look of pity in his people's eyes. And she would not look at Wolf's father with pity.

Drawing her horse to a halt in front of Wolf's lodge, Jo felt faint of heart when her eyes met and held those of the Ottawa chief. Never in her life had a man affected her in such a way. When she had agreed to marry Max, it had been a decision born of a friendship that began when they were children. But those young promises of the heart had gone sour when she had been crippled by the train wreck.

If she was honest with herself, their feelings

had gone sour long before that. She had lost respect for Max years before and had been searching for a way to tell him that *she* couldn't marry *him*.

At least the train accident had taken care of that unpleasant chore for her. She was still lying in the hospital bed when Max callously broke it off with her.

"Good morning," Jo said as Wolf took her horse's reins. She realized that her voice sounded different with her heart thumping so hard inside her chest.

She blushed, smiled awkwardly, and cleared her throat as Wolf's eyes spoke volumes to her.

"I am glad that you came," Wolf said, his eyes finally shifting away from her as he glanced at the wheelchair. "*Nee-may-nan-dum-wah-bum-eh-na-wa.*"

When he looked up and saw the confusion in her eyes, he realized that she did not understand his language.

"I said I am glad to see you," he explained, smiling. "And it is good that you brought the wheelchair. I told Father about it."

He didn't go on to say that his father had already refused to accept her chair or use it. It was Wolf's intention to take the wheelchair inside his father's lodge and place it there for him to actually see. He hoped his father would be intrigued by an invention that would transport a person easily from place to place.

He hoped that if his father saw it actually working, his curiosity would be aroused. Wolf hoped that Jo wouldn't mind demonstrating it for his father.

He turned to Jo again. "After I take the chair inside my father's lodge, would you join us?" he asked. "Could you possibly show my father the ease with which you can get from place to place in the chair?"

"I would be happy to," Jo said, smiling at him. "I will have to demonstrate that to him in *this* chair, for I didn't bring my own. I . . . I . . . wasn't sure how long I would be staying."

"You did not think I would invite you to stay for a visit?" Wolf asked, realizing just how awkward she might feel in the presence of his mother and father. "Mother has prepared a sweet drink and small cakes for your visit with us. She does this to show her appreciation of what you are doing for my father."

"I don't need payment for helping someone," Jo murmured, yet she was touched deeply by the kindness of Wolf's mother to go to so much trouble just for her.

She felt less apprehensive about meeting his parents, especially since they already knew that she couldn't walk.

And, of course, his parents wouldn't have any idea that this crippled woman cared deeply for their son.

If they did, she wondered how welcome then she would be at their village . . . in their home?

She reminded herself that she wasn't even sure if Wolf was married, or had children. Jo looked past Wolf at his cabin, then questioned him with her eyes.

Wolf was well aware of the way she had glanced at the cabin and then looked at him in question. Something deep inside told him what she was wondering.

"*Gah-ween*, no, there is no wife or children to join us this morning, to have drinks and cakes with my parents," he was quick to say.

He smiled when he saw relief rush into Jo's deliciously blue eyes. How sweetly she smiled to know that he was quite available for the right woman.

Jo was at a loss as to what to say to him. She realized that he had somehow read her thoughts and responded to questions she had not spoken aloud.

"I will take the chair inside my parents' lodge and then return for you," Wolf said.

"Thank you," Jo replied, sighing contentedly as she took a deep breath and allowed herself to relax and enjoy these moments of awakening love between her and Wolf.

She thanked the good Lord above that Wolf didn't see her as less of a woman because of her disability.

At this moment she felt *all* woman. The wondrous desire she felt for this man was something she had never experienced before.

She felt her heart begin to pound just to look at him. And when he smiled at her, her insides melted.

When Wolf came back out of the cabin, he

was no longer smiling. He was moody, even brooding, as he stopped beside the wagon.

"What's wrong?" she dared to ask.

She was afraid that she knew the answer. Surely his father was unhappy about the wheelchair.

If so, would Wolf's father also be unhappy about her being there?

"My father does not welcome the chair in his lodge," Wolf said apologetically.

"When you first told him about it, did he react against it then?" Jo asked softly.

"*Ae*, but I thought that when he saw the usefulness of it, he would change his mind," Wolf said, heaving a deep sigh.

"But you see, Wolf, he hasn't yet actually *seen* its usefulness," Jo said softly. "He has only seen the *chair*, not me in it, moving easily from place to place. Take me inside. I will show him. Surely he will change his mind."

"He is a man of great pride," Wolf said, gently lifting Jo from the seat. He drew her close in his arms. He gazed down at her. "He has resented having to be carried everywhere. But now I am afraid his pride goes farther than that. If he sees the chair as something made solely for white people's use, he will never use it."

"The chair was made for anyone who has need of it," Jo said. "The skin color or race doesn't matter." She twined an arm around Wolf's neck, in heaven being this close to him. She could feel his heartbeat against her body.

She could smell the manliness of his flesh. She savored how his breath warmed her face as he leaned down closer to shift her to a more comfortable position in his arms.

Having Jo so close, her breasts only inches away from his hands as he held her tenderly against his chest, and hearing the sweetness of her voice, Wolf felt as though his knees might buckle with the wonder of the moment. No woman had ever stirred such feelings inside him. He had never wanted or *needed* a woman as he needed her.

And he would protect her from his father's reaction to her kind offer of her wheelchair. His father had two ways of reacting when he was disturbed by something.

Silence was one way.

Speaking loudly against whatever bothered him was the other.

Wolf hoped that his father chose the silent way today.

And surely he would, especially after he saw the utter sweetness and gentleness of the woman who was there to offer him help.

When an Indian woman came from the lodge wearing a buckskin skirt, blouse, and moccasins, her black hair tied in a knot behind her head, Jo knew that she was in the presence of Wolf's mother.

Wolf carried Jo to Blue Moth and stopped. "*Gee-mah-mah*, Mother, this is Jo, the woman who so kindly brought the chair for Father, and who has agreed to represent our people in the issue of fishing rights," he said.

He was so glad when his mother's eyes didn't shift downward to Jo's legs. He didn't want Jo to have any reason to feel uneasy in the presence of his gentle, beloved mother.

"It is good to greet the woman whose heart is kind toward the Ottawa," Blue Moth said softly. She gestured toward the open door. "Come inside. Have refreshments with us."

"Thank you, I'd be delighted," Jo murmured. She was still held so close to Wolf's body that she could feel the hammering of his heart.

After she was inside and settled in a wooden rocking chair close to the fireplace, where a warm fire wrapped its flames slowly around a stack of logs on the grate, Jo's gaze went immediately to Wolf's father. He appeared much older than Blue Moth, and he had chosen to sit on a cushion of pelts on the floor before the fire instead of in a chair.

Jo tried not to take it personally when he didn't cast her even one glance. He kept his back to her, his old eyes on the fire, watching, his bony hands clutching a blanket around his frail shoulders.

"*Gee-bah-bah*, Father, we have a visitor," Wolf said as he sat down in a chair beside Jo.

When his father still acted as though he wasn't aware of anyone's presence, Jo gave Wolf a quick, questioning glance.

Wolf looked apologetically at Jo. "My father, Sleeping Bear, is stubborn sometimes when he should not be," he said. "In time he will soften in his mood. You will then know the gentle man who is my father."

Blue Moth brought in a wooden tray on which were stacks of cakes cut into squares, and wooden cups filled with some sort of red liquid, with steam spiraling from it.

"Strawberry tea," Blue Moth said as she caught Jo studying the drink while Wolf placed it in her hands. "I dry fruits and have them for use the year round. The tea was made from this year's strawberries."

"Thank you," Jo murmured, smiling at Blue Moth as she placed a small wooden dish with a piece of cake on it on Jo's lap.

"This, too, was made from strawberries," Blue Moth said, then gave Wolf a cup of tea and a saucer of cake.

"It all looks and smells so delicious," Jo murmured. She gave Wolf's father a slow gaze. She wasn't surprised when he shrugged off his wife's offer of refreshment. Jo could tell that he was being stubborn on purpose and she wanted to believe that the wheelchair, not her presence was the cause.

She ate the cake with her fingers and drank the tea along with Wolf and Blue Moth, and then set her empty cup and saucer on a table beside her.

Again she looked over at Wolf's father. "Sleeping Bear, please allow me to show you how handy the wheelchair can be to someone like you . . . and . . . me," she murmured. "Please watch me wheel myself around inside your cabin after Wolf places me in the chair. Surely you will want to use it so that you can do things for yourself that you now cannot do."

When he still stared at the fire, not showing any sign of having heard Jo, she looked with uncertain eyes at Wolf. "Should I do it?" she whispered.

Blue Moth rose from her chair and went for the wheelchair. Her jaw tight, her eyes determined, she wheeled the chair over to Jo. "My husband must see to know," she said. "Please demonstrate its use. Even if he is not looking directly at you in the chair, he will see your activity in it out of the corner of his eye."

Jo nodded and slid from the wooden chair over onto the wheelchair.

As Wolf and Blue Moth stood back and watched, glancing often at Sleeping Bear to see his reaction, Jo maneuvered the chair easily around the room.

When Jo realized that Sleeping Bear wasn't going to budge or look her way, she knew that it must be his pride that was causing him to refuse to even consider using the chair.

Stung by Sleeping Bear's adamant rejection of the wheelchair, Jo couldn't prevent her hurt from showing as she looked at Wolf.

Seeing her hurt, Wolf bent low and gently swept Jo from the chair.

Without glancing again at his father, and only nodding a silent goodbye to his mother, Wolf carried Jo outside to her wagon.

"I will go for the wheelchair," he said, turning on his heel and walking back toward the house.

"No, don't," Jo said, her words stopping him in mid-step.

He turned and gave her a questioning look.

"Leave the chair with your father," she suggested. "Perhaps he'll change his mind and use it later. He might practice using it when no one is there to watch him."

"*Ae*, perhaps," Wolf said, sighing heavily. He went back to the wagon. "Can you stay awhile longer? We can go to my cabin. We can talk."

The mere thought of their being alone together sent waves of rapture through Jo. "I'd love to," she murmured. "But only for a short while. I need to get back to the office." She smiled. "I've a special case to prepare for."

"My people's?" Wolf asked, raising an eyebrow.

"Yes, your people's," Jo said, again twining her arm around his neck when he lifted her from the seat.

Wolf carried her inside his lodge and seated her gently on a soft pallet of furs close to the fireplace. While she waited for him to add more logs to the fire, Jo looked around at how he lived. It was a masculine place devoid of anything that a woman might put in a cabin. There were pelts hung along the walls, a cache of weapons leaning against another wall, and bags stored beneath a bed made of logs, with blankets and thick pelts spread over what appeared to be willow branches stretched over the top of the bed.

There were no visible cooking utensils. Probably someone cooked for Wolf and brought him food.

The cabin was spotlessly clean, the wooden

floors mopped and swept, and Jo guessed that someone also took care of those chores for him.

The thought of a woman coming and being so intimate with Wolf's things caused Jo a stab of jealousy.

But this was quickly forgotten when Wolf sat down beside her on the pelts and they talked and talked as though they had known each other forever.

Just as Wolf reached over to draw Jo into his embrace to kiss her, his mother came into his lodge carrying a huge tray of cooked meats and sliced fruits.

"The cakes were not enough nourishment," Blue Moth said, setting the tray on the pelts between Jo and Wolf.

"Why, thank you," Jo said, touched deeply by the continued kindness of this woman. "Please stay and join us?"

"*Gah-ween*, no, not this time. My husband awaits my return," Blue Moth said, brushing a soft kiss on her son's brow.

Blue Moth stopped long enough to give Jo a gentle, affectionate touch on the cheek, then left.

"She is so sweet and kind," Jo said, not even surprised at the woman's gesture of affection. She was a woman of great gentleness and kindness.

Truly not hungry after having eaten the cake and drinking the sweet tea, Jo eyed the food somewhat wearily.

"You do not look any hungrier than I am,"

Wolf said, the thought of food the last thing on his mind.

"No, I don't think I could eat a bite," Jo murmured, suddenly feeling awkward, so very aware of the sexual tension between them.

"Then I insist that you take the food home and share it with your father," Wolf said, pushing himself up to go and get a wicker basket.

Jo watched him place the food in the basket. Then her breath was stolen away as he put the basket aside and knelt before her. His hands framed her face as he lowered his mouth to hers and gave her a soft, yet deep kiss.

When he leaned away from her, their eyes locked, their hearts pounded. He held her hands and smiled at her. "I have wanted to do that since the moment I allowed myself to see you, *truly* see you, that first time," he murmured.

"When you realized that the wheelchair made no difference to you where I was concerned?" Jo murmured, breathless from the kiss.

"*Ae*, yes, then," Wolf said, his eyes reaching deeply into Jo's soul for understanding.

"I'm so glad that you could," she said, flinging herself into his arms, reveling in his closeness.

But then she pulled away from him. "I think I'd best leave now, don't you?" she said, afraid that things might go farther. To herself she admitted that she was afraid her body might not cooperate.

Although she was filled with many sensual feelings, she was afraid that they were only on the surface. Would her body allow her to feel the actual act of lovemaking?

Or was that part of her dead, also, leaving her incapable of being with a man in such a way?

"Will you come again?" Wolf asked huskily. "Or better yet, let us go horseback riding."

Jo lowered her eyes. "I . . . haven't . . . been on a horse since the accident," she murmured. "Since my legs are dead, I don't think—"

"I do not mean that you should ride alone on a horse," Wolf said, interrupting her. "I will carry you on my lap."

She looked quickly up at him. "You would do that for me?" she murmured, loving him more dearly as each moment passed.

"I believe you need to do more than just sit in that chair," Wolf said thickly. "I am here to see that you do."

She twined her arms around his neck and drew his lips to hers.

Her heart sang as he kissed her again, his hands straying to her breasts, cupping them.

She sighed at the exquisiteness of the moment. Never before had a man touched her there. The sensation was sheer heaven.

But afraid that things could get quickly out of hand, and that she might discover she could never be a whole woman again, she eased herself away from him.

"I truly must leave," she said, her pulse racing, her face hot with a blush.

Wolf's own pulse had gone wild. His loins were on fire as never before in his life. His need of this woman was an ache inside him. "Yes, I know," he said, his voice drawn.

He handed her the basket of food, then swept her into his arms.

As their eyes held as though in a trance, he carried her out to the wagon.

"I hate to see you go," he said as he placed her on the seat. "Are you certain you must?"

"Yes, I truly have to go," Jo murmured, inhaling a quivering, deep breath.

She placed the basket on the seat next to her, grabbed the reins and snapped them against her horse, then smiled over her shoulder at Wolf as she rode off in her wagon.

"I shall see you soon," she said, then looked away from him least she change her mind and go back and stay with him forever!

Chapter Seven

Roy Bates was stacking wood away from the large piles of lumber at Max Schmidt's lumber company on the outskirts of Lone Branch. His eyes gleamed as he struck a match and threw it into the wood. As the fire caught hold, reflecting the lenses of his glasses, his pulse raced and his loins grew hot. As the fire burst into bright, wild flames, Roy's body shuddered with gratification.

Max was drawn to the window of his office when he saw a burst of flames outside. Panic seized him, for he knew that if the fire got out of hand, his entire business could go up in flames.

"Damn that Roy Bates," he snarled as he ran from his office. He almost tripped down the outside steps as he took them two at a time. "Why do I put up with him?"

But he knew the answer to that question. Roy Bates was useful to him in many ways. He was not only his personal attorney, he did other little jobs for Max that no one else would do.

"Grab buckets of water!" Max shouted at his lumberjacks who were just bringing in a wagon of lumber. "Damn Roy. He's started another fire! And this time it's on my premises, not someone else's."

A bucket brigade was formed and soon the fire was out.

Max searched for Roy, who had gone into hiding among the thick forest of trees at the far side of Max's lumber camp.

"Damn you to hell, Roy," Max shouted when he found his attorney and grabbed the squat little man by his arms and shook him. "Don't you know you could have put me outta business by setting that damn fire? If you've got to set fires, do it elsewhere. Do it where it profits not only your twisted desires, but also me. Put your obsession to use where it will do us some good."

Roy's thin lips twisted into a sneer. "Sure, Max," he said. "Sure. Whatever you say, Max. You pay me well. I'm here to please."

"You sure as hell have a funny-ass way of showin' it," Max said. He gave Roy a shove, forcing him to walk ahead of him. "You're sick, Roy. Sick, sick, sick!"

"I get my kicks my way, you get your kicks *yours*," Roy said, shrugging.

Chapter Eight

It was as though Jo were floating in a mid-summer's dream as Wolf cradled her on his lap while they rode his black stallion across a wide meadow dotted with autumn flowers.

He had surprised her by coming for her early in the afternoon, just when her eyes were feeling tired from poring over law books since dawn.

But if she hadn't already found the answers she needed to win her case for the Ottawa, she wouldn't have let Wolf take her away from her studies, no matter how tired her eyes were. She had much to prove to many people, perhaps herself most of all. She had stayed away from her practice for so long, she had begun to wonder if her reasons for doing so were valid, or if she had just lost interest in law.

Luckily Wolf had arrived in her life just in time for her to find her way back to the living again. Certainly, she could never feel more alive than she felt now. She couldn't believe this man's gentleness toward her . . . his understanding about her being disabled.

How she was enjoying the feel of the wind in her hair, the warmth of the afternoon sun against cheeks that had grown too pale from hiding indoors.

And while she was with Wolf, the pleasure of being on a horse and being outdoors was doubled. Even though she had only just met this man, she was in love with him.

But no matter how attentive he was toward her, she could not help fearing that he might not be able to love her as much as if she had the use of her legs. She took what he gave her, thankful for it, but prayed that the day would come when she could go to him as a whole woman again.

His arm felt so wonderful about her waist, his breath warm on her cheek when she turned sideways to glance up at him! Jo relished these moments, wishing they would never end.

And her fascination with this man had only increased, for today she was seeing yet another side of his character. When they had stopped to rest, or to get a drink from a stream, she had noticed with awe how the woodland creatures came up to him as though they had been tamed by his gentle hand.

Even the ugly buzzards sweeping and soaring overhead seemed to be his special friends.

When she had asked Wolf about this, he had explained that his grandfather had been a mystical man, a shaman. He had introduced Wolf to the animals and birds. None were afraid of him.

Wolf had told her that because of his mystical connection with the animals and birds, the hunt for food was hard for him. He feared that when he downed an animal, he was slaying a friend. Because of this, he always offered prayers and apologies over the animals that sustained his people.

Jo's thoughts were interrupted and she was momentarily distracted when for a moment she thought she had seen a flash of white in the shadows of the forest. It looked like several wolves rushing from place to place.

"Wolf, did you see them?" Jo cried, pointing where she had seen the flashes of white. "I truly believe white wolves are there in the forest. It is as though they are keeping up with us. Wolf, did you . . . did you . . . see them?"

"No, I did not see anything," Wolf said, hating having to lie, for he *had* seen his friends bounding along in the forest's shadows.

He hated not sharing his wolf friends with Jo, yet felt he must wait until he knew more about how she felt about animals. He truly believed that someone as gentle as she would love his animal friends as much as he.

Ae, in time he would tell her. When he felt

87

the time was right he would tell her everything about himself, as he hoped she would share her life's story with him.

He hoped to bring sunshine into that part of her life that had been struck by tragedy.

He rode onward through the Ottawa heart- land. The land was part of an old coastal plain that was covered with dark clay loam in the south and light sandy loam in the north, and drained by thirty primary river systems into Lake Michigan and Lake Huron.

Wolf steered his horse to the right and soon saw the spectacular shoreline of Lake Michi- gan ahead of them. Soon he was riding with Jo beside the mystical lake, where there were great sand dunes and beaches.

When he heard Jo sigh and felt her shifting her weight on his lap, he glanced at her. He wasn't sure if she had sighed because she was enjoying the sights, or because she was tired.

Just to be sure not to overtire her, he drew a tight rein and stopped, then slid her from his lap onto the saddle, and dismounted.

"We shall rest awhile here," he said, reach- ing up and placing his hands at her waist. Gently he took her from Midnight, reveling in how she always twined her arm around his neck so trustingly . . . so sweetly.

"It is so beautiful here," Jo murmured as he placed her in the shade of a multicolored sandstone cliff. "This is where I often gathered seashells with my mother."

For Jo, the mention of her mother took away the magic of the moment. It reminded her of the tragedy she was trying so hard to put in her past.

But until she walked again and quit dreaming of the train wreck over and over again at night, battling it as if it were some dark monster consuming her, she knew that tragedy would cling to her like an ugly leech.

"I have spent much time on this lake with my father fishing for whitefish, alewife, catfish, and perch," Wolf said. "One day I would like to take you in my canoe and show you my skill at bringing fish from the water."

"I'd love that," Jo said, smiling, again captivated by his presence and pushing aside thoughts that ruined the moment. "As a child I fished often with my father."

She laughed softly. "I am an only child, so of course father taught me things he would have taught a son," she said. "My parents named me Josephine, but my father called me by the more boyish name Jo."

"You are anything but a boy," Wolf said, chuckling as he gave her one of his long, appreciative gazes. "Of that *I* am glad."

Jo felt herself blush, a rarity for her. But while she was with Wolf, so much about herself was foreign and strange to her. Especially emotions that made her feel peculiarly giddy, yet deliciously sweet.

She felt they were dangerously close to kissing again. Afraid of where kisses might eventually take them, she hurried to talk about something far removed from intimate subjects.

"You said earlier that your grandfather was a shaman," she said, smiling a thank you to him when he took a blanket from his saddle and gently spread it around her shoulders to ward off the damp, cool breeze that wafted in from the lake. "Please tell me something about your religion. I've always been intrigued by things I have heard about your . . . *Manitou* I believe it is called?"

Wolf settled more comfortably on the sandy shore beside her. He leaned back and rested one elbow on the sand, then stretched a leg out before him as he drew the other one comfortably up before him. His free hand began sifting sand through his fingers.

"My people are firm believers in our *Manitou*," he said. "All the good things my people attribute to the *Gitchi Manitou*, which is known as the Great Spirit, and the bad things to *Motchi Manitou*, known as the Bad Spirit. Every animal and bird-being in the Ottawa world possesses an unseen power, or *Manitou*, which is separate from its physical form. Life depends on a proper relationship with all the powers of the natural environment. Every being is treated as though it is a member of our families. My people even address the more important animals as 'mother,' 'father,' 'brother,' or 'sister.' "

"It all sounds so beautiful and spiritual," Jo murmured.

"Daily life holds many dangers, and every Ottawa, beginning in childhood, needs a *Man-*

itou who will be a special personal protector to lend its power to help control certain forces of nature," Wolf continued. "All Ottawa children of the proper age observe a special ceremony of fasting and prayer. His or her *Manitou* then appears in a vision in the form of an animal or bird. From then on the *Manitou* can be summoned to give extra strength in times of trouble."

"Your name, Wolf. Was that given to you after your time of fasting and vision quest?" Jo asked, again thinking about what she had thought were white wolves running through the forest close to where she and Wolf had been riding. She could not help feeling there was some connection between those wolves and Wolf, yet he had denied seeing them, so surely she was wrong.

Wolf's throat tightened, for he was getting dangerously close to wanting to tell her everything about his time with the wolves and how they still came to him, as brothers.

But that must be said later, when he was sure she deserved to know such a private thing about himself that he had shared with no one but his mother and father.

"Yes, I earned the name Wolf and carry it with me proudly," he said. Then when he saw her shiver, he scooted nearer to her, swept an arm around her shoulders, and drew her close.

His heart beat like a thousand drums within his chest when her eyes moved up and she gazed intensely into his. He recognized sexual hunger when he saw it, and his own hunger, which had not been fed for so long, caused his lips to go to hers, trembling and hot.

Taken heart and soul by the kiss, Jo slid her arms around Wolf's neck and pressed her breasts against his chest. The mere touching of their bodies sent a spiraling pleasure through her. She heard someone moaning and soon realized that it was herself as Wolf inched a hand up beneath her travel skirt.

Legs that she had thought were totally dead came alive beneath the warmth of his fingers as he moved them slowly upward.

And the place that she thought might never come alive beneath a man's touch tingled with pleasure as Wolf's fingers crept up into her undergarment and soon swept over the blond patch of hair that covered her throbbing woman's center.

Jo's face became hot with an anxious blush and her breath came in short rasps as he stroked her and brought her more alive with each touch.

She tried to move her legs, to open herself more fully to his fingers, but soon found that, although there had been feeling there moments ago, her legs were still like dead weights and wouldn't budge.

Sensing what she wished to do, Wolf drew his mouth from hers and turned so that he could ease her down on her back on the sand. Then as he gazed with passion-hot eyes at her, he slowly drew her legs apart and lifted her skirt up to her waist.

"This is the first time for me," Jo whispered, almost swallowed whole by her want.

His hand cupped over her, he felt her heat and her wetness against his palm. That confirmation of her readiness made it hard for Wolf to stop now that he had gotten so close to having her.

But her words "This is the first time for me," and her looking at him so innocently through her thick veil of lashes made him realize that this wasn't right. His need, his *hunger*, had to wait, for he did not want Jo to think that this was the only reason he had taken her for a ride today . . . to take advantage of a woman who did not have the ability to walk away from the situation should she desire to.

No, he would not make love with her today. He wanted their relationship to be one of restraint and slowly escalating passion born of innocent kisses and touching. Their passion would be all the sweeter if they went through the tantalizing preliminaries and foreplay.

"I must return to my duties at the village," Wolf said, unable to think of any other excuse that might seem valid to her. He slid his hand away from her. "Lovemaking should not be something rushed into. There is a time. There is a place."

Stunned that Wolf had decided not to make love after getting her so emotionally ready, Jo did not know how to respond. Was it her inability to move her legs that had caused him to draw away from her so abruptly?

Oh, Lord, she despaired, his rejection was almost as blunt and ugly as Max coming to her in the hospital room and telling her that he couldn't marry her.

It was like living the shame and degradation all over again.

But there was no way she would allow this man to know how she felt. Her pride was too strong to allow her to do what she wanted to do . . . shout at him that he was a heartless coward!

"I understand," Jo murmured, pulling her skirt back down over her lifeless legs as he rolled away from her, then sat up beside her. At least two wonderful things had been proven to her . . . she *did* have *some* feelings in her legs and she *could* make love like a normal person. She still throbbed sensually where his fingers had kneaded her.

Jo slowly sat up as Wolf stared out at the water, seemingly in another world, and most certainly one that did not include her. She could hardly wait to return home and be away from such embarrassing moments as this.

And never would she be so willing with a man again. She had learned in the cruelest of ways not to allow any man such liberties.

"I need to get back to my studies," Jo said, handing him the blanket that had fallen from her shoulders.

Yes, she would still fight his battle in the

courtroom. She was not the sort to go back on her word, even though she felt that in a sense he had betrayed her.

But had he gotten involved with her only to make sure that she would do the job for him and his people?

If so, he had gone about it in the wrong way.

She fought to keep her voice steady, pretending that nothing was wrong. Her anger at him might even *help* her tomorrow. When she appeared in the courtroom, her temper would be fueled by thinking of today and the humility of it. She would be her old self when she fought for the rights of those who were being mistreated.

Yes, tomorrow she would prove many things to this man. No matter how foolish and unwanted he had made her feel today, she would be more the woman tomorrow!

Wolf gently lifted Jo into his arms.

When their eyes met and held he winced, for he saw something there that didn't seem right. It was certainly not the way she usually looked at him.

Jo sensed that he could read her feelings in her eyes and forced herself to smile and look down, for she didn't want him to know how deeply he had hurt her.

At least not now.

Tomorrow?

Yes, tomorrow she would show him just how cold she could be toward him, but only after she had won his case for him and made him feel humble in her presence.

"The air has become so cold," she murmured. "And it's blowing sand in my eyes."

"I'll get you away from here quickly," Wolf said, relieved that what he had seen in her eyes was only caused by the sand stinging them. For a moment he had felt a coldness.

But now there was her usual sweet smile, the twine of her arm as she clung to him while he carried her toward the horse. It had been hard to stop short of making love with her. He wanted her more than ever now. He could not help envisioning how it would be to finally have her!

Jo sat on his lap as he rode away from the lake. She tried hard, but she couldn't get that moment of rejection from her mind. She felt empty, dejected, and sad, yet she did have tomorrow to help erase the hurt. Tomorrow at the court hearing she would show this man exactly what she was made of!

She would give her all for this man who could not give his all to her. She would prove to him that she was a stronger person than he.

Chapter Nine

Jo was proud of how well she was being received by Judge Smyser, who had listened intently to every word she said. For the moment forgetting that she was in a wheelchair, Jo summed up her argument for the Ottawa's right to fish freely in the Grand River.

She was aware of how quiet the courtroom was, even though it was packed full of both Indian people and whites. She knew that for the most part the white people came only because they were curious about a white woman, one in a wheelchair at that, who was going against the system to defend Indians.

She had spoken up in behalf of Indians before, mainly the Chippewa, but never had she actually argued a case before a judge and a crowd of curious onlookers.

97

As she continued to speak, she was keenly aware that one pair of eyes in particular were watching her.

Wolf's.

He had hardly taken his eyes off her since he had arrived with his family and friends to see Jo speak up in their behalf, to fight for the rights that had been theirs since the beginning of time.

Jo would not allow herself to be unnerved by Wolf's presence. Whenever she started to recall that instant when he had drawn away from her in the throes of passion, she would blink her eyes and the thoughts would be gone. It was as though a hypnotist had ordered her that whenever she blinked her eyes she would forget Wolf and her feelings for him.

When she had seen Wolf for the first time today, he had smiled and nodded at her. For that brief moment she had become a prisoner of his magnetism again.

Then she had pulled herself together and turned her back to him, but not before she saw a quick questioning in his eyes. She hoped that her cold behavior toward him would make him aware of how he had hurt and humiliated her.

There were other eyes on her as well. Max's.

She had only moments ago discovered him sitting at the back of the courtroom glaring at her. His being there proved that he was a part of the conspiracy against the Ottawa.

Yes, in time, even though she no longer had

good feelings for Wolf, she might find herself fighting for the Ottawa's rights where their lumber was concerned. She would get much delight in discrediting Maximilian Schmidt.

Jo felt other eyes on her and grew warm and mellow inside as she glanced at her father. She could see his pride in her as he sat so square-shouldered and smiling.

She was proud of herself and now wished that she hadn't waited so long to return to work. Now that she was in court, arguing the Ottawa's case, she was alive again inside. Never again would she allow herself to wallow in self-pity, not even over having been made a fool of by the handsome Ottawa chief.

"I have offered proof according to the laws of the United States that the Ottawa should retain legal ownership of the fishing rights in the Grand River, and that they should be able to fish for rainbow trout, or whatever other fish they catch, in whatever way they wish to fish, be it with nets, spears, or hooks," Jo said, her voice filled with determination. "Judge, I have cited a body of treaty law that proves the Ottawa's rights. My clients, the Ottawa, were tricked by the white government when the government told them that no signatures were required on many of the fishing right treaties, that a verbal agreement between the government and the Ottawa was binding enough. Verbally the Ottawa were given the rights to all of the Grand River's fish. Sheriff Gowins has wrongfully taken it upon himself to go into the Ottawa village and make demands of these proud people. Sheriff Gowins and his men wrongfully seized the fish that the warriors took from the Grand River."

She turned her wheelchair and smiled smugly at Sheriff Gowins, who sat in the front row of the courtroom, one hand slowly rubbing his badge as though it might be a way to remind Jo of the power that came with being a lawman.

She knew that most people might crumple beneath such a threat, for everyone knew that Sheriff Gowins was devious and heartless.

But she didn't budge.

She wheeled her chair around and again faced the judge.

"Judge Smyser, as I see it, the Ottawa should never be required to have a fishing license to fish in the waters of their ancestors. There should never be another dispute about this matter brought into your courtroom, Judge Smyser. It is a waste of your time, as it is mine and the Ottawa people's. Also, there should be no fine paid."

She wheeled herself to one side and watched as Roy Bates, the attorney who represented Sheriff Gowins as well as the United States government, took his place before the podium. She smiled as the weasel tried to discredit what she had said, but in the end he only proved that her arguments were the more valid.

When it was all said and done, she would win the Ottawa a victory. She was saddened, though, by the fact that she had lost an important personal battle. Surely Wolf couldn't find it within himself to love a woman who was crippled.

Her thoughts were brought quickly back to the present when Judge Smyser slammed down his gavel so hard that it rattled the panes of the windows behind him.

There was a hush in the courtroom as the judge spoke his mind, saying that Jo had made it clear who was in the wrong here. He ruled in favor of the Ottawa and then dismissed the case, slammed down his gavel again, and left the courtroom.

"Hurrahs" filled the courtroom as the Ottawa showed their happiness over the outcome of the quick, but effective trial. They came and crowded around Jo and her wheelchair.

As she wished them luck in the future, some hugged her as they thanked her.

Others shook her hand.

But when one hand in particular reached out and took hers, his fingers intertwining with hers, Jo's breath caught in her throat. She gazed at Wolf as he dropped to his haunches before her and gazed into her eyes.

"My people thank you," he said thickly. "I thank you. Because of you, my people are free to fish again."

Wolf paused and looked deeply into Jo's eyes, then said, "Jo, tell me what is wrong . . ."

His words were stilled when someone stepped up beside him.

Slowly Wolf rose to his full height and, his jaw tight, turned and stared back at Max Schmidt.

Jo wheeled her chair back from both men, her eyes filled with loathing when Max turned to her and gave her a mock salute.

"Good job, J. T.," Max said sarcastically. He glanced down at her lifeless legs, then smirked. "I see that being crippled has its advantages. It got the judge's sympathy so much, he leaned in your savage friends' favor. Were you standing on your two feet like a normal person who practices law, you wouldn't have had a chance in hell of winning today."

One glance at Jo's face told Wolf how the man's words had hurt her. Seeing red, Wolf doubled up a fist and smacked it into Max's jaw, knocking him to the floor.

Jo was stunned by Wolf coming to her rescue in such a way. It was then that she knew she had surely misread what he had said to her on the shores of Lake Michigan. He had even then, in a sense, defended her, though in a much different way from today. He had not wanted her to rush into lovemaking when she might later regret having done so.

She couldn't understand why she hadn't realized that earlier!

The hurt, that was why. She had been too hurt to think logically about why Wolf had turned away from her when he did.

"You sonofabitch," Max growled, drawing a gasp from Jo. He had directly insulted Wolf's mother.

102

Jo looked quickly around the courtroom and found Blue Moth sitting beside her husband in the front row. It was obvious that Blue Moth hadn't heard herself being referred to in such a vulgar way.

Jo's gaze was brought back to Wolf when he reached down and grabbed Max by the shirt collar and brought him back to his feet.

"Get out of here," Wolf growled. "And you had best be more careful of who you insult in the future, be it my mother, or my woman."

"The 'educated beast' speaks not only with his fist, but with his tongue," Max said, still rubbing his jaw. He flinched when Wolf doubled up a fist and waved it before his face again.

Educated beast? Jo thought, paling at the mockery in Max's voice as he referred to Wolf in such a despicable manner.

She felt so much for Wolf at this moment that all her own anger and hurt were forgotten.

She started to reach out for him, but lurched in her wheelchair as she was suddenly wheeled out of the courtroom by her father.

"I'm going to get you home," Addison said, pushing her outside. He determinedly headed for their horse and wagon. "You've had enough for one day. I'm afraid of what the strain might do to you. And, Lord, I'm glad to get out of that courtroom. It had become nothing but a circus."

Having been whisked away from Wolf so quickly by her father, Jo was at a loss for words. It was at this moment that she realized just how helpless she was. If someone decided to take control of her wheelchair, he could take her anywhere. She looked over her shoulder and up at her father.

"Father, I wasn't ready to leave yet," she said, her voice drawn. "I . . . I . . . had something to say to Wolf."

"Daughter, I think enough has been said today," Addison said, stopping just beside the wagon. He stepped around in front of the wheelchair and knelt down before Jo. "Daughter, I saw what happened in there. Yes, you made a powerful case for the Ottawa and won it. But what came afterward was uncalled for. You shouldn't have been put in the position of witnessing such a thing as a fistfight between two men. That is something a lady should never have to witness."

"Father, Wolf *had* to hit Max," Jo argued. "Damn it, Father, had I been able to get out of this wheelchair, *I* would have clobbered Max myself, for insulting me and then Wolf. He even insulted Wolf's mother."

"See? That's what I mean," Addison said, sighing. "Just listen to yourself. What you are saying is not the way a lady should talk."

"Well, just maybe I'm not feeling much like a lady right now," Jo said, her voice breaking. "How can I when I am confined to this . . . this . . . damn contraption."

"I'm taking you home, Jo," Addison said, gently lifting her from the wheelchair. He set her on the seat of the wagon, then placed her wheelchair in the back.

"Now, young lady, I have something more to say to you," Addison said, settling down on the seat beside her. He lifted the reins and flicked them, sending the horse in a brisk trot down the center of the street.

"What else, Father?" Jo said. She looked over her shoulder to see if she could see Wolf as he stepped out of the courthouse, but was disappointed.

Only half listening to what her father was saying, Jo turned her eyes straight ahead. Her heart was being left behind, with Wolf.

"Young lady, I don't think you should enter a courtroom again, even though I am very proud of your triumph there today," Addison said, his voice tight. "You aren't strong enough—"

Jo interrupted him. "Father, I am strong enough to do anything I wish. And nothing will keep me from what I feel is my salvation. My law practice means everything to me. It is the very center of my being."

But deep down, where her desires were formed, she knew that there was something else, some*one*, who was equally important to her.

Wolf.

How could she have ever thought she didn't love him?

The very thought of him made her insides melt.

Chapter Ten

His father in his arms, Wolf stepped from the courthouse and stopped long enough to look down Main Street. He was just in time to see Jo's father taking her away from the courthouse by way of horse and buggy. Wolf had felt the strain between himself and Jo today. He vowed to find out what was bothering the woman he loved. He had to know what was wrong to be able to make things right between them.

Today he had been more impressed by her than ever before. He was so proud that she did not let her affliction stand in the way of her pursuing the things she felt a passion for. He knew of afflictions. Before his father had become crippled with the joint disease, Wolf's grandfather had been downed by it.

Wolf knew that being crippled did not have to stand in the way of someone's deepest feelings and dreams. One of the reasons he loved Jo so much was because of her courage to face the public, despite the fact that her legs refused to work.

He carried his father to his wagon and gently placed him on the seat, then helped his mother up next to him.

In Wolf's mind's eye, he was remembering the ease with which Jo had gotten around in her wheelchair today.

He hoped that in time his father would understand how much easier it would be for him to get around using the same type of chair.

He wished that his grandfather had had the same opportunity.

Wolf climbed onto the wagon and snapped his reins. Their smiles broad with triumph, the Ottawa followed behind him in their wagons and on their horses.

But Wolf could not keep his mind from moving to Jo. Tomorrow he would truly thank her for all she had done. He could hardly wait to be with her again, but this time away from a courtroom and people. He would not take no for an answer when he asked her to go riding with him again!

Chapter Eleven

Still feeling proud over her victory the day before, Jo wheeled herself over to the wooden file cabinet in her small Lone Branch office, which she used when she did not want to travel into Detroit.

Smiling, she thumbed through her file folders and slid one in place among those labeled with the capital "O." In it were the papers she had used in the courtroom yesterday.

When she heard the creak of the door behind her, she stiffened. She knew the rage that many felt over her having won the case for the Ottawa. She now realized that she should have not left herself so accessible to those who held a grudge against her. She should have locked the door.

Wheeling herself quickly around to see who

the intruder was, Jo caught her breath. It was Wolf, his dark eyes silently questioning her.

Yesterday, when her father had whisked her away in her wheelchair, it seemed that Wolf was about to make things right between them. She had even expected Wolf to follow her home and talk things over with her there.

The fact that he hadn't done so made her think that she might have misconstrued his feelings for her again.

And now, as he silently gazed at her, Jo was tongue-tied. She wasn't sure how to approach him, whether or not he had come merely to thank her again for her performance yesterday, or for the reason she prayed for.

She loved him so much.

"Why are you here?" Jo blurted out, sitting stiffly in her wheelchair, her hands tightly gripping the wheels.

Now that the ice had been broken between them, Wolf walked into the room and closed the door behind him.

He went to Jo and went down on a knee before her wheelchair. He reached up and gently touched her cheek. "I have come to tell you I love you," he said, his voice soft and endearing and, oh, what he was saying so welcome and wonderful.

"Can we begin anew?" Wolf asked, his eyelids heavy over his midnight dark eyes. "Can we forget whatever it was that made you wear hurt in your eyes yesterday?"

"You . . . love . . . me?" Jo said, her voice breaking, her heart thudding.

The touch of his hand against her face made her head spin with desire for him, yet she fought the tumultuous feelings.

"More than any man could ever love any woman," Wolf said huskily. He reached up and framed her face between his hands.

Jo could only stammer as she tried to talk to him. "But . . . but . . . the other day, when . . . when . . . we were alone together beside the lake, you—"

Wolf slid a gentle hand over her mouth and sealed the words behind his palm. "So that was the reason for the hurt in your eyes yesterday?" he said, his voice drawn. "That is the reason you are having trouble believing my words of love for you today? Because I did not make love to you?"

She reached up with a hand and slid his away from her lips. "Because you started to, then stopped, and I found it hard to believe the reason you told me," Jo murmured. "I thought you were having second thoughts about your feelings about me. I thought . . . when you were lying with me, you were seeing the wheelchair in your mind's eye. I thought you could not look past that wheelchair to let yourself make love to me."

"Do you not know that we share something so special that nothing can come between us?" Wolf said, taking her hand and holding it over his heart. "Do you feel my heart beating within my chest?"

"Yes," Jo said, her own heart beating as loudly.

"Its every beat is whispering to me of my love for you," Wolf said, smiling at Jo. "It is speaking your name to my soul."

His vow of love for her made Jo gasp softly. A sensual shiver rode her spine. "But why *did* you draw away from me when we were so close to making love?" she asked, wanting to hear him say it.

Yes, after her initial hurt, she needed to hear his explanation about that day when she had come so close to knowing the true mystery of lovemaking.

"I told you why then," Wolf said thickly. "It was because I felt we were moving too fast into something you might not even want. I felt it was not right to make love so soon after meeting one another. I . . . wanted . . . you to be sure. It is not an easy thing for a woman if she makes love and then regrets it."

"How could I have ever regretted making love with you?" Jo murmured, deeply touched by his explanation. Her insides were warmed by a delicious feeling that was spreading through her. "Our love is something that was meant to be. Our love for one another is something written in the heavens."

She was content now to know why he had not made love to her that day. It *was* as she had finally concluded . . . that he had been considering her feelings!

She should have been more hesitant, herself. He could have seen her as a loose woman if she had made love with him on their very first outing together.

But today? She knew that if he initiated lovemaking again, she would welcome it. She wanted him so badly her insides ached.

"But how will it look for such a powerful chief as yourself to love a woman who cannot walk . . . who must get around by way of a wheelchair instead of her legs?" she said, her voice breaking. "Can't you see it, Wolf? You having to wheel me everywhere? People will gawk even more than when my father wheels me around. You are a powerful leader. People will expect you to choose a woman who can walk tall and proud at your side."

"You do not know, do you, that when most people see you, they do not see a woman in a wheelchair?" Wolf said thickly. "They see a woman of much courage . . . a woman who is more beautiful than the stars!"

Jo giggled and blushed. "I wish that were so," she said softly.

Wolf swept a hand beneath her lustrous, long blond hair and gripped her gently at the nape of her neck and softly drew her lips to his. "It *is* so," he whispered as he brushed a series of kisses over her warm lips. "Tell me that you are mine . . . that you will be mine, *ah-pah-nay*, my people's way of saying forever."

"Yes, oh, yes, I am yours," Jo whispered. "I am yours *ah-pah-nay*." She closed her eyes, and her heart sang as she twined her arms around his neck and got lost in a kiss so deep and passionate, she felt as though her body had left the wheelchair and was soaring in the heavens with beautiful eagles.

When footsteps were heard outside the closed door, Jo was brought down to earth. She untwined her arms as his lips moved away from hers.

"Come with me today," Wolf said, his eyes meeting and holding Jo's. "Ride with me again. Did you not enjoy it before? I can take you places today that you do not know exist."

Jo smiled up at him. "Yes, I would love to go with you," she said, her hands already on her wheels. "But where are you taking me? From my years of horseback riding, I know this land pretty well. I doubt that you can take me to many places that I haven't been before."

Wolf's eyes sparkled. "You shall soon see," he said, leaning down to whisk her from the wheelchair and into his arms.

He kissed her softly on the lips, stood there for a moment longer as he gazed with adoration into her eyes, then laughed softly from happiness as he went to the door. He opened it and walked proudly down the corridor, paying no heed to those he passed who stared at them.

Jo giggled as people hurried out of the way when Wolf headed toward the door at the end of the corridor. She nodded hello to those she knew, amused at their incredulous looks over how she was being carried, and by whom.

Jo knew there would be much gossip about her at many supper tables tonight and she smiled at what people might say.

Surely the women who gawked today were

jealous that Jo had captured the heart of such a handsome, virile man as Wolf. Although most white people spoke against relationships with redskins, Jo knew that many women fantasized about being with a handsome warrior.

Even she was guilty of such daydreams, especially after she had met her first Chippewa warrior. She had been riding past the Chippewa village one day when out of a clearing came a handful of Chippewa warriors on horseback.

It was on that day that she had made friends with Fast Horse, who was then considering becoming a Methodist minister. She had sat among his people and had enjoyed making their acquaintance. She had formed a lasting friendship then with the Chippewa people, as she now wanted to do with the Ottawa.

Sitting in front of Wolf on his horse, riding down the street away from her office building, she was lost in wonder at being with him again.

And she could hardly wait to see where he was taking her.

If it was a place she didn't know, surely it was special and secret!

The only thing that concerned Jo was the time. It was late afternoon. Soon it would be night. She ought to have sent word to her father where she was going, and with whom.

Yet she had told her father that she would be working late. She had much to catch up on due to the many months she'd been away from her offices. She hadn't expected her father to come and pick her up in the wagon until much later.

Jo's thoughts came back to the present and her curiosity about Wolf's destination. Soon she saw the outskirts of his village coming into view in the shadows of the quickly falling dusk. She could see smoke spiraling from the many log cabins. She could even see the glow of a huge outdoor fire.

She had seen such a glow in the sky before from her own house and knew that it originated at the Ottawa village. She had never asked why they kept a fire burning at night, having concluded that the fire was to keep wild animals from straying too close to the Ottawa village at night. It was their horses the Ottawa wanted to protect from predators, for they owned few and valued them highly.

Then, as Wolf rode into his village, Jo recalled his having said that he was taking her to a place she had not known existed. She turned questioning eyes up at him and saw his smile when he caught her looking at him that way.

"You question why we are here at my village instead of a more mysterious place?" Wolf said, riding on past the log houses and the huge fire.

Jo was quickly aware that no one was about. Even the dogs seemed to have deserted the village.

"Yes, and . . . and . . . where is everyone?" Jo asked, now gazing from cabin to cabin, still seeing no signs of life except for the smoke spiraling from the chimneys.

"You will soon see," Wolf said, now riding past his larger house, and then his father's. "I vow to you, my woman, even though we are here among my people, you will still travel to places unknown to you. Be patient. Soon you will understand."

"So you are just coming to your village for a short while and then you will take me to the special place?" Jo asked, again questioning him with eager eyes.

"No, the special place is here, in Wolf's village," he said, causing Jo's eyes to widen.

She sighed, then again looked at the quiet village.

"Where is everyone?" she asked softly. "Have . . . have . . . they, by chance, gone to that special place you are taking me to?"

"In a sense, yes," Wolf said, chuckling.

"You sure are creating an atmosphere of mystery for me," Jo said, laughing softly. "But I am game. I will patiently wait and see what this all means."

She settled herself more comfortably against him, trusting that what he planned would, indeed, be special. Wolf rode onward until he came to the far end of the village, which was unfamiliar to her.

She gazed at a huge longhouse that sat deep in the trees, smoke spiraling from two chimneys, one on each end of the lodge. As Wolf drew a tight rein beside the building, Jo became aware of someone talking inside the longhouse.

"Come inside with me," Wolf softly urged, sliding from the saddle, then reaching up to get Jo. "You are moments away from many intriguing places."

Jo gazed at him with silent questioning, then looked around as he carried her inside the huge longhouse. It was crowded with Ottawa people sitting on blankets in a circle, facing a lone elderly man who sat on a platform in their midst.

Jo became aware of large trays of food set beside one of the two fireplaces.

Beside the trays of food were jugs, which Jo surmised were filled with something special to drink. It looked as though the people were involved in a special ceremony which would surely be followed by feasting.

Afraid to speak, to ask Wolf anything about this place lest she disturb the ceremony, Jo only smiled awkwardly.

As Wolf worked his way across the crowded floor, Jo clung to him. When he reached his mother and father, he put her down gently, then seated himself beside her.

"Welcome to our time of storytelling," Blue Moth whispered as she leaned closer to Jo. "Our storyteller will take you to places you never knew existed."

Hearing the same words that Wolf had used when describing where he was taking her, Jo turned to him and gave him a slow smile. Now she knew! He had been referring to the stories. The *stories* would take her to those places! And, oh, how she loved stories. She could hardly wait to become immersed in them.

Her heart melted when Wolf slid an arm around her waist and drew her closer to him.

"I love being here," she whispered to him. "Thank you for bringing me. I know that I will love the stories of your storyteller."

"I, too, will tell stories tonight," Wolf whispered back to her.

Jo's eyes widened in anticipation.

Chapter Twelve

Jo was entranced by the storyteller as everyone sat by the light of the two crackling fires in the longhouse. The stories being told were about the Indian's kinship with the animals and the earth, and of their people's war parties of the past, of their heroes of the past and present, and of the humorous events that had colored their lives. Jo knew that many of the stories had been passed from generation to generation of storytellers.

In these stories, Jo discovered that animals were often personified and their actions were used to explain natural phenomena or the meaning of some part of Indian life.

She listened to Old Iron Hawk as he began another story. In order to watch his hand gestures and his facial expressions more closely, she leaned forward, unaware of Wolf watching her, enjoying her reaction to each new story that was told.

"The turtle has special meaning to all Ottawa people," Old Iron Hawk said, his gray hair lying in long swirls around his bare, thin shoulders. "At one time the Ottawa were threatened by a big flood and none of the people could swim. Along came the turtle. The people all hooked up to the turtle and the turtle took them to land. Some of our Ottawa people respected the turtle so much for that deed that they adopted his name for their clan."

Old Iron Hawk looked around the room. He smiled and nodded at one child and then another, then reached over and placed a bony hand on the head of a young brave of eight winters.

"Beaver Tail, tell me the story you wish to hear, for I will tell only one more and then our chief will tell his," Old Iron Hawk said, his brown eyes squinting through shaggy gray eyebrows that hung low over them.

"Tell us about the beaver and how it builds a dam," Beaver Tail said, his round copper face alight with a smile. "I was named after brother beaver. I enjoy hearing all about him."

"Then I will tell you the story as I have many times in the past," Old Iron Hawk said, chuckling.

Again he looked slowly around the room, still focusing on the children, who sat attentively watching and listening. "As I have told you before during other story times, originally beavers had narrow tails," he began. "One autumn the beaver was gathering sticks to build his home. When he stopped working, he noticed that the muskrat had a wide, flat tail. Coveting the muskrat's tail, he offered his own in exchange, which the muskrat accepted. With his new tail, the muskrat could swim swiftly through shallow water and could build his home near the shores of lakes and rivers. From that day on, the beaver, with his flat tail, had to build dams to make the water deep enough for him to travel."

"Please tell us about the owl before you end your storytelling tonight," another young brave begged, moving to his knees anxiously.

Old Iron Hawk glanced questioningly at Wolf.

Wolf smiled and nodded his approval.

"When I was a mere child, my mother quieted me at bedtime by saying, *Ko-ko-ko-qusa-be-ki-yon*, which means 'owl will get you,'" Iron Hawk said. "From then on I was afraid of the owl as most of you also are afraid of the owl, because your mother has used this same story to get you to behave and go to bed at night."

Old Iron Hawk smiled at Wolf, then drew his blanket up around his shoulders and watched his chief rise to stand above everyone. "Children, it is time now for our chief to weave his own tale and enchant you," he said.

Anxious to hear what Wolf was going to say, Jo watched Wolf intently, her pulse racing.

She was quickly entranced by not only the story, but by his voice, which was so deep and affectionate as he looked from child to child, smiling.

She knew then that he would be a wonderful father. She would not allow herself to ruin this moment by worrying about the possibility of her not being able to have children. Now that she knew that her body could come alive at Wolf's mere touch, surely there was a chance that her body would allow her to have children!

She held that thought as she listened to Wolf begin his story.

"I tell you today the 'Rainbow Legend,'" Wolf said, smiling from child to child. "When *Gitchi Manitou* created the flowers, they were all the same white color. Not satisfied, he retired to his favorite hillside and made a mixture of colors for the flowers. When he was at the task of painting all of the flowers, two small birds began arguing. This kept up until they began to chase one another. Jabbering and squawking, they flitted about in the trees and bushes. They swooped back and forth, close to where *Gitchi Manitou* was painting. He was kept busy chasing them away. He had the pots of colors all set out when the birds landed nearby. He quickly shooed them away, but when the birds tried to get out of his way, they accidentally stepped into the pots of paint. They flew up in the air, one chasing the other, and landed across a small pond. As they flew, the colors of red, blue, and yellow dribbled from their feet and formed an arc of colors. With Brother Sun shining on them, the colors seemed to glow. So today, when rain-clouds gather and Brother Sun plays hide-and-seek among them, you can still see the rainbow of colors. Now when you all see the rainbow and its many beautiful colors, you will know how the flowers, and those two pesky birds, made the colors in the sky."

Jo laughed softly as the children swarmed around Wolf, hugging him. He sat down and gathered many onto his lap, their eyes looked adoringly at him.

"My *nin-gwis*, son, is a man who steals children's hearts," Blue Moth said, drawing Jo's eyes to her. "When Wolf talks, the children, especially, listen, for they learn things from him their mothers and fathers have never told them. And when he talks, it is straight from the heart."

Jo turned her gaze to Wolf again. She recalled when he had drawn away from her that day of wondrous passion, and how she had misconstrued his motivation. If she had listened then with an open heart, she would have not put herself through the misery of feeling rejected by him. She now knew that he *did* speak from his heart, and that he had her welfare at heart in everything he did.

"I know," Jo murmured. "Your son is a very special man."

"He will make a good *mee-kah-wah-diz-ee*, husband," Blue Moth said, reaching over to pat Jo's knee.

Jo looked quickly at the middle-aged woman. She wanted to ask Blue Moth if she could approve of a crippled woman for her son's choice of wife. She wasn't sure if Blue Moth knew that her son cared that much for Jo. Or did his mother possibly think that Wolf had brought her there today only out of gratitude for having won the case for his people?

Jo felt a welcome reprieve from having to discuss Wolf any further with his mother when several women got up and began handing out wooden dishes of food to everyone.

Jo gladly took hers. She was famished. She had worked the long day through without stopping to eat.

When Wolf sat down beside her and rested his plate on his lap, Jo smiled at him as he hungrily ate the fruit and meat.

After the feast was over and the people had departed to their own lodges, Wolf first carried his father to his parents' lodge. He then went back for Jo and took her there to spend some time with his parents.

Jo noticed how quiet Wolf's father was as he sat before the roaring fire on a thick pelt. He had already lit his long-stemmed pipe. As before, when she had been there to introduce him to the wheelchair, he had his back to everyone as he stared at the flames and smoked.

Jo questioned Wolf with her eyes. When she

saw that Wolf wasn't going to offer an explanation about his father's attitude, she tried to focus her thoughts elsewhere. She nodded a thank you to Blue Moth, who brought her a cup of steaming brew.

"This is coffee but unlike what whites drink," Wolf said, sitting down in a chair next to Jo's. "It is made from the roots of the hickory tree."

"Oh?" Jo said, arching an eyebrow as she stared at the brown liquid.

"Drink," Wolf encouraged, placing a gentle hand beneath the cup and bringing it to her lips. "You will find it more pleasant than white man's coffee."

Jo sipped it. Her eyes widened in surprise as she found herself enjoying the drink. It wasn't bitter like the coffee she drank at home. It was sweet.

"It's delicious," she murmured, then took another sip.

Blue Moth smiled and nodded a silent thank you, then sat down beside her husband on the pelts. Unlike her husband, she faced away from the fire as she spread a piece of buckskin across her lap and proceeded to sew beads onto it.

"Mother is a skilled seamstress," Wolf said softly. "By sewing the beads, moosehair, and porcupine quills in various shapes and designs my mother weaves her own tales."

"Blue Moth, what are you making tonight?" Jo asked, leaning down to set her empty cup on the wooden floor.

"A new bag in which to carry my sewing

127

materials," Blue Moth said, her hands working moosehair in and around the porcupine quills that she had already sewn on the buckskin. "I also make jewelry. I enjoy using the tiny bones from the inside dew claws of the deer." She glanced over at Jo. "It is a matter of pride for the Ottawa craftmaker to do the work herself though it is a long procedure."

"I would love to learn these things from you," Jo said, finding this to be a wonderful way to possibly bond with Wolf's mother. She felt it was almost as important to bond with her as it was to have Wolf love her.

"I will gladly teach you," Blue Moth said, smiling at Jo.

Then Blue Moth's smile faded as Wolf got up, left the room for a moment, then came in again pushing the wheelchair that Jo had left there for his father.

"Wolf, why are you doing that?" Blue Moth asked, laying her sewing aside. "Your father—"

"My father is being too stubborn for too long," Wolf said thickly. "Life would be so much easier for both you and Father if he would use this chair to get from place to place."

Now Jo understood why Wolf had come to his parents' lodge instead of going on to his as she had thought they were going to do. He wasn't going to give up on his father using the wheelchair.

She glanced over at Sleeping Bear. He was still sitting with his back to everyone. His back was stiff. His hand was trembling as he held on to the stem of his pipe, sucking deep whiffs of smoke into his mouth.

At first she had thought that it was because of *her* that he had turned away from everyone in the room.

Now she knew that he had known all along that Wolf was going to encourage him again to use the chair. Jo expected Wolf to ask her at any moment to demonstrate it again.

"Jo, would you mind showing my father again the ease with which you get around in the chair?" Wolf asked, wheeling the chair on over to her.

"I would be happy to," Jo murmured, but she was afraid that her role in this might turn Sleeping Bear against her.

Still, she knew the worth of the chair and would not allow herself to be afraid of his feelings toward her. It was worth the risk of alienating him, if he would eventually use the chair.

Certainly it would make Wolf's mother's life much simpler. She was the one who had to go for someone to carry her husband every time he wanted to leave their lodge.

Yes, Jo had to try again to persuade him that the chair was a worthwhile thing and should be a part of his life.

Wolf lifted her gently into his arms and placed her in the chair.

She scarcely breathed when Wolf went to his father and placed a hand on his blanket-wrapped shoulder.

"*Gee-bah-bah*, you taught me as a child that

129

stubbornness was frowned upon by *Gitchi Manitou*," Wolf said. "*Gee-bah-bah*, I listened well to your teachings. Today I hope that you will remember that it is wrong to be stubborn."

"*Nin-gwis*, you talk to me as though I were the child, you the father," Sleeping Bear said, not turning to look at Wolf. "Where is the respect that I taught my son?"

Jo swallowed hard and her eyes widened in horror when she saw how his father's scolding had affected Wolf. He had dropped his hand from his father's shoulder and had taken a step away from him, a look of shock in his eyes.

Blue Moth got to her feet and went to Wolf. "Son, do not take to heart your father's words tonight," she said. She placed a gentle hand on Wolf's arm. "He does not mean to hurt you. Leave with Jo. Go on about your evening without any more worries about your *gee-bah-bah*. He will do as he pleases no matter what you or I say."

"I'd best take the chair home with me," Jo said, drawing both Wolf's eyes and his mother's. "Wolf, don't you think so?"

Blue Moth went to Jo and knelt down before her. She took both of Jo's hands in hers. "Leave the chair," she murmured. "I do see the worth of it even though my husband does not. He has always valued what I think about things. He will soon value how I feel about the chair and will use it."

"If you truly believe so, then I won't take

it," Jo said. She melted inside when Blue Moth reached her arms around her and gave her a tender hug.

Blue Moth moved away from Jo as Wolf came and swept Jo into his arms. He smiled down at his mother, then carried Jo from the cabin. He said nothing to her until they were inside his own cabin, where the closed door separated them from the outside world.

Chapter Thirteen

"I'm so sorry about your father," Jo murmured as Wolf placed her on thick pelts beside the fireplace where the fire had burned down to smoldering coals.

"It is he who suffers the most by not using the chair," Wolf said, lifting a log onto the grate. He fanned the coals with a hand and when flames began to caress the log, he turned and sat down beside Jo.

"What I regret the most is how my father's coldness affects you," he said. He reached up and brushed strands of Jo's golden hair back from her eyes. "It is not like my *gee-bah-bah* to be so cold to others."

"He must resent me as much as the wheelchair," Jo murmured, her voice catching.

"No, it is not you he resents, it is his son

who insists on something he does not want to do," Wolf said, frowning. "In time he will see the wrong in his behavior toward both you and me. I am sure that he will somehow discover how much easier his life would be if he used the chair."

"I so enjoyed the stories," Jo murmured, purposely changing the subject, for she knew the hurt his father had inflicted on Wolf by not trusting his son's judgment about the chair. "Yours, especially."

"There is one about a Garden of Eden that is told between husbands and wives when their children are asleep in their beds," Wolf said, his eyes dancing when he saw a look of recognition come into Jo's eyes at the mention of the Garden of Eden. "You are familiar with that story?"

"Yes," Jo murmured. "But I didn't know you knew about it. It is written about in the white man's Bible. Is that how you know about it?"

"The Ottawa have their own story about the Garden of Eden," Wolf said softly. "But I am aware of yours. I read the story in one of Fast Horse's Bibles one day."

"Do both stories have the same meaning?" Jo dared to ask, feeling the sexual tension rise between them again.

She hoped that this time would be much different than the last. Although she was not a woman who had spent much time thinking about such things as sex, now that she had felt the stirring of desire within her, it was hard not to think of sharing such moments with the man she loved.

Her body hungered to know the true meaning of lovemaking!

Even now, while thinking about it, she could feel herself get strangely warm and wet where Wolf's fingers had awakened her to passion. He had stroked her in a private place that no one had ever touched before.

"Are you asking me if the Ottawa story tells of a man and woman discovering love?" Wolf asked, his hands sliding down from her hair, to cup both her breasts through the cotton fabric of her dress. "*Ae*, it speaks of unbridled passion between two people who until that moment were forbidden to be with one another."

Jo closed her eyes and a wondrous thrill soared through her when Wolf kissed the hollow of her throat.

Her breath caught when she felt his fingers pulling her blouse free of the waistband of her skirt.

When he slid a hand up inside her blouse and touched a bare breast, his thumb circling the nipple, Jo drew a ragged breath of rapture and then moaned when she soon felt her blouse lifted. His tongue found her nipple, flicking it.

Cradling her close, Wolf eased her down on her back on the blankets and pelts that he had purposely prepared for this moment. He had planned it well, this night when they would find total bliss within each other's arms.

135

Jo opened her eyes and gazed at Wolf when he moved away from her and stood up.

Her heart pounded when Wolf slid his fringed buckskin shirt over his head and dropped it to the floor, revealing a powerful, muscled chest.

She scarcely breathed when he untied the thongs at the waist of his breeches, knowing that he would soon drop them, revealing to Jo a man's total anatomy for the first time in her life.

She had felt the full length of his manhood before when he had pressed his body against hers and she had realized that he was aroused.

She knew how large he was, yet she wasn't sure how that part of a man's body looked.

When he finally dropped his breeches to his ankles and she saw how large he *was*, and how his manhood jutted up so stiffly erect from his black patch of hair, Jo was stunned to speechlessness. Never had she expected that part of a man would be so intriguing. It made a strange sort of ache in the pit of her stomach. She wanted Wolf. With every fiber of her being . . . she . . . wanted him!

When Wolf wrapped a hand around himself and knelt down before Jo, that part of him so close to her now, she was overcome with a strange sort of feverish heat.

"*Mee-kah-wah-diz-ee-gee-wee-oo*, my woman, touch me," Wolf said thickly. "Stroke me."

Jo's eyes widened.

Her throat went dry.

136

Her breath caught again as she stared at that part of him that he was offering her.

"You want me to . . . to . . . touch and stroke you?" Jo asked, her voice scarcely a whisper as she now gazed into Wolf's eyes.

Wolf smiled at her and reached out to take one of her hands.

Jo's face grew hot with a blush when he brought her hand to himself and urged her to wrap her fingers around him.

When he began moving her hand on his sex, and she saw the fire of pleasure leap into his eyes, she became lost in a passion she had never known possible.

Suddenly he took her hand away.

His steel arms enfolded her as he stretched out over her, his one hand shoving her skirt up past her thighs, his one knee parting her legs.

When he kissed her she felt his hunger in the hard, seeking pressure of his lips, and the probing of his sex where her heart seemed centered at the juncture of her thighs.

"Relax," Wolf whispered against her lips. "Let it happen."

Again he kissed her.

She became dizzy with rapture when she felt him sliding slowly inside her, and then she winced when a sharp pain cut through the pleasure.

"Do not think about the pain, for it will be erased by pleasure," Wolf whispered into her ear. Then he moved his lips to her mouth and kissed her again, long and deep.

When he was finally entirely inside her and he began his rhythmic thrusts, Jo soon learned that nothing on this earth could feel as wonderful. A euphoria she never knew before swept through her.

And when he slid his mouth downward and once again flicked his tongue around her nipple, his hand now caressing her woman's center, Jo felt something happening she didn't understand, but welcomed. It was as though she was losing conscious thought of everything but the passion she was sharing with Wolf.

"Let it happen," Wolf whispered huskily against her lips. He placed both hands beneath her buttocks and lifted her closer to his heat. "Feel it, *mee-kah-wah-diz-ee-gee-wee-oo*, my woman. Feel the licking flames of pleasure spread through you."

"I've never felt such joy," Jo whispered back to him. She twined her fingers through his long, black hair, her eyes closed as the pleasure mounted. "I can feel everything, Wolf. Oh, such passion and rapture!"

He bent his head to her lips and kissed her as he took one last, deep thrust inside her which brought them both to the peak of pleasure they sought.

She clung and rocked with him.

He held her as though in a vise as he continued to move within her.

She cried out as her body exploded in spasms of desire.

Stunned by the intensity of the bliss he had

138

brought her, Jo clung to Wolf as he thrust over and over inside her, then moaned sensually as he shuddered his seed deep inside her.

They lay there for a long while, their bodies pressed together.

"I was able to feel everything," Jo said as Wolf leaned over her on an elbow to gaze with passion-heavy eyes at her. She looked adoringly at him. "My body actually allowed me to feel the wonders of lovemaking."

"As it will one day allow you to walk," Wolf said, brushing a kiss across her lips.

She closed her eyes and enjoyed being with him for a moment longer, then her father came to mind, jolting her back to the present and how worried he might be about her.

"I must go," she said, sitting up, smoothing down her blouse and rebuttoning it. Frowning, she smoothed her skirt down across her legs. "Oh, what if my father guesses what we did tonight just by looking at me?"

"There is nothing wrong with what we shared tonight," Wolf said, combing his long, lean fingers through her hair, straightening it around her shoulders. "We love each other. We will be married."

"Married?" Jo said, looking quickly up at him.

"You will marry me, will you not?" Wolf asked, his eyes imploring her.

"You . . . you . . . truly want me even though I . . . am . . . a cripple?"

"How can you ask that after what we have just shared?"

139

"It all seems so unreal."

"I would hope not," Wolf chuckled, sliding on his breeches. "Everything was real tonight. Everything."

"Yes, I know," Jo said, laughing softly. "It is just that—"

"We will make plans soon to marry," Wolf said, interrupting her. "But for now I must see that you get home safely."

"I will never forget tonight," Jo said, sighing as he grabbed her up into his arms and walked toward the door.

"It is the beginning of all our tomorrows," Wolf said, stopping to kiss her before going outside.

Hating to leave, Jo clung to him.

But she knew that she had been gone from home for much too long. She hoped her father wasn't so worried about her that he had sent a posse out to look for her.

The thought of Sheriff Gowins looking for her for any reason made her shiver with disgust.

"You just shivered," Wolf said as he carried her outside to his horse. "Are you cold?"

"I could never be as warm as I am now," Jo murmured, brushing a kiss across his lips before he sat her in the saddle. She was glad that his people were in their homes, so there was no one to see her kiss their chief. She had been accepted up until now. But would they accept her when they realized that she would soon be a part of their lives forever?

She settled herself comfortably in front of Wolf when he got into the saddle. She leaned against his powerful chest and let nothing get in the way of her contentment, for this moment was so precious she wanted to savor it forever.

He guided his black stallion out of the village, then rode at a gentle lope beneath the moon and stars until Jo saw the outline of her home silhouetted by the silver moonlight. She could smell her father's prize roses. She could hear the last crickets of autumn.

Wolf drew a tight rein before her house, then carried her up the porch to the front door. Her father was quickly there, opening it.

"Father, I'm sorry if I worried you," Jo murmured, unable to see his face since it was shadowed by the porch's roof. "I went to Wolf's village. I listened to the storyteller telling stories. It . . . it . . . was so much fun."

Still her father didn't speak. She knew by his silence that she had worried him. She should have thought to at least send word about her plans to go to the Ottawa village. But it had all happened so fast.

"Please take me in to my wheelchair, Wolf," Jo asked softly. She kept a wheelchair at home as well as at her two offices. She felt the tension between Wolf and her father as Wolf brushed past him and went into the parlor, where lamplight sent a golden glow around the room.

Wolf gently placed Jo in her wheelchair, bent low to kiss her brow, locked eyes with her for a moment, then again brushed past Jo's father in the corridor and left.

When her father came into the parlor, Jo's guilt at not sending word to him was replaced by anger at his unfriendliness to Wolf.

"Father, how could you behave like that to Wolf?" she said, their eyes meeting and holding in a silent battle. "You have good reason to be angry at me. But treating Wolf so coldly was uncalled for."

"Jo, while you were gone, threats were made against your life," Addison said, clasping his hands tightly behind him as he continued to stare down at her.

Jo's eyes widened. Her throat went dry. "Threats?" she said, her voice drawn. "How? What kind? Who did it?"

"I'm not sure who," Addison said thickly. He reached over and grabbed up a piece of crumpled paper from a table top. "This note was tied to a rock. Someone threw it through our kitchen window."

"Good Lord," Jo said, paling. She took the note as he handed it to her. Her eyes quickly went over the few words that had been handwritten on the paper. The note referred to her as an Indian lover and warned her against taking their side again.

Jo's spine stiffened with anger, for no one would tell her what to do, especially when it had anything to do with the Ottawa. She would fight to the end for them, for her heart belonged to their chief.

She tore the note up into tiny pieces, wheeled herself to the fireplace, and tossed them into the fire.

"Jo, you'd better take the threat seriously," Addison said, going to lean an arm against the fireplace mantel and staring at the flames.

"Father, anyone who is too cowardly to tell me to my face how he feels is too cowardly to carry out any threats," Jo said, then sighed and welcomed her father's arms around her neck when he knelt down and hugged her.

"Father, I'm sorry that I worried you tonight," she murmured. "I promise not to be so careless in the future."

"As long as I hold breath within my lungs, I'll worry about you," he said softly. "You are all I have left, you know."

"Yes, I know," Jo murmured, wondering how he would feel when she told him she was going to get married and leave him. For it *was* going to happen. She *was* going to marry the man she loved! No threat would keep her from speaking vows with Wolf!

Chapter Fourteen

Jo was jerked from sleep by the sound of thundering hoofbeats outside her bedroom window. When she bolted upright in the bed and saw the reflection of fire on the ceiling, an instant fear leaped into her heart.

The note!

The threat!

Surely whoever had sent it was trying to impress on her how seriously she should take the warning!

"Jo!" Addison cried as he ran into the room in his robe. He hurried to her window and looked out. "Several men are outside on horses. They have torches! Lord, are they going to set fire to our house?"

Jo scooted over onto her wheelchair and wheeled herself to the window.

Cassie Edwards

Coldness rushed through her veins when she saw how many men were out there, and how many torches were being waved in the air.

"I know you're in there watchin' us," a man shouted. "J. T., you'd better quit sidin' with the redskins. By doing so, it makes you no better than a heathen yourself. If you don't stay away from the savages, you'll pay. You *and* your father will pay!"

Taking the torches with them, the men rode off.

Addison lit a lantern and knelt down before Jo. "Jo, those men mean business," he said, his voice shaking with fear. "You've got to stay away from Wolf and his people. And, by God, pass on any court cases that have to do with Indians. Don't you have enough trouble already in your life without adding any more to it? Damn it, being crippled is enough for you to have to contend with, much less a bunch of crazed white men who are out for blood . . . *yours.*"

Jo said nothing, only twined her arm around her father's neck and gently hugged him. But there was anger in her eyes, for she was even more adamant about helping the Ottawa should they ask her assistance again.

And, by damn, where Wolf was concerned, no one would tell her what to do. She would never let herself be bullied by anyone.

They'll pay, she thought angrily to herself. *Somehow . . . some way. . . .*

Chapter Fifteen

"I don't like leaving you alone," Addison said as he gazed down at Jo, who had wheeled herself to the door to say goodbye.

"Father, we can't let those threats last night change our lives," Jo murmured. "You have your meeting in Detroit. Please go on. I, for one, will not stay in hiding at home like a scared rabbit. When I'm not at the office, I plan to spend as much spare time as possible with Wolf."

"Jo, I wish you would reconsider and stay home where you have a loaded shotgun ready in case of a repeat performance of last night," Addison said, lifting his hat from the hat tree and putting it on.

He then took his topcoat and slung it over

his arm. His gray wool suit and starched white shirt with a matching gray tie made him look the successful man of business he had been until the train wreck.

"Father, I let my disability hold me back for far too long, as you allowed it to put a halt to your life," Jo said, reaching over to take his hand. "Just look at you. If mother were here she would say you looked 'spiffy.' And you do. Go on. Please go on to Detroit."

"Very well," Addison said, squeezing her hand affectionately. Then he bent low and gave her a tender kiss on her brow.

He walked to the door and opened it, then turned to Jo again. "You are going in to work today?" he asked, his voice drawn.

"No, I'm playing hooky," Jo said, laughing. "Wolf will be here soon. We're going horseback riding."

"You mean *he's* going horseback riding and you will be on his lap," Addison grumbled. "That sight should be enough to cause a few more rocks to be thrown through our windows."

"And if so, I'll put some lead into the seat of someone's breeches," Jo said. She was skilled with firearms, her father having taught her as soon as she was old enough to hold a rifle and aim it.

"Jo, please don't do anything reckless," Addison said, sighing. He shook his head and gazed at the floor. "I think I'd better not go today after all. I—"

"Father, please get out of here and stop worrying so much about me," Jo murmured. She wheeled toward him. "Please?"

Addison's eyes wavered as he gazed at her, then he nodded, gave her another kiss on her brow, and left.

Sighing heavily, Jo listened to her father leave in his horse and buggy, then wheeled herself into the dining room and began to clear the table. It was Harriet's day off.

She had loaded the dishes onto a tray that rested across her wheelchair and taken them into the kitchen when she heard hoofbeats outside the window. She knew it wasn't Wolf because she could hear more than one horse.

Thinking it might be the men who had come last night with their torches and loud threats, Jo clenched her jaw with anger. Her eyes flashing, she wheeled herself to the gun rack and grabbed the loaded shotgun.

With it resting on her lap, she went to the door and swung it open.

Relief rushed through her when she wheeled herself out onto the porch and saw Wolf sitting tall and handsome on his black steed. A brilliant white stallion trailed behind him, secured by a rope tied loosely around its neck.

"Are you ready for that ride today?" Wolf asked, his eyes twinkling as he smiled at Jo. His smile faded when he saw the shotgun on her lap. He stared at it for a moment, then looked questioningly at Jo. "Who did you expect? Why do you feel the need of the firearm?"

Jo explained about what had happened the night before, first about the threatening note, and then about the men with torches.

"It is not safe for you to live here any longer," Wolf said, sliding from his saddle. "Come with me. Stay in my village."

"I can't do that," Jo murmured as he came up the steps, then knelt on the porch beside the wheelchair and took one of Jo's hands. "Wolf, it is not only I who was threatened. There is also Father, and I know that he won't abandon this house which has been his since he married my mother." She swallowed hard. "And he certainly wouldn't stay at your village."

"Because he has feelings against redskins?" Wolf said thickly. "He has prejudices?"

"No, it's nothing like that," Jo said. "It's because the threats were about my involvement with the Ottawa. I was warned against being involved in Indian affairs. So my father believes I should be more careful with the cases I take in the future. Also, he thinks I shouldn't be seen with you. It's all because he fears for my life. Not because he has anything, personally, against you or your people."

"Has he forbidden you to see me? To be with me?" Wolf said, his voice low and drawn.

"He did ask me not to," Jo murmured. "But I told him that no threats would dictate my life. I told him that nothing would keep me from seeing you."

She looked past him and gazed admiringly at the white stallion. "Why did you bring the white stallion with you today?" she asked, then looked again at Wolf. "It's so beautiful, Wolf. So very beautiful."

"I am glad that you are taken by it," Wolf said, his lips lifting into a soft smile. "For the horse is now yours."

"Mine?" Jo gasped, her heart leaping, her eyes widening. "Why? Why are you giving it to me?"

"It is not a gift from me alone," Wolf said. He looked over his shoulder at the magnificent steed with the big, friendly brown eyes. He gazed at Jo again. "It is a gift from my people. It is their way of thanking you for saving their fishing rights."

"A gift?" Jo murmured, staring at the beautiful horse. "Mine? This horse is mine?"

"Yours, Jo," Wolf said, nodding. "And today you are going to ride it."

Jo looked quickly at Wolf. Her heart skipped a beat when she saw that he was serious. "But I can't," she said. "I would never take payment for helping your people during their time of trouble." Her voice broke. She spread her hands out on her legs. "And I can't go riding on the horse because of my legs, Wolf. You know they won't allow me to ride."

"This is not payment. This is a gift," Wolf said. He gently framed her face between his hands. "Have you tried to ride since the train wreck?" His eyes searched hers. "Have you?"

Almost hypnotized by his eyes, she slowly shook her head.

"There is no reason why you can't sit in the saddle and ride White Cloud," Wolf said, taking the shotgun from her lap and placing it just inside the front door.

Closing the door behind Jo, he swept her into his arms and carried her to the horse. Gently he placed her in the leather saddle. "This horse is yours *ah-pah-nay*. You will ride White Cloud today," he said. "I will fit your feet into the stirrups. You take up the reins. And that is all that is required of you to ride White Cloud."

Jo's heart thumped wildly as she reached for the reins and gripped them tightly. She gazed down at her legs where the skirt of her lacy cotton dress was hiked up past her knees. She tried to move them, but they were like dead weights. She couldn't even feel her feet in the stirrups.

Feeling unsteady in the saddle, knowing that if she couldn't control her feet in the stirrups, she might slide sideways at any moment, Jo scarcely breathed.

"We will ride at a slow lope," Wolf said, encouragingly. He untied the rope that held White Cloud in place behind Midnight. He wound the rope up and hung it from his pommel, then reached up and took one of Jo's hands from her reins. "You will enjoy the ride today. Do not be afraid of anything."

"There is one thing," Jo murmured, glancing toward the front door. She reached inside a pocket of her dress and handed a key to Wolf. "Please lock the front door."

"There are no locks on the doors of the Ottawa houses," Wolf said, gazing at the key in his hand.

"You might want to reconsider that," Jo said, her voice dry. "This area is no longer as safe as it was only a few years ago. Father and Mother never locked our doors. But as the town of Lone Branch grew, so did the dangers."

Wolf nodded and went and locked her door, then gave her the key and mounted his steed.

"I still am not sure about this," Jo said, holding herself stiffly in the saddle. "I do so badly want to enjoy it. But I know how easily I could slip from the saddle."

"I will be right beside you," Wolf said, sidling his horse as close to the white stallion as he could get it. "And we will not go far this time." He nodded toward a bluff. "We will go there. From there we can see many things to enjoy . . . the river, the autumn leaves, the wildflowers dotting the land. It will be a time for enjoying nature as we enjoy being with each other."

Jo was feeling more secure by the minute. She relaxed when Wolf gave her an encouraging smile and urged Midnight into a gentle trot. She flicked her reins and rode alongside Wolf. Each moment was more wonderful than the last, for she had always loved horseback riding. And it was something she had thought she could never dream of doing again, not as long as her legs refused to cooperate with the rest of her body.

When she saw shadows of wings on the

ground moving along with White Cloud and Midnight, she looked quickly upward and gasped when she saw several buzzards sweeping around in a circle overhead. They seemed to be following Jo and Wolf as they rode up the winding, travel-worn path that would take them to the bluff.

"I've been seeing those buzzards lately," Jo said. She gave Wolf a quick glance, glad that the path that led up the side of the hill to the bluff was not a steep one.

Even so, she was fighting the pull of gravity, but she would not let Wolf down by falling off the horse. She was so glad that he had encouraged her to do something she had longed to do for so long. While on the horse, she felt normal in all respects.

"Isn't it unusual to see buzzards like this?" she asked.

"I often see buzzards, and also eagles," Wolf said as the trail leveled out on the flat land that led to the bluff's edge. He sidled his horse closer to Jo's again, having been forced away from her while riding up the incline.

"But eagles are beautiful and noble in appearance, and buzzards are so ugly," Jo murmured.

Finally at the bluff's edge, Jo drew a tight rein as Wolf stopped his steed. She waited for him to dismount, then reached her arms out for him when he came to take her off the horse.

He carried her to a thick bed of moss and set her on it, then secured both horses' reins by laying heavy rocks on them on the ground.

"*Ae*, the buzzards' appearance is not as

noble as the eagle's, but there is a reason for that," he said, settling down beside Jo. He reached for her hand and twined his fingers around it. He gazed up at the buzzards which still soared overhead. "Look closely at them, Jo. Do you not see something majestic about them? Do you not see something similar to an eagle when you look at them?"

Jo looked up and studied the large birds. "Well, yes, there is *some* resemblance to an eagle, yet there is such a vast difference in the plumage of their heads," she said. "In fact, there is hardly any plumage at all on the buzzards' heads."

"I will tell you a story about that," Wolf said. He snaked an arm around her waist to draw her closer and again watched his friends, the buzzards. "Long ago, the eagles of this land decided to see who could fly the highest in the sky. There were two brothers. The older went up first. Up and up he flew, catching the wind currents and getting higher until he was just a speck in the sky. When he slowly descended, the other eagles cheered him loudly and greeted him upon his return. The younger eagle, jealous and angry, started up on *his* flight. Determined to win, he went straight up into the sky. As he picked up speed, getting higher and higher, he could hardly see the other eagles below on Mother Earth. Just a little farther, he thought, and he would beat his older brother. One last big burst of speed took him higher than he had ever been before. He knew he had finally won."

He gazed over at Jo. "Just as he was getting ready to turn back, a sudden updraft caught him and carried him still higher," he continued. "He tried to fly down, but he couldn't. The wind was pulling him toward the sun. He was getting hotter, and *still* the updraft swept him up. His flight was helpless and out of control. The heat became unbearable and soon he blacked out. When he came to, he was tumbling toward Mother Earth. Nearing the crowd of eagles, he could hear them laughing at him. The beautiful white feathers on his head were singed off by the heat of the sun. His head was naked."

Wolf brushed a soft kiss across Jo's lips, then said, "The Great Spirit told him that this was a punishment for his jealousy, that from this day on, his head would be naked and he would be a scavenger of the dead animal brothers and sisters. This would be his means of existence. So from that day on, the eagle who flew too high became a buzzard, and ever since then he has been feeding on the carrion of Earth Mother."

"That's such an interesting story," Jo said, loving Wolf's colorful way of explaining things. She smiled at him, but then her attention was drawn elsewhere when she saw great plumes of smoke coming from somewhere far below the bluff.

Her pleasure changed to horror when she realized that she could see her house from the bluff, and that the smoke was coming from it.

"Wolf, my house!" she cried, pointing. "It's

on fire!" But she felt a measure of relief when she saw the fire wagon arriving.

Wolf grabbed Jo up and placed her on the saddle of his horse, then swung himself up behind her. "We will come back for White Cloud later," he said, wheeling his horse around and riding down the side of the hill.

As Wolf's arm held Jo protectively against him, she was lost in thought. She knew that the fire had not started on its own. Those men who had threatened her in the middle of the night had set it. And surely they thought she was inside the house, helpless in her wheelchair, which meant they had wanted her to die in the fire!

She hated to think that those men could be so angry at her for fighting for the rights of the Ottawa people, yet they had proved it by this fiendish act.

When they arrived at the house, the fire fighters had put out the blaze, and only a portion of her home had been damaged. Everyone in the neighborhood had congregated to talk about the fire. As the fire wagon pulled away, Jo saw that someone had managed to get her wheelchair out of the house.

Wolf carried her to the wheelchair and placed her in it. In a state of shock, she gazed at the portion of the house that had burned. It included both bedrooms. The firemen had managed to stop the blaze from consuming everything else.

"Jo, oh, Jo, at first I thought you were inside," her next-door neighbor said as she came and hugged Jo about the neck. "When the empty wheelchair was brought out of the house, I expected to see you brought out next."

"I was lucky this time," Jo murmured, returning the hug, shivering at the thought of anyone being vicious enough to set a fire that could have killed both her and her father.

"I am taking you home with me," Wolf said, ignoring the stares of the people as they turned their eyes to him.

"No, I can't do that," Jo murmured, glad when her neighbors started returning to their homes. "I'm afraid I'll bring trouble into your people's lives by being there. At this time, I seem to be the true target of the fiends."

"But you cannot stay here," Wolf said, dropping to his haunches before her. He reached up and gently touched her cheek. "Come home with me. You will be safe. Your father can come there as soon as he knows what has happened."

"It's best that I get a hotel room in town," Jo said. "I just can't risk being responsible for your people being drawn into my problem."

She reached out and took his hand and held it. "Please take me to the hotel," she murmured. "I shall return later when things have cooled down in the house and get what Father and I will need until the house is repaired."

"Your father," Wolf said. "When is he expected home?"

"Not until later tonight," Jo said. "I want to be here when he arrives. When he sees the house, I don't want him to think I was harmed in the fire."

"I will take you to the hotel, but I refuse to leave you there alone," Wolf said, taking her up into his arms. "I want to take my wheelchair with me," she said. "Would you please go and get the wagon from the barn? The horse I use is in the stall."

As Wolf walked away from her toward the barn, Jo gazed past the house and at her father's rose garden and orchard. None of the trees had burned and the roses were still thick and beautiful.

"Thank God, at least they were spared," she whispered, a tremor racing up her spine when she thought of how this might have turned out if the men had come in the night and set the fire.

She knew now that she should have been more alarmed by the torches last night. She should have gone to the sheriff and reported the threat. She hadn't though, because she knew that he was too corrupt to trust.

"I wonder what those fiends will do next," she whispered. "I wonder just how involved the sheriff is with those men."

When Wolf came back to her with the wagon, leading her black gelding by the reins, Jo smiled. "Thank goodness the barn was spared," she murmured. "Had Old Tom died in the flames, I'd be out for blood."

"Old Tom?" Wolf said, raising an eyebrow as he dropped the reins and reached up for Jo.

Jo slid easily into his arms and gave Old Tom a pat as Wolf carried her past the horse to the wagon. "That's my gelding," she murmured. "He's as old as Methuselah but as dependable as the sunrise."

"Old Tom can retire now," Wolf chuckled as he gently placed Jo on the seat. "White Cloud can replace him."

"I'd rather reserve White Cloud for horseback riding," Jo said, taking up the reins. She turned and looked up at the bluff, then frowned down at Wolf. "I can get to the hotel safely enough. Don't you think you'd better go and retrieve White Cloud? If someone found him—"

"I will see that you get to the hotel safely, and then I'll go for White Cloud," Wolf said, swinging himself into his saddle.

"I don't think I should stay at the hotel for long," Jo said, flicking her reins. "I'll register and then come back to the house. If Father decides to come home early, I do want to be there."

Wolf nodded.

Jo looked around her for signs of men lurking in the alleys, wishing now that she had gotten a better look at those who had arrived last night with their torches. Unfortunately, the light of the torches hadn't given her that opportunity.

But she had her suspicions. She hated to think that Max might have had anything to do with this, but his anger toward her might have caused him to become involved. As for Sheriff Gowins, she could expect anything from him!

But she had no proof. When she did, some- one would have hell to pay!

Chapter Sixteen

Having worried all day about Jo being home alone, Addison slapped the reins and turned his horse and buggy down a street that would get him to his house more quickly than going through the downtown area.

It was just growing dark. Lamplight was beginning to glow in the windows of the houses that lined the street. He hoped he would soon see lamplight in his own house, proving that Jo was alright.

He had made a decision today.

He had decided not to go back to work until this present crisis was past and he felt it was safe enough for Jo to come and go without his being around to keep an eye on things.

He would never get the threats off his mind.

His daughter was much more vulnerable now than she had been before the wreck.

Should someone truly want to harm her, it could be easily done.

She would not be able to run, or walk away, from trouble.

"She'd better be safe," he grumbled beneath his breath as he urged his horse to a faster gait. "Lord, why did I choose today to go into Detroit? If anyone saw me leave . . ."

As he made a flying turn that took him onto the street where his house stood, the color drained from his face. He instantly saw the one charred side of his house. The bricks were still standing, but the bedroom windows had been blown out from the fire, leaving blackened holes like empty eye sockets staring back at him.

He stared at the other windows in the house. There was no lamplight. There was no sign of life anywhere!

"Jo," he whispered, and an ache circled his heart. Had she been injured in the fire, perhaps . . . perhaps . . . killed?

Cold inside, he rode up the small gravel lane and stopped in front of his house. His nose twitched with the strong stench of smoke, ashes, and burned wood.

Dropping the reins, he hurried from the wagon and limped up to the house.

The utter, tomb-like stillness of the house made tears rush from his eyes.

"Jo, my Jo," he sobbed, reaching a hand out toward the house. He just knew that she had died there.

Then out of the corner of his eye he saw a movement in his rose arbor; a moment later he saw another movement among his apple trees.

"Jo?" he whispered, hope rising within him that she was there, checking on things, and that she would wheel herself out into the open at any moment.

But what happened next sent spirals of fear through him. Whoever had made the movement among his roses and apple trees was not his daughter! It was someone who had just set fire to the trees; the flames were quickly spreading into the roses!

"No!" he cried, limping as quickly as possible to an outdoor well and bringing up a bucket of water from its depths.

Panting, his heart pounding, he ran with the bucket of water. But just as he started to throw it into the flames, he felt a blow to the back of his head.

As he fell to the ground, the water from his bucket spilling and pooling around him, he saw a man running away from him. And then Addison found himself being sucked into a black void of unconsciousness. The fire spread on all sides of him, fed by the roses and the autumn-dried grass and fallen leaves. A throaty, sinister laugh wafted through the smoke and flames.

Chapter Seventeen

Jo had signed the register for two rooms in the hotel. Just as she left the hotel and was helped into her wagon by James, the hotel owner, she jumped with alarm when the fire wagon with its team of horses and jangling bells rushed past.

Jo's head turned automatically in the direction the fire wagon was traveling. The color drained from her face when she saw great plumes of smoke rising into the sky from the direction of her house.

"No!" she cried, growing cold with panic. "Please don't let it be my house again."

She thanked James, then slapped the reins hard against Old Tom's back and traveled at a great speed down Main Street. She didn't want to think that whoever had set the earlier fire had returned to finish the job.

But she now realized that anything was possible if someone hated someone enough. And it was certain that someone was out to get *her*.

She noticed a crowd of horses and buggies and men on horseback on both sides of her and behind her, all of them following the fire wagon.

And she understood. It was unusual for this town to have two fires in one day. This would make the headlines in *The Lone Branch Sentinel* tomorrow.

She was just glad that neither she nor her father would be a big part of those headlines since they had escaped the wrath of the flames.

"Father!" Jo whispered harshly. Fear swamped her at the thought that perhaps her father had arrived home early and was the target of this newest fire.

Her heart pounding, praying that she was wrong, Jo hurried onward.

When she made the turn that took her onto her own street she knew that she had been right to suppose the fire had something to do with her. But this time it wasn't the house. Her father's precious rose arbor and apple orchard were going up in flames.

Tears streaming from her eyes, she rode onward, then drew a tight rein on the opposite side of the trees away from where everyone else was standing.

The men were just unwinding the hose from the fire wagon. People were forming a bucket brigade from her father's well.

Wiping tears from her eyes, Jo looked into the flames, then her heart stopped dead inside her chest when she saw something that no one else had seen.

It was a body!

It was her father!

And the flames were so close they threatened to set his clothes afire!

The only thing that seemed to have thus far saved him was the water that had surely spilled from a bucket lying at her father's right side.

He had probably been carrying the bucket of water to put out the fire when he had either fainted or . . .

Not taking the time to think any more, only wanting to get her father safe from the fire, Jo leaped from the wagon, and before she realized it she was actually running to her father.

Just as she reached him, Wolf rode up on his horse. He had gone to retrieve White Cloud from the bluff, and had seen the flames from there.

He had then seen Jo riding toward them. . . .

As Wolf drew his horse to a halt, he saw a miracle at work as Jo ran to her father and bent low to grip him beneath his arms and drag him free of the fire.

Jo's legs had taken her to her father!

She had actually been able to run!

To stand!

To walk!

Astonished, Wolf ran into the smoke and grabbed Addison up into his arms.

"Follow close beside me!" Wolf shouted at Jo, who was coughing and grabbing at her throat. "Hurry!"

Jo nodded and ran beside Wolf until they were free of the smoke and flames.

Wolf laid Addison down on the far side of the inferno.

Her throat parched, her eyes burning from the smoke, Jo knelt down beside her father and gently smoothed his scorched hair back from his eyes. "Father, oh, Father, please be alright," she sobbed. Joy filled her heart when his eyelashes began fluttering open.

She leaned low and clutched him in her arms. "Father, Father," she sobbed.

"Jo, are . . . you . . . alright?" Addison breathed out. He could barely speak, and his eyes stung so much he could barely see his daughter.

"Yes, and thank God I think you're going to be alright, also," she cried, seeing that he had only been blackened by the smoke, not burned.

Addison reached up and gently touched Jo's face. "Daughter, daughter," he choked out, tears of relief rushing from his eyes.

"When I saw you lying there, Father, I died a slow death inside," Jo said, half choking on a sob. "I thought you were dead. And, Father,

I . . . I . . . didn't realize it at the time, but . . . but . . . I *ran* to you. I . . . actually . . . *ran* to you. My legs *worked! I* can *walk* again! I . . . can . . . run!"

Addison's eyes widened, then he grabbed her and brought her down for another fierce hug. "Out of tragedy always comes some good," he said, sobbing. "Thank the good Lord, something wonderful came out of this one."

"And you, Father?" Jo said, leaning away from him, studying him more carefully.

"Someone set the fire and then hit me over the back of the head," Addison said, wincing when he reached up and found the lump on his head. He then laughed goodnaturedly. "I can expect a headache tomorrow, don't you think?"

"I'm glad that's all," Jo said, then smiled sweetly at Wolf as he knelt down beside her. There was something in his eyes that she had never seen before as he gazed in wonder at her.

"What is it, Wolf?" she murmured. "Why are you looking at me like that?"

"You walked," he said thickly. "*Mee-kah-wah-diz-ee-gee-wee-oo*, my woman, you *ran*. I saw you run to your father. The pain of seeing your father so close to dying made you forget the pain of your mother's death. It brought life back to your legs. You can walk again."

Tears streaming from her eyes, Jo nodded. "Yes, walking came that easily in the face of danger," she murmured, ecstatic over being able to walk again.

"It's so wonderful," she murmured, wiping tears from her face with the back of a hand as people came and stood around them, staring. The fire had been extinguished. "I can walk and . . . Father . . . is alright."

Addison slowly sat up. He shook one hand and then another as people leaned down to tell him they were so glad he and Jo were alright.

Then when the fire wagon and the people left, Wolf and Jo got on each side of Addison and helped him up from the ground.

Addison's head spun. He grabbed at Jo for more support, and then the lightheadedness was gone. He stepped away from Jo and Wolf, limping his usual limp, and gazed sadly at his destroyed rose arbor and apple orchard.

He then looked at his house, again seeing how badly it had been burned.

"Someone means business," he said thickly. He turned to Jo. "Jo, I truly see the danger we are in. We've got to think things through and make sure nothing else happens. We both could be dead, Jo. If not for you, I'd certainly be lying dead now amidst the charred trees and roses. The smoke was so thick on the one side, no one could see me. Had you not ridden up on the other side, where the smoke was blowing away from you, I would not have been rescued."

"You should both come and stay at my village. There you will be safe while I send warriors out to search for those who are responsible for what has happened here," Wolf said. "Or stay at least until your house is repaired. Sentries are posted around the reservation. No white man can come anywhere near you while you are there among my people."

Jo remembered the hotel rooms that she had already paid for, yet believing they would be much better off at the reservation, she decided not to tell her father about them.

He looked uncertain, as though he was ready to agree to go to the reservation. Although she knew that he was thinking their troubles would stop if she would stay away from Wolf and his people, he also knew that there was more to her feelings for the Ottawa than altruism.

He knew now that her feelings for their chief had gone far beyond admiration. He surely knew that she was in love with Wolf and understood that he had to find a way to accept her feelings.

Going to the Indian village would be his first step toward accepting the inevitable.

Just as Addison started to give his answer, the sound of horses arriving made them all turn abruptly.

Jo's insides went cold when she saw Sheriff Gowins and two of his deputies ride up.

"I heard about the fires, Addison," Sheriff Gowins said, looking past him at the charred remains of the orchard and arbor. His eyes shifted to the house, then he looked with a half smile at Jo. "Damn sorry, Jo. Damn sorry."

"About as sorry as I was glad that you were elected sheriff," Jo said sarcastically. She stepped away from Wolf and her father and placed her hands on her hips as she glared up at the sheriff. "Now, what are you going to do about this, Sheriff? Two times in one day someone has come on our private property and set fires. Someone tried to murder my father. The lump on his head is proof of that. Whoever set the fires hit him over the head and left him to die in the fire."

Addison stepped up next to Jo. He slid an arm around her waist. "I demand that you find the fire starter," he said hotly. "When you find *him*, you will find the man who tried to kill me today. It's your duty as sheriff to keep things like this from happening in Lone Branch."

Sheriff Gowins stared disbelievingly at Jo, obviously stunned to see her standing up away from her wheelchair. He gripped the pommel of his saddle and leaned down into Jo's face. "Got your legs back, huh?" he said mockingly. "I'd say the timing is good, for you see, Jo, none of what's happened can actually be blamed on the man who set the fire." He then shifted his eyes to Addison. "Your daughter is to blame, Addison. What happened today should be message enough to your daughter that it's not good to side with Injuns."

Wolf clenched his hands into tight fists at his sides as Sheriff Gowins looked at him and laughed throatily. It took all of Wolf's willpower not to drag the evil sheriff from his saddle and make him pay for his behavior toward Jo.

But he knew that nothing would please the sheriff more than Wolf losing his temper and going against a white lawman. That would give the sheriff the right to put Wolf in jail and throw away the key!

Instead, Wolf held himself under tight control as he glared back at the sheriff. When the sheriff realized that Wolf wasn't going to comment one way or the other about what he had said, he gave one last laugh and rode off with his deputies.

"He's not going to do anything about what happened today," Jo said, stunned to realize just how corrupt the sheriff of Lone Branch was.

She turned and gazed at Wolf. "I've never felt as helpless as now," she said, her voice breaking. "Not even when I couldn't walk!"

He gripped her shoulders gently with his hands. "My woman, I insist that you and your father come to my village," he said thickly.

"But, Wolf, don't you see how that would be bringing danger to your people by my mere presence there?" Jo asked. "I don't want to do anything that would harm your people. This is my battle. I must stand up for my rights and fight this to the end. But I don't want to make it your battle, as well."

"Anyone who goes against you is automatically my enemy," Wolf said tightly. "Anyone who goes against you automatically goes against me, for you and I are as one, my woman. We are of the same heartbeat."

Out of the corner of her eye Jo saw her father flinch at those words. But she couldn't worry about that now, for Wolf was now her protector, not her father.

"Yes, we'll go with you," she blurted out, ignoring her father's gasp behind her. She turned to her father. "I'll go inside and gather up a few things. I just hope that no one comes and takes what is left. There is no way to take everything with us."

When they left the charred remains behind them, Jo was in her wagon with White Cloud tied behind her, her father was in his buggy, and Wolf was riding alongside Jo.

Jo felt a little guilty at taking charge today by deciding for both her and her father what was best for them. She hoped that sometime down the road he would understand her action and might even thank her for it.

One thing she didn't want him ever to know was just how frightened she was for them. With Sheriff Gowins ignoring what had happened today, she knew just how vulnerable she and her father were.

One day her father would realize that Wolf was their only salvation. . . .

Chapter Eighteen

Max sat on his horse in the far shadows away from the smoking rubble of the burned arbor and orchard. He had seen everything that happened after Roy Bates struck the matches that started the fire.

Even now Roy was on his horse beside Max, striking one match after another, staring into the flames, obviously hypnotized by them.

Max leaned over and slung an arm around Roy's shoulders. "You did good today," he said, laughing. "You put the fear of God in the Stantons."

Max's smile waned when, in his mind's eye, he again saw Jo rush into the smoke and rescue her father. Obviously in the heat of the moment she'd forgotten that she had lost all use of her legs.

To have seen her walking again, to see her as that whole woman he had fallen in love with even before she had become a woman, made Max's desire for her as strong as it had been before the damnable train wreck.

Yes, she *was* a whole woman again.

Yes, he could not *help* wanting her again!

And, by God, he would have her!

Chapter Nineteen

Deciding not to allow anyone to chase them from their home, Jo and her father stayed at Wolf's village for only one night.

"Lady Unafraid" Wolf had called her when she had told him of her decision to return to her home and fight fire with fire.

Touched deeply, she stood back from the house now and watched the Ottawa warriors working together to rebuild that portion of her father's house that had been destroyed by the fire.

Her gaze went to Wolf and her father, who were working together, side by side, as they fit a pane of glass into one of the bedroom windows.

It was wonderful to see her father and the man she loved coming together as friends.

Wolf had told her that this was the way of

the Ottawa. When tragedy struck, everyone worked together to make things right again.

He had said that now that she was a part of his life, it was only right that his people work alongside Jo and her father to make things right for them.

It was this act of friendship from the Ottawa that had changed her father's mind about Jo helping the Ottawa in the courtroom should the need arise again.

It made tears swell in her eyes to know that he had even accepted the love she had for Wolf. He had told her that it did his heart good to see his daughter's eyes shine with happiness again. He had not seen her so full of life since the day her mother died.

Her fingers sore from hammering so many nails, Jo welcomed this momentary reprieve from her labors. Everyone had been working since dawn. Not much was left to do before the house would be like new again.

She gazed down at her legs and smiled, for she had never known just how much it meant to be able to walk until the ability to get around on her own had been taken from her. Before the accident, she had taken for granted the ability to rise every day and go about her daily activities.

Now she felt blessed with every step she took.

She looked over at the wheelchair that sat just inside the open door of the barn. Although at first she had hated having to use it, she had come to see it as her special friend.

Now that she would have no more need of it, she was going to donate it, and the others that were at her offices, to the orphanage. Too often crippled children were brought to the orphanage by parents who did not want to be bothered by having to care for someone who required more work than the average child. It made her heart ache to think of one such child: sweet Judith Lynn, an eight-year-old girl who had been abandoned at the doorstep of the orphanage when she was just the age that children learned to walk. It was apparent that when the parents discovered that Judith Lynn couldn't walk, they discarded her like some old shoe.

It was Judith Lynn who had drawn Jo often to the orphanage. Feeling deeply for the child, Jo spent as much time with her as possible.

She smiled when she thought of Judith Lynn sitting in one of Jo's wheelchairs. The one that Judith Lynn had was tiny, cramped, and hard to get around in.

Jo's moved with ease.

Yes, Judith Lynn would have one of the chairs and would discover the ease with which she could get from place to place.

The child with the golden curls and sweet smile would even be able to wheel it around herself, whereas now she had to be pushed by an attendant at the orphanage.

The sound of a horse arriving pulled Jo

from her deep thoughts. She turned and shaded her face with a hand so that she could see despite the bright afternoon sunlight.

She stiffened when she saw that it was Max riding up on his strawberry roan, a bouquet of flowers in his right hand, his reins held in his other.

As Jo's mother would label him, he was "spiffy" today in his fancy dark suit, his golden hair combed to perfection, his boots shining from a fresh "spit-shine," as Max had always termed his way of shining his boots with spit.

In the sunlight the freckles across the bridge of his nose were more prominent, making Jo recall those days of their youth when she teased him about his freckles even though she really loved them, thinking they made him even more handsome.

Today she resented even his freckles, and especially his wide smile as he drew a tight rein close to her.

The flowers again caught her gaze; she knew that a man only brought flowers to a lady if he was interested in courting her.

She recalled the day when he had told her that he no longer wanted to marry her.

Then she remembered how he had not only mocked her in the courtroom after she had won the case for the Ottawa, but also had mocked Wolf.

Yes, she hated this man with a vengeance, and she was sure that he was in on the plot to ruin the Ottawa.

She even suspected that he had had a part in her house being burned.

His gift of flowers was surely only a ploy . . . a smoke screen of sorts . . . to take suspicion away from him.

He surely couldn't be stupid enough to think that she had any feelings for him other than seething, silent loathing.

"Mornin', Jo," Max said, sliding out of his saddle. He held the bouquet out to her. "I heard about the tragic fire." He glanced over at the busy workers.

The only ones who stopped to glare at Max were her father and Wolf.

Jo saw how Wolf took a step forward, as though he was going to come to her and protect her, but then he stepped back to her father's side and waited.

And she was glad. She could take care of this problem herself. Max would never get the best of her again.

"Max, don't pretend to care about the fire, or me," Jo said, sighing heavily.

She could see his smile turn into a glower.

"The Ottawa are helping Father repair the damage," she went on. "Father and I will be able to sleep in the house again tonight. And, by damn, should anyone come again and cause us any trouble I, personally, will shoot them."

Max's blue eyes snapped angrily as he turned them on Jo; then he forced himself to smile. "I'd be glad to do the honors for you, Jo," he said, his voice tight. "I'll come and stay this first night at your house with you and your father. I'll keep watch. I'll not let anyone hurt you or your father."

He glanced over at the orchard and the ruined roses. "And damn it all to hell, why'd the sonofabitches have to go as far as that?" he said, motioning toward the arbor with the bouquet he still held in his right hand. "I know how much your father loved those roses. And he had the best apples in town. Now the children at the orphanage won't be able to have their usual autumn apples from your father. What a shame. Yep, what a damn shame."

"We'll still be taking apples to the children," Jo said smugly, wanting to laugh out loud when Max's eyes jerked back to her in surprise. "Yes, Max. God must've sent Father into the orchard only a couple of days ago. He picked all that were ripe enough for picking. The apples are stored safely in baskets in the barn."

"Your father always was one who thought ahead," Max said, shuffling his feet nervously. "That's nice, Jo, that you can still take apples to the orphans."

His gaze swept down to her legs. His eyes then roamed slowly upward again until he was gazing into her eyes. "Jo, I'm so damn glad you're able to walk again," he said thickly. "I thought you'd be crippled forever."

"I have a way of surprising a fella, now don't I, Max?" Jo said, her eyes gleaming. She placed her hands on her hips. "Let's quit the small talk. Why are you here?" Her gaze went to the flowers. "And why on earth do you have those flowers with you?" She laughed sarcastically as she looked up at him again. "Now, those couldn't be for me, could they? A woman who turned your stomach only a few hours ago because she couldn't walk?"

"Jo, I never felt that way about you and you know it," Max said, paling. "I . . . I . . . just didn't see how it'd work for us, that's all. But now that things have turned around for you, and *you* have a different attitude about things, I think it would work after all. How's about us thinkin' on marriage again? I'd love to have you for my wife, Jo. You know how long I've loved you."

He paused, then said, "Jo, marry me, and I'll see that nothing ever happens to you and your father again," he said smoothly.

"Max, no," Jo said, holding back what she truly wanted to say to him. She knew that everyone was watching her and Max now, for everything had gone quiet behind her. Because of this she was trying hard to maintain her ladylike composure. But it was hard not to say things to Max that should never leave the lips of a lady.

"Why not, Jo?" Max said, swallowing hard. "You wanted me as a husband before. Why not now? Is it because I broke off with you after the accident? If so, I humbly apologize. I never stopped loving you, Jo. Never."

"Max, you never *ever* loved me," Jo said, her voice breaking. "You just loved the idea of

185

marrying me. Though we were close as children, and foolishly promised ourselves to each other, it is not the same now that we are adults and know so much about each other."

When Max saw Jo slide a slow gaze over to Wolf, he was stunned speechless.

"Jo, you can't have feelings for a savage Indian," he blurted out, drawing Jo's eyes quickly back to him.

She stepped closer to Max. She held her hands to her sides in tight fists. "Savage?" she hissed. "You call that man a savage? Max, *you* are the true savage."

She stopped and sucked in a deep, quivering breath. "And, Max, I wouldn't marry you if you were the last man on earth," she spat out rapidly, as if her words were bullets shooting from the barrel of a gun. "I despise you, utterly despise you. You are nothing like the young boy I loved as a child. You are despicable. You are loathsome. And, Max, if ever I can prove your role in what has happened to me and my father, *and* the Ottawa, I'll bury you."

Max gasped.

His eyes widened.

The flowers fell from his hand to the ground as he stepped slowly away from Jo.

Then he spun around on a heel and mounted his horse.

He gazed down at Jo with contempt, gave Wolf a look of hate, silently vowing to himself that he would take care of that Indian, then sank his heels into the flanks of his horse and rode off.

Jo was left trembling from the experience. She sighed deeply, then felt better when Wolf came to her and took her hands.

"He said things to you that upset you," he said flatly. "I did not interfere because I know you are a woman who can speak well enough for herself and would want it that way. But perhaps I was wrong. I feel your hands shaking. I see the uneasiness in your eyes."

"I'm alright," Jo said, laughing somewhat awkwardly. "I'm still Lady Unafraid."

She looked away from Wolf for a moment, swallowed hard, then looked into his eyes once again. "He wants to be a part of my life again," she explained. "Of course you know that I refused him."

When her father stepped up to her, she quickly explained things to him.

Then she looked at Wolf again. "Max guessed what my feelings are for you," she murmured. "I saw him look your way. I saw the hate in his eyes. He even called you . . ."

She stopped short of telling him that Max had called Wolf a savage. There was no need to inflict hurt in such a way, for she knew that no man or woman wanted to be labeled a savage.

But the one thing Wolf needed to know was the danger Max presented to Wolf and his people. She knew that the Ottawa had much to fear from the dark, sinister side of this man she'd adored as a child.

"Wolf, now that I've rejected Max, he may seek vengeance by harming your people," Jo said, her voice catching. "I think you should prepare them for whatever he might decide to do."

"They already are prepared," Wolf said thickly. "Sentries have been doubled around the reservation. They are now keeping watch, both day and night. No one should be able to get past them."

Jo didn't want to say she doubted that anything would keep Max from having his vengeance. If he had to kill the sentries to achieve what he was determined to do, she expected that he would.

But she didn't say anything else to Wolf about it. She didn't want it to look as though she didn't trust his judgment. He had been chief for too long to need her advice.

Wolf stepped to Jo's side and slid an arm around her waist. He turned her so that she could see the house. "It is all but done," he said proudly.

"How can we ever thank your people enough?" Jo murmured, smiling up at him.

"Tomorrow you can thank *me* by going fishing with me for brook trout in the Grand River," Wolf said softly.

"Your warriors will be with us?" Jo asked, eyes wide. "It will be a big fishing expedition to replace those that were taken from you?"

"Tomorrow the fish will only answer to me and you," Wolf said, chuckling. "It will be a day of leisure, my woman, a day for only us."

Jo glanced over at her father. "Will you need me tomorrow?" she asked softly.

"No, but I thought you were going to work," Addison said, thinking she would be safer there than out somewhere fishing alone with Wolf.

"I've plenty of time to catch up on what I neglected," Jo murmured. "Because of my legs, I was held back so long from doing things I loved to do. Tomorrow, Father, I would love to take at least one more day of fun before getting down to brass tacks at my office."

"Then, daughter, do it," Addison said, smiling from her to Wolf. "But, Wolf, don't let her outdo you while fishing. When I've taken her with me she's doubled everything I ever caught." He chuckled. "Seems I taught her too well, doesn't it?"

"I think you did everything right where your daughter is concerned," Wolf said, his eyes twinkling down into hers.

Jo felt deeply content, yet she couldn't help thinking back to Max and how angry and humiliated he was when he rode off.

She knew to expect anything from him at any time.

Chapter Twenty

Sitting beside the river on a blanket, watching Wolf preparing brook trout for cooking in the fire that she had helped him build, Jo was lost in thought. Never had she had such a fun, carefree day as today.

First, it had been absolutely wonderful to ride beautiful White Cloud to Wolf's reservation. Gently she had squeezed the sides of the horse with her legs to prove that she *could* feel the horse with them. She had felt giddy when she discovered that, yes, she could feel the horse's muscled body with legs that worked!

And, ah, how quickly she had bonded with the beautiful white stallion. It was as though they were one soul.

She felt so lucky that she had feeling back in her legs, and that she had a special, adorable man in her life. It was as though she were beginning life all over again, but this time with much more meaning.

Of course, there were things that troubled her—the Ottawa's continuing struggle to live a life without the interference of white people.

And there was the fiend whose love of fires kept all of them on their toes at night, with shotguns loaded beside their doors!

And . . . then . . . there was Max.

Jo knew that he would find a way to devise some scheme to make her pay for having humiliated him, especially since she had done so in front of the Ottawa warriors who had seen her turn down his proposal of marriage.

And something else troubled her. She was finding such joy being with Wolf, she no longer saw her career as something she wanted to pursue as avidly as she had in the past. Being with Wolf was all she thought about.

And when she married him, she would definitely give up her career to make him a good wife and eventually a good mother for their children.

And, ah, there *would* be children!

Many of them!

She would never raise a single child as she had been raised. She had learned early in life that an only child was a lonely child.

"And so you see how it is done?" Wolf said, dropping to his haunches before her as he began wrapping a cleaned fish in one of the

manhood was stretched to its limits, a pearl-bead of wetness shining on its tip.

She didn't have to be told what to do next. Her fingers trembled as she slid her blouse free of the waistband of her skirt.

With eagerness she unbuttoned it and cast it and the rest of her clothes on the ground beside her.

Her heart thundering, her senses already reeling, Jo stretched out again on her back on the blanket and reached her arms out for Wolf.

"Come to me," she said, the huskiness of her voice making her sound strange and unfamiliar to herself. "Wolf, oh, how I love you. How I *need* you."

Wolf knelt down beside her instead of stretching out over her. His eyes feasted on her body as his hands moved softly and gently over her, her every secret place becoming his.

He smiled when her eyes closed with pleasure as he cupped both of her breasts with his hands, his thumbs slowly circling her nipples.

And when he knelt lower and flicked his tongue over the nipples, drawing a gasp of pleasure from Jo, his one hand slid downward across her flat tummy and soon cupped her where she ached almost unmercifully.

"Oh, Wolf, how can it feel so wonderful?" Jo whispered, gazing at him as he now sat up and watched her reaction to his caresses.

When he thrust a finger inside her and she flinched, he withdrew the finger and again only caressed her.

He could see the pleasure building in her eyes, and this time when he slid a finger inside her, she didn't flinch. She moaned and arched her body upward, her hips moving as he rhythmically moved his one finger, and then two, within her.

Finding herself becoming lost, heart and soul, Jo reached out for Wolf. "Please . . . ?" she whispered.

Her eyes flaring with hungry intent, she beckoned him to lie down with her.

As he gave her a meltingly hot kiss, he moved his body over hers.

Groaning huskily and holding her within his arms, he found her softness with his throbbing shaft and ground into her, her low cry of passion proving her pleasure.

As his body moved, Jo drew a ragged breath. Then he kissed her with a fierce, possessive heat, and she writhed beneath him, breathless now with building rapture.

A raging hunger consumed Wolf. Waves of heat pulsed through his veins with each thrust inside her. Wolf slid his mouth down and showered kisses over Jo's breasts, his tongue flicking the nipples, one by one.

He slid a hand down between their bodies and found her swollen nub.

His thrusts continued inside her as his finger now moved insistently over her woman's center, each caress bringing new, long gasps of pleasure from deep within Jo.

Wolf watched her now as her head thrashed back and forth, her hair billowing around her face like golden strands of silk from freshly picked corn in summer.

Ah, he thought to himself, she was such a vision, her pretty face flushed pink, her long, thick lashes like dark veils over her closed eyes, and her lips slightly parted and still wet from his kiss.

He moved sideways over her and cradled her now in one arm, his own breath short and raspy as his pleasure built.

Her head was no longer tossing, but now lying at a slight angle to his. He buried his face next to her neck and closed his eyes. He savored how her body moved with his, as he moved within her now with faster, quicker, surer movements which would soon bring them both to the brink of ecstasy they were seeking.

"Wolf," Jo cried, reaching out for him, bringing him again above her.

She strained her body up against his.

She pressed her throbbing center against him, so that his each and every move brought her closer and closer to the moment of fulfillment.

His mouth came down hard upon hers. His muscled arms swept around her and held her close as he kissed her long and deep, his thrusts now insistent. His tongue swept through her lips and into her mouth. Her tongue touched his in a dance that was new to her, yet wonderful.

A series of tremors soared through Jo's body, and then her body exploded in spasms of desire just as he groaned and lunged over and over again into her, his own pleasure having peaked.

When they came down from that place of wonder and joy, Wolf still did not move away from her. He buried his face between her breasts, trembling anew when her hands ran slowly down his back and then circled around and enfolded his shrunken, spent member within her warm fingers.

Wolf's body jerked with her first touch.

Then he fell away from her on his back and let the feelings begin anew as her fingers brought him back to life and the heat filled him and his heart soared.

He closed his eyes and ignored the wonderful aroma of the fish baking in the hot coals. He had been anxious to eat his favorite fish. But now he didn't care if he ever ate, or even if he ever left this place where he and his woman were away from the rest of the world and its troubles.

For now he would just believe they were the only two people on the earth.

Theirs was a love all-consuming!

Nothing and no one could ever take it away from them!

When Wolf felt Jo's warm mouth close over his engorged sex, her tongue flicking, his whole body vibrated with pleasure.

Chapter Twenty-one

Pacing in his plush, oak-paneled office, his hands clasped behind him, Max sucked feverishly on a fat, freshly lit cigar. Several gazes were on him, especially that of Roy Bates, whose beady eyes squinted through the thick lenses of his glasses.

"Max, can't you stop pacing and get down to brass tacks?" Roy said, pushing his chair back. He impatiently took his glasses off and wiped the lenses with a handkerchief. "Why'd you call this meeting? For us all to just watch you silently brood over something?" He slid his glasses back in place on the bridge of his nose. "What's got you so riled up? Is it Jo? Did she turn you down when you asked her to marry you?"

The sun sent splinters of light through a

window behind Max. It outlined him when he stopped and glared first at Roy, and then at the other men under his employ who sat around the room.

He yanked his cigar from his mouth and laid it in an ashtray on top of his large oak desk. "This meeting is about Jo, alright," he spat out as he glared from man to man. "It's about downing her and anyone who's associated with her."

"So she *did* say no, huh?" Roy said, laughing sarcastically. "I told you not to bother with her, Max. I told you she only had eyes for that damn savage."

Max stamped from behind his desk. He stopped before Roy, leaned down and grabbed him by the collar at his throat. He hissed out his answer. "I don't need no advice from the likes of you," he said. "I give the orders around here. Not you."

"Max, *God*," Roy said, gripping Max's hand and forcing it away from his shirt. "There is no need to get so hot and bothered, now is there? Tell us your plan. That's why we are here. Not to fight amongst ourselves."

"Then watch your mouth if that's the way you want it," Max said. He cleared his throat and walked away from Roy. His thick blond hair glistened in the sunlight as he went back to his desk and sat down behind it. He leaned his elbows on his desk and placed his fingertips together before him. "Now, fellas, here's what I have planned. I'm giving orders to all of my lumberjacks to move farther onto Indian land for more lumber. I'm tired of pussyfooting around with them. They know the law's on our side." He laughed. "Sheriff Gowins wouldn't lift a finger against me, you know."

"Yes, but I know who would," Roy said, nervously removing his glasses again. "That damn broad. That's who. She'll take you to court, Max, and fight for the Indians' rights again. She won once for the savages. As smart and educated as she is, she'd probably get the best of you again."

"She might *think* she won," Max growled out. "No matter what transpired in that damn courtroom, I still see the fish and the land as the white man's."

"Yeah, but thinking it doesn't matter a damn," Roy said sourly. "She made a fool of me once, Max. Don't let her best me twice in the same courtroom. I'd lose face, Max."

"You'd lose more face if you let people know you're afraid to go up against a lady," Max said, then snickered. "Roy, you'd best just listen and do as I say when I say it. I'm the one paying your bills, now aren't I? Don't you think I'm the one you've got to worry about most?"

"Yeah, sure," Roy grumbled.

"Then pay attention when I say the lumber will be mine," Max said. He nodded toward his men. "Now get out there and spread the word that trees are to be cut."

"I've heard that the Ottawa have placed

many more sentries everywhere," one of the men said, standing. He frowned. "I don't think I want an arrow stuck in my behind."

"If you don't do as I say, you'll have more than arrows piercing your ass," Max threatened. "Now get out of here. All of you, except Roy. Roy, I have something else to discuss with you."

The men filed out of the room, leaving Roy to stare questioningly at Max.

"What else is on your mind?" Roy asked warily.

"Roy, I want to make Jo pay for humiliating me, and in the same breath I plan to take the Ottawa's confidence down a notch or two," Max said tersely. "The corn crop is ready for harvesting at the Ottawa reservation. Go and take care of it in the way only you know how. The importance of the corn to the Ottawa people cannot be overstated. They depend on it to get them through the long, cold winter. If we put fear into their heart about one thing, namely burned corn, they will forget to worry about another, leaving the lumber at my disposal. And they'll begin to wonder what is next. People of all kinds, red or white skinned, can take only so much before they give in."

He went to the window and gazed in the direction of the Indian reservation. "Yep, one way or another I'll get back at the Ottawa chief *and* Jo for having interfered too many times in things that are important to Maximilian Schmidt."

His eyes gleaming, his coat pocket full of matches, Roy left Max's office.

Chapter Twenty-two

The day had been so sweet, so complete, Jo hated to leave Wolf, yet she knew that she must get back home. She didn't want to worry her father needlessly.

For the first time in her life, she didn't want to travel after dark, not even while she was with Wolf. Ambushes were much easier under the cover of dark.

Patting White Cloud on his muscled neck, her golden hair flying in the wind behind her, Jo gazed over at Wolf as he rode beside her on his own magnificent steed. She smiled to herself when she saw a look of utter contentment on Wolf's face and knew she was responsible. Only moments ago they had made love again.

If the truth were known, she would have made love still more, for she was becoming addicted to loving this handsome Ottawa chief.

When she thought of being married to him, waking up every morning in his arms and being beside him all night every night, she could hardly believe it might come to pass.

He loved her!

He wanted to marry her!

She glanced down at her legs. Tears came to her eyes every time she thought about how lucky she was to be walking again. She felt blessed because of it.

Her eyes jerked away from her legs when she got a sudden scent of smoke in the air.

Her spine stiffened and fear crept into her heart when she saw smoke spiraling into the sky from somewhere ahead of her.

"My village!" Wolf cried. "The smoke is coming from the direction of the reservation!"

Not saying anything else, or waiting for Jo to reply, Wolf sank his heels into the flanks of his horse and rode off in a hard gallop. He couldn't believe that anyone could have made it past his sentries!

Catching up to Wolf, Jo sidled her horse closer to him. "You do believe it's your village, don't you?" she shouted over the thundering of the horses' hooves.

"My village is the only thing in the area," Wolf shouted back at her. He cast her a dark, worried glance. "It never ends . . . the suffering my people must go through at the hands of whites!"

Those words stung Jo's heart because she felt she was responsible for whatever had happened to the Ottawa people now. Surely this fire had been set to drive her away from Wolf and his people.

If so, she knew more than one person to point an accusing finger at.

Most prominent in her mind was . . . Max!

She would never forget that look in his eyes when she refused to marry him, and then how he had looked over at Wolf, obviously realizing that Jo and Wolf had deep feelings for one another.

Suddenly speechless, Jo looked straight ahead and rode onward.

The closer they got to the fire, the thicker the smoke became. It was so intense it burned Jo's throat and eyes. She wiped at her eyes with one hand while struggling to hang onto the reins with the other.

And then finally they broke through the smoke enough to see what was on fire.

It wasn't the Ottawa houses.

It was their corn field!

Flames were lapping hungrily at the dried stalks that were just ready for harvesting.

From what she could tell, none of the corn would survive the fire, even though many Ottawa people were carrying wooden buckets of water from the river and throwing it into the flames.

The flames were an inferno, unstoppable.

Just as Jo and Wolf rode up to the crowd

alongside the flaming corn field, the people stepped aside and set their buckets on the ground. Jo flinched when she saw the look of defeat in the Ottawa's eyes. She knew now that the importance of the corn crop to the Ottawa people could not be overstated. Corn was one food source that could be preserved and eaten through the lean months of the year.

And they could only grow one crop of corn because of the short growing season. They couldn't even be sure that the time and effort invested in planting would yield a harvest because the soil of the region was rather infertile.

Nonetheless, their survival depended on their corn crop, along with hunting and fishing.

Wolf drew a tight rein and brought his horse to a halt. He slid from his saddle and gazed from one smoke-blackened face to another.

"The fire had to have been set," he said, his eyes narrowing with anger. "Did anyone see who did it? And how about our sentries? Has anyone checked on them to see if they are alright?"

Red Hawk stepped away from the others. "The sentries came quickly when they saw the smoke," he said. "They helped with the effort to extinguish the fire."

"They saw no one?" Wolf said, searching through the crowd for the sentries he knew were supposed to be posted today. He saw none of them and had to surmise that they had returned to their duties.

"No one," Red Hawk said somberly. "Who-

ever did this, Wolf, is as tricky . . . as sneaky
. . . as a weasel."

Hearing that description, Jo raised her eyebrows. Weasel. She knew a man who fit that
description. Roy Bates.

Her eyes widened when she remembered
something about Roy that made her suspect
even more strongly that he might be the one
setting the fires. She had seen him playing
with matches more than once as he waited for
Max in various places.

It gave her shivers to recall, now, the look in
Roy's eyes as he watched the match burn
down almost to his fingers. It was a look of
bliss, as though he got some sort of sexual
gratification from watching fire burning.

Yet, no, surely not. He was a man who had
spent many years studying law. He even grad-
uated from law school at the top of his class.
Surely he wouldn't lower himself to commit-
ting such crimes. Surely she had just imag-
ined it when she watched him toying with
matches.

No, Jo thought, as Wolf and Red Hawk continued to talk about the matter at hand, while
others added their own ideas to the debate,
surely it was someone besides Roy.

"Max," she whispered to herself. Surely Max
had something to do with this. He could have
offered a good sum of money to any man who
was down on his luck, and surely someone
like that would be glad to set a fire for the
money.

And Max was clever. He would know exactly how to pick a man who was able to move past the sentries without being seen.

There were many of Sheriff Gowins' deputies who would fit the bill and who knew the country well enough to know where to look for the sentries and how to elude them.

"Jo?"

The sound of Blue Moth gently speaking her name brought Jo out of her reverie. She turned her eyes to Wolf's mother and gave her a look of apology, for Jo *did* feel responsible for what had happened today. Her association with the Ottawa had brought them trouble, as she had feared it might.

"Come with me out of the smoke to my lodge," Blue Moth murmured, smudges of ash on her copper cheeks. "Wolf will be busy with the warriors. Come. Let us get away from the smoke. And I must get back to Sleeping Bear. When the shouting began about the fire, I rushed from the cabin, leaving Sleeping Bear behind, alone."

"Please go on without me," Jo said, reaching down from her horse to gently smooth away the ash from Blue Moth's face. "I . . . I . . . have something that needs to be done."

"And what is that?" Wolf asked, stepping up beside Jo just as she made the statement. He gazed questioningly at Jo. "What needs to be done? Where are you going?"

Jo's eyes wavered as she gazed into Wolf's. "Wolf, what happened here today is because of me," she said, her voice breaking.

He reached up and took her reins from her. "My woman, trouble from enemies, mostly whites, began before I ever knew you," he said thickly. "Trouble from whites is what brought us together. I will not let it tear us apart. Someone has been out to destroy the Ottawa for some time now. If it isn't the fishing rights, then it is the lumber companies wanting the Ottawa's trees. I noticed this morning that lumberjacks have moved even closer to our land with their axes and saws." He doubled his fists at his sides. "They had best heed my warnings not to go too far."

He unfolded his hands and turned and gazed wistfully at the destroyed corn crop. "Today, though, the main concern is the loss of our crop," he said sorrowfully. He gazed up at Jo again. "My warriors must work doubly hard at the hunt now, and must return to the river for fish."

As he was talking, Jo's thoughts went again to Max. Wolf had said that the lumberjacks were moving closer to his land.

Max.

Yes, he was the sort of man who would do anything to get back at someone who wronged him.

And she was the sort of person who would not hesitate to stand up to him.

"Wolf, I have something to do," she said, giving him a look of apology. She felt so terrible about what had happened to his people today. She gazed at Blue Moth. "Thank you so much for inviting me to your cabin. I hope you understand why I can't go with you. I truly have something that needs to be done. And now. Today."

"Come anytime," Blue Moth said, smiling up at her. "My door is always open to you."

"You are so kind," Jo murmured, then again gazed at Wolf. "I truly must go."

Wolf questioned her with his eyes, for he felt deep inside himself that she had a mission, one that he perhaps should stop. Yet he knew that she was a woman with a strong will, and chose not to interfere.

Besides, his people needed him. He had to find a way to calm their fears.

He nodded at Jo.

She returned the nod, then swung her horse around and rode off at a hard gallop.

Wolf watched her until she was lost in the low-hanging smoke, then turned to his people and thought hard about what he would say next. How could he calm their fears?

He sighed heavily, then stood tall before his people and began to speak encouraging words. Instantly their eyes lit up. Obviously they still had great trust in their young leader.

Chapter Twenty-three

Jo rode up to Max's two-storied brick mansion. It had tall columns gracing the front like the palatial Georgian homes she had seen while traveling with her parents before entering law school.

They had gone south to see historical spots made famous by the Civil War. She had seen then what greed could do to people. That was what had spurred her interest in law . . . her hopes of defending people whose lives were torn apart by greed.

Whipping herself out of her saddle and stamping up the steep steps that led to the long front porch of Max's mansion, Jo was aware of eyes on her from a downstairs front window. She knew it was Max standing in his study. She had been in his house many times and knew the house well enough to go on inside and find Max without announcing herself to Max's butler.

She went to Max's plush office and came face to face with him immediately as he met her at the door.

"Well, what have we here?" Max said, circling her, his eyes taking in her smoke-stained attire. He chuckled, then went and stood before her, clasping his hands tightly behind him. "Where've you been, J. T.? To a bonfire?"

Jo was so angry she could hardly find the breath to talk.

She swallowed hard, drew in a quivering breath, then challenged him with an angry stare. He was wearing an expensive suit, with a diamond shining from the cravat at his throat, and his hair was combed to perfection. The familiar scent of his after-shave on his smooth cheeks reminded her of times long past when she had not seen him as an enemy.

Before he had changed into a rogue, he was such fun to be with. She had enjoyed being seen with him at dances and outings. Yes, she had been so proud to be escorted by him, the gracious man that he had been back then.

When Jo had been seventeen and he nineteen, ah, how he had charmed the ladies, rich and poor alike.

But all that had changed when she had become embarrassed to be seen with him. He had changed and gradually she began to realize that he cared nothing for anyone but himself and the riches he could amass in his private bank account.

"You know damn well where I got this smoke that you see on my face and clothes," Jo spat out, her eyes flashing angrily. "Although you didn't set the fire yourself, I know that you gave the orders. And I imagine you are even responsible for the fire at my house, and in my father's rose arbor and orchard. You not only wanted to put me in my place, but also the Ottawa."

"How can you accuse me of such things as that, Jo?" Max said, a nervous twitch beginning on his right cheek just below his ocean-blue eye. "Why, I'd say that's mighty unkind of you."

"You just can't stand it that I'm in love with an Indian, can you?" Jo said.

Suddenly Max's smile changed to a look of rage. He yanked his hands from behind his back and grabbed Jo by the wrists. Growling, he wrestled her to the floor and straddled her.

"No Indian is going to have you," he said, his eyes becoming glassy with a dark hate. "When I get done with you, I'll have made sure that none'll even want you."

He held her in place with the force of his body, his one hand holding her wrists against the floor, his other whipping up the skirt of her dress.

"What do you think you're doing?" Jo screamed, trying to wrench her wrists free. "Lord, Max, stop and think of what you're doing. Raping me will only make me hate you more. And Wolf will kill you once he learns of it."

"I'm not going to rape you," Max said between clenched teeth. "I don't even want you in that way any longer." He released her hands, flipped his coat tail aside, and yanked a knife from a sheath at his waist. "I'm going to make it so *no* man can make love to you *ever*."

"What?" Jo cried, her face gone pale with the realization of what he was about to do to her. "You can't, Max. Oh, God, Max, what's happened to your mind? Surely it's not you saying and doing these things."

He sneered and flashed the knife before her eyes. "Just you watch me," he said, then slowly began lowering his knife down to where her skirt was hiked up past her knees.

Realizing now just how mad this man was, and knowing that she had to find the strength to stop him, Jo did the only thing that came to her mind. As he leaned slightly away from her, she thrust a knee up into his groin as hard as she could.

When he dropped the knife and rolled away, grabbing his private parts and yelping with pain, Jo scrambled to her feet.

Panting, she reached down and grabbed the knife. Holding it between herself and Max as he lay there, groaning and glaring up at her, Jo frowned down at him.

"I ought to report you to the sheriff, but I know that would be a waste of time because the sheriff is your buddy," Jo hissed out. "So

the next best thing is to warn you, Max. If you
get near me again, or do anything else to the
Ottawa, I'll beat you in the best way possible.
I'll take you to court. I've already proved that
the judges in this town aren't corrupt. I'll fight
you and win."

Through his pain Max found the strength to
laugh at Jo.

"Max, you know I'll have the last laugh if
you cross me again," Jo said, then turned on a
heel and left his house, her knees growing
weak only when she stepped outside into the
fresh air and sunshine.

Trembling, she went down the steps and
leaned heavily against White Cloud.

"White Cloud, take me away from this
place," she sobbed, pulling herself into her
saddle.

She looked at the knife that she still held in
her hand like sin itself, then shuddered and
dropped it to the ground.

When she looked toward the house, Max
was standing in the doorway, still holding
himself and glaring at her.

She swallowed hard, wheeled her horse
around, and rode off. She knew that she had
sounded convincing when she had threatened
Max, but deep down inside herself she was
scared to death of what Max's next move
would be. . . .

Chapter Twenty-four

Jo had scarcely slept a wink after her confrontation with Max. She kept waking with a start, sweat beaded on her brow, after dreaming over and over again about what Max had tried to do to her. The knife had been in the dream, so close, so threatening.

She had finally gotten up and paced the floor as she wrestled inside her mind over what she should do about Max. She almost knew for certain that he would find some scheme, *soon*, to go farther onto Ottawa land, although he had to know that she would fight him tooth and nail in the courtroom.

Her decision about what to do to stop Max had come in the wee hours of the morning. She saw no choice other than to do exactly what she was planning to do today.

As she rode White Cloud toward the court-house, she knew that she was right to begin fighting for the Ottawa's land rights even before she knew what scheme Max would come up with.

"Judge Harper," she whispered to herself. Yes, she was right to seek Judge Harper's help. He was powerful enough to make *any* wrong right.

She nodded a morning "hello" to one man on horseback and then another as she rode past them down the middle of Main Street. Everyone knew her, and by the smiles on the men's faces, she knew they were happy to see her able to ride a horse again, and walk.

She was so proud she sometimes felt as though she would burst. But then things would happen, like yesterday, that brought her down to earth again and made her realize that she was still vulnerable. When men like Max hated her, she had to be on guard one hundred percent of the day and night.

Bringing her horse to a stop before the courthouse, Jo stared at an upstairs window. She prayed to herself that Judge Harper would be there in his private office already preparing for his long day in the courtroom.

She knew that he had arrived a few days ago for some serious hearings. He was a federal judge who had clout and who was admired by everyone. He was called upon when it looked as though things might be too tough for the local judges.

She knew he wasn't corrupt and weighed each case fairly before setting down judgment.

The only thing that worried Jo was the fact that Judge Harper had been close friends with Max's father. They had attended school together in Springfield, Illinois, the town where Judge Harper resided when he was not called away to other courtrooms.

When Max's father had died, Judge Harper had been the first to arrive in town for the funeral.

Because of Judge Harper's sentimental feelings for Max's father, Jo just might find herself up against a brick wall this morning. Would he be swayed by his longtime friendship with Max's father?

But she had to believe the moral side of Judge Harper's character would prevail.

Dismounting, Jo wrapped her horse's reins around a hitching rail. She took a satchel from her saddlebag, then rushed up the steps and into the courthouse.

Private meetings with a man of such distinction were rare, but Judge Harper knew of Jo's success as a lawyer and admired her. He had even sent her letters of congratulation from time to time when she had won a grand battle in the courtroom.

He had sent a card after the recent victory for the Ottawa, which she had discovered in her mailbox yesterday.

It was while reading this card that she had begun to consider going directly to Judge Harper to seek help.

She didn't need several weeks to prepare for this case. While studying the Ottawa's fishing

219

rights, she had also learned everything that had to do with the lumber on their land.

She smiled when she thought of how clearly it was stated that Max couldn't set one foot on Ottawa land with his lumberjacks.

Because she had not seen Judge Harper for some time now, she felt somewhat nervous about going to him for private counsel. It wasn't that she didn't trust him. It was just that he was so powerful, so important, she didn't want to waste even one minute of his time.

"But fighting for the Ottawa is not a waste of anyone's time," she whispered to herself as she walked along marble floors until she reached a staircase at the back of the building.

Lifting her skirt, she hurried up the steps, again marveling that she could do this when only a few days ago she would not have been able to get up the stairs without being carried.

Carrying her satchel, she walked down the corridor past many closed doors, then stopped and drew in a deep, nervous breath when she came to the office that was reserved for Judge Harper's use when he came to town.

When she heard him clearing his throat inside his office, she smiled. She knew him well enough to know that was a nervous habit that had begun many years ago while he sat in the courtroom during boring hearings.

Jo knocked on the door and waited with a racing pulse for him to open it.

She could hear his heavy footsteps as he came toward the door.

She could hear him clear his throat once again just as he swung the door open.

"J. T.?" Judge Harper said, his eyes widening as he saw she was standing.

"Yes, I can walk again," Jo said, smoothing her hands down the front of her skirt as she gazed down at her legs.

She felt a warm glow when his large, bulky arms swept around her and hugged her. "Damn good to see you, Jo," he said thickly. "Damn good to know that you've finally been able to put that train wreck behind you."

"Yes, me too," Jo murmured, returning his hug.

Then he stepped away from her, walked across the floor, and motioned toward a comfortable leather chair. "Sit, Jo," he said, going to sit in a chair behind his grand old oak desk. "Tell me all about yourself. And how is your father?"

Jo sat down in the chair and placed her satchel on her lap. She wanted to get past the small talk and get right down to business, for she was anxious to leave the building knowing she had again bested Max. She hoped that would be the case!

But there was that one nagging thing that worried her . . . Judge Harper's past association with Max's father.

"Father?" Jo said, sitting stiffly in the chair.

As Judge Harper peered at her, Jo proceeded to tell the judge everything that had happened lately, not only to her and her father, but also to the Ottawa.

She left one important incident out. The way Max had accosted her yesterday. It was just too painful to discuss.

"So life's been kind of rough these past days, huh?" Judge Harper said, running his hands over his clean-shaven face. "When I heard about your recent success in the courtroom, I thought that would be the end of the trouble for the Ottawa, at least for a little while."

"As long as Max gets away with it, he'll never give up trying to take things from the Ottawa, or attempting to discredit them," Jo said, trying to blot out the memory of how close she'd come to being harmed by Max for life.

The more she thought about it, the more she knew that she should tell the judge and gain some sort of protective order from him against Max.

"Max?" Judge Harper said, raising an eyebrow. "Are you speaking of Max Schmidt, your betrothed?"

"Judge Harper, I most certainly am talking about Max Schmidt, and he is most certainly no longer my betrothed," Jo said, her jaw tightening. "Sir, I'm not sure how much you've been around him since his father died, but if you did have the opportunity, you would see someone quite different from the boy he was. He's become a greedy, heartless man. He is the main cause of the Ottawa's problems. And now it is he who is threatening to send his lumberjacks onto land that is not his."

"But Max is an intelligent man and knows that the state's native people have legitimate rights guaranteed by treaty," Judge Harper said, moving aside a law book that he had been going through prior to Jo's arrival. "I don't understand how he thinks he has the right to go against the treaty."

"Sir, you know as well as I do that the land now held by the Ottawa belonged to Max's family before the government purchased it for the reservation," Jo said. "Of course, when Max's great-grandfather got paid for the land, he was pleased enough with the price. Even Max's father never objected. It's Max who feels the price was not enough and so it should still rightly belong to his family."

"Young lady, you go back to the Ottawa people and tell them that I, personally, will see to their rights, and that they need not worry about Max uprooting them from land that is rightfully theirs. Nor shall they lose one tree to Max, or anyone, for that matter," Judge Harper said, rising from his chair. He went and sat on the edge of his desk close to Jo. "I admire your spunk, young lady. Your father must be very proud of you."

"Yes, I believe he is," Jo said, laughing softly. She rose from the chair, reached out to shake the judge's hand, then stopped and turned with a start when Max stormed into the room. His eyes narrowed angrily as he glared from Jo to the judge and back again to Jo.

The color drained from Jo's face as she backed slowly away from Max. "What are you . . . doing . . . here?" she stammered.

"I saw you come into the courthouse. I

knew Judge Harper was in town. I *knew* you'd go crying to him about what happened," Max said, stopping to nod toward the judge and give him a quick, less than cordial, "good morning."

With Max so close she could almost smell his anger, Jo was reminded all over again of what he had almost done to her yesterday.

How did he have the nerve to come in here like this when she was meeting with Judge Harper?

Perhaps he thought that his father's past friendship with the judge might protect him against anything she could tell Judge Harper.

It *would* be Jo's word against Max's.

"Max," Judge Harper said, eluding Max's handshake. "Jo here has been telling me some incredible things about you. I doubt your father would be proud of such behavior, Max."

Max gasped and blood rushed from his face as he took an unsteady step away from the judge. He lowered his hand to his side and looked quickly over at Jo. "How could you . . . tell . . . him . . . ?" he said, his voice breaking.

Jo was puzzled for a moment to know what he meant, and then it came to her in a flash that he had misconstrued what the judge had said. He thought that she had told the judge the unspeakable thing he had tried to do to her.

The judge looked from Max to Jo.

Judge Harper went to Jo and took a hand. "Was there more to what has transpired between you and Max than what you've told me?" he said, his voice low and comforting. "I can judge a person's behavior, and I see that something terrible must have happened between you and Max, and I don't mean a simple thing such as your arguing for the Ottawa's rights."

Max gulped hard. He ran a trembling finger around the stiff collar of his white shirt as he stared dumbfoundedly at Jo. "You didn't tell him, did you?" he said thickly. "I . . . I . . ."

"No, not that," Jo said, sighing heavily. "But perhaps now is the time to let him know the worst about you, Max."

"Jo, by God if you ever tell him that, I'll . . ." Max said, then looked at the judge again when he realized that the judge had understood his threat.

Max glared at Jo, then turned on a heel and ran from the room, stopping just short of the door as he turned and looked at Jo again. "So help me God, if you tell him, Jo, I'll never forgive you," he said, then bolted away from the door and ran down the corridor.

Jo's heart was racing, for she knew that now, no matter what she did, Max would not stop at anything to make her pay for today's embarrassment in front of Judge Harper.

She turned her eyes to the judge.

When he gave her a slow nod, she knew that he was waiting for her to open up to him.

"If I tell you, I'm afraid of what he'll do," Jo blurted out.

"Does he deserve to be locked behind bars?"

Judge Harper said, now gently holding both of Jo's hands. "Jo, it doesn't matter one iota to me that Max's father was my best friend. You know that I would never protect Max if he is guilty of some terrible sin. I chose my profession because I wanted to protect the innocent, not the sinners. Jo, tell me. If it's as bad as I think it is, I'll see that Max is behind bars before sundown today. I'll even be the judge that will see that Max has to pay for whatever he's done to you."

"It's not so much what he did, it's . . . what . . . he attempted," Jo said, gently sliding her hands from his. She went to a window and stared down at the street from the second story.

A chill raced up and down her spine when she saw Max standing across the street with Roy Bates. They were both staring angrily up at the window.

When Max saw her standing there, he shook a finger at her and mouthed something.

This helped her make the decision about what to do.

With a tight jaw and angry eyes she turned and faced the judge. "Judge Harper, sir, that man tried to disfigure me yesterday," she blurted out. The judge's gasp proved his utter shock.

She continued until everything was said.

Strangely, she no longer felt threatened by Max. She was relieved to have gotten the terrible secret out into the open. And she knew that the judge would keep his word and make sure that Max never threatened anyone again.

"I'll go to the sheriff and see that a deputy goes for Max this morning," Judge Harper said, walking toward the door. "Jo, do you want to accompany me there?"

"No, I think I'll hurry on home and tell father everything," Jo said. She had not yet told her father about Max's nightmarish behavior.

She picked up her satchel and hurried toward the door. When she stood side by side with the judge before leaving, her eyes wavered.

"If you are trying to make things right in the town of Lone Branch, Sheriff Gowins and several of his deputies should be replaced," she said firmly. "They are Max's friends. If you don't accompany the sheriff personally to arrest Max, I doubt Max will spend one night in the jail."

"If that's what must be done, by God, I'll do it," Judge Harper said, walking down the corridor with her. He stopped and turned to her. "Do you feel safe enough to go on home alone?"

"Yes, I doubt Max would try anything in broad daylight, especially with you here in town to hear about it," Jo said. "I'll hurry home, Judge." She reached a hand out to him. "Good luck. I'll rest much more easily tonight if Max is behind bars . . . and the sheriff and the deputies are no longer in charge in Lone Branch."

"I can't rush things through that quickly

about getting a new sheriff," the judge said. He took her hand and patted it. He then released it and went down the steps beside Jo. "There are certain procedures I must go through. But I'll take care of it as soon as possible."

When they got outside on the brick walk, Jo looked slowly around her, up one side of the street and down the other. Max was nowhere in sight. She was suddenly afraid of traveling even the short distance it would take to get home, but knew that she could not hide like some scared mouse forever.

And surely Max would be behind bars soon!

She turned to Judge Harper. "Thank you so much for everything," she murmured.

"I'll see you in court," he said, laughing. "When you are there to put the last nails in Max's coffin."

Jo's face drained of color, for she hadn't even thought about having to testify against Max before the whole community. The thought of telling everyone about what he had tried to do made her feel sick to her stomach.

But she would do anything to put a stop to his underhanded ways. And finally she would be free of him, as would the Ottawa people.

"Yes, I'll be there," she said, then watched the judge walk on down the sidewalk toward the jail.

She looked at the hitching rail for the sheriff's horse in front of the jail. Yes, it was there. She smiled at the thought of the surprise he had coming to him!

Wanting to get safely home, Jo slid her

satchel in her saddlebag, mounted White Cloud, and rode off down Main Street toward home.

She kept feeling as though eyes were following her, yet when she surveyed the area, she could see no one looking her way.

It had to be Max, she concluded.

He was hiding somewhere, scheming . . . scheming against *her*!

Chapter Twenty-five

When Jo arrived home, she found that her father wasn't there. She had left before he had risen from bed. When he had awakened and found her gone, surely he had thought that she had left early and was safely with Wolf.

But now that her father wasn't there, she had mixed feelings. In a way she had wanted to get all of the sordid details about Max behind her, yet she absolutely dreaded telling her father and welcomed this momentary reprieve.

Thinking about Max brought Judge Harper to mind. She went to the window and gazed out it, straining her neck to look toward town. By now the judge should have talked to Sheriff Gowins. If the sheriff was going to cooperate, he should have arrested Max.

The thought of the rage Max would feel at

being locked behind bars made shivers go down Jo's spine. She knew what Max was capable of even while incarcerated. He had friends. His friends would do Max's dirty work for him while Max was locked up and unable to do it himself.

Feeling vulnerable at the window, even though it was broad daylight, Jo whirled around and walked briskly away from it.

Now worrying about her father, wondering where on earth he could have gone, Jo walked back to the study and gazed at the desk. Nothing seemed changed from last night when her father had closed his journals and gone to bed.

She went to his bedroom and slowly opened the door. The bed was made, as it was her father's habit to do upon first arising on those days when the housekeeper wasn't there.

"Where are you?" she whispered, going out into the corridor.

Unsure of when to expect her father, Jo went into the kitchen to make a fresh pot of coffee, but stopped at the sound of a horse coming up the small graveled lane to the house. It wasn't her father, for she would also be hearing the wheels of his buggy crunching rock beneath them.

Her throat went dry when she thought of the possibility that Max had eluded arrest.

Or just perhaps the sheriff was even more corrupt than everyone suspected and hadn't arrested Max at all.

Or he might have agreed with Max to make the arrest later, after Max had had the chance to take care of the person responsible for the arrest.

Her pulse racing, Jo hurried from the kitchen and headed toward the gun rack in the study. She stopped when she saw Wolf through the front-door window and knew that she no longer had anything to fear. The horse she had heard was bringing her beloved to her.

So glad to see him, Jo ran to the door. Just as she jerked it open, she caught sight of her father, who had just turned into the lane and was now headed toward the house in his horse and buggy.

But even though she was relieved that Max wasn't a threat to her at this moment, she was again uncertain what to do concerning her father. She had almost decided not to tell him about Max's assault on her. There were enough other reasons for Max's incarceration without her having to disclose the worst to her father. That would only enrage him.

And there had been enough happening of late that had caused him so much alarm. He didn't need anything else to upset him.

Yet, there *was* the trial. Everything would be brought out into the open then. It was best that she prepare her father ahead of time.

Now that Wolf was there, she would tell her father and Wolf at the same time and get it over with.

Jo flung herself into Wolf's arms. "I'm so glad to see you," she murmured. "I'm sorry I didn't come back to your village yesterday. I . . . had . . . things to tend to."

Recognizing the desperation in Jo's hug, Wolf held her close, then gently put her away from him.

Their eyes met and held, but there was no time for anything to be said between them. Addison had tied his reins to the hitching rail and was coming up the steps, a deep frown creasing his brow.

"Father?" Jo said, paling when he came up the steps to the porch and stopped beside Wolf.

"Does he know?" Addison said thickly as he looked at Jo, yet nodded toward Wolf. "Jo, did you tell him and not me?"

"Tell him what?" Jo asked, puzzled by his behavior.

"Jo, come on inside," Addison said, brushing past Wolf to take her gently by an arm. "There's much you must tell your father, isn't there?"

Jo was forced to go back inside the house. She looked over her shoulder at Wolf, who stood quiet and stiff on the porch, his eyes filled with puzzlement as he watched Jo being ushered away from him.

Addison stopped and turned to gaze with heavy eyelids at Wolf. "Come on inside, Wolf," he said hoarsely. "I think we've got some things to settle among us all."

Jo's heart was racing and she felt weak in the knees as she looked from her father to Wolf, and then back at her father. "Father, please tell me what's wrong," she said, swallowing hard. "Why are you behaving like this? Where have you been?"

Addison gave her a downcast look, then nodded at Wolf again as he stepped away from Jo and opened the door more widely so that Wolf would realize the invitation to enter was a serious one.

Jo watched it all, her thoughts scrambled. Her heart sank when she finally realized what might be troubling her father. If he had run into Judge Harper, would the judge have confided everything to him?

Oh, Lord, did her father already know what Max had attempted to do to her?

She wished with all her heart that he could have been spared that, and felt bitter toward Judge Harper for having told her father, if he had done so. Yet, in a way, perhaps the judge had thought this best for her, so that she wouldn't have to tell her father herself.

"Come on into the parlor," Addison said, stepping aside so that Wolf could walk with Jo. "I'll go and put coffee on the stove. I'll be there in a minute. We'll get this talked over, Jo." His eyes wavered. "Daughter, I'm damn sorry it had to happen to you. Damn sorry."

He looked at Wolf, then questioned Jo with his eyes. "Did you tell Wolf everything you told Judge Harper?" he blurted out, seeing her wince at the realization that he *had* heard about the brutal attack yesterday.

"No, I . . . I . . . haven't had the chance," Jo said, tears filling her eyes. "I . . . I . . . had come home this morning to tell you, and then I was going to go to Wolf's village and tell him."

Addison went to Jo and took her hands. "Jo, I hate to tell you, but Max Schmidt eluded arrest," he said, his voice hollow. "And not only has *he* disappeared, Sheriff Gowins and several of his deputies can't be found anywhere. Nor does anyone know where Roy Bates is. After the judge told Sheriff Gowins what had happened and insisted that the sheriff arrest Max, all of those men who work for him disappeared."

"It's like a nightmare," Jo said, heaving a sigh. She slid her hands from her father's. Then she twined an arm around his neck and gently hugged him. "I'm so sorry you had to be brought into the nightmare with me."

He patted her back. "Daughter, surely you know I'd die for you if that meant you would be alright," he said, his voice breaking.

He slipped away from her and nodded toward Wolf. "I think he deserves to be told everything," he said softly. "I'll stay in the kitchen long enough for you to tell him."

Jo nodded, glanced at Wolf, then waited for her father to leave before telling the man she loved about the terrible incident with Max.

When she was finished telling him, she saw rage in his eyes. "Please don't involve yourself in this," she murmured, knowing that he was thinking of vengeance. "It's in the hands of the law. Lawmen will be brought from neighboring towns. Wolf, they'll form a posse. Everybody will be caught and things will be alright again."

"I would get much joy in squeezing the breath from that evil white man," he growled. "But I will wait before involving myself in the hunt for Max Schmidt. I cannot promise for how long."

"Just give the lawmen a chance to do what they are paid to do," Jo said, then hugged him fiercely. "I love you so much. It's so good to be with you. I *was* going to come today and share this latest unfortunate incident with you. For you see, Wolf, when Max is found and put behind bars, I . . . I . . . will have to testify against Max in a courtroom. Everyone will eventually know everything that transpired between me and him."

Then she thought of something positive that she could tell Wolf. She hurried into the explanation about how Judge Harper would see to it that the treaties were upheld. There was no danger of white men logging the trees on Ottawa land.

She could see Wolf's eyes brighten the more she said. When she was finished, he grabbed her into his arms and gave her a fierce hug.

Before he could say anything, though, her father came into the room carrying a tray of cups of steaming hot coffee.

"Here, here, let's have none of that," Addison said, chuckling as Wolf and Jo eased from each other's arms and turned to smile at him.

"That smells delicious," Jo said, going to

take the tray from her father. She set it down on a table, but just as she started to hand Wolf one of the cups of coffee, he started walking briskly toward the door.

The color drained from Jo's face as she watched him leave the room. She flinched when she heard the door close and she knew that he had left without saying goodbye.

She turned questioning eyes to her father, then looked again toward the door that led out to the corridor when she heard the front door open and close again. Wolf had not left after all. When he entered the room carrying a buckskin bag on which were sewn many beautiful beads, she raised an eyebrow.

"I have brought gifts today," he said, laying the bag on a table and slowly untying the thongs at the top. He stopped and smiled at Jo, and then her father. "There are presents for both of you."

Wolf's smile faded as he looked with deep seriousness at Addison. "I have brought what my people call a bride price for your daughter," he said. He then looked at Jo. "My gift for you is something I wish you to wear on our wedding day . . . tomorrow. Jo, will you marry me tomorrow?" He shifted his gaze to her father again. "Will you give your daughter to me in marriage?"

Jo was so stunned by the suddenness of all this, she was speechless. She looked quickly at her father and saw a look of utter disbelief in his eyes. She wasn't sure how to interpret that. Was he glad or angry over Wolf's proposal?

Surely her father had known it was coming. But neither she nor her father had expected it to come so suddenly, and so soon.

"Do not speak until you see the gifts," Wolf was quick to say. "Both are special. They were made by my mother's hands and she is known to be the best at beading among my people."

Jo's heart thudded wildly within her chest when Wolf brought from the bag a necklace made from two strands of tubular beads.

A joyous feeling came over her as he gently placed the necklace around her throat. She lifted her hair and waited for him to fasten it at the back, then she reached down and ran her fingers over the beads as she admired them.

"They are so beautiful," she said, sighing. "The color of the beads is so unique and soft looking."

"These beads were made by my mother's hands from the white and purple marine shells I found washed up along the shore of Lake Michigan," Wolf said. He stepped around in front of Jo and gazed admiringly at the necklace.

Then he placed a finger beneath Jo's chin and lifted it so that their eyes could meet. "This is what is known to your people as 'wampum,'" he explained. "Strings of shell beads have been used by generation after generation of Indians to declare war or to sue for peace, or to legitimize deeds. Today my use of them is for gentler reasons . . . to legitimize my proposal of marriage to the woman I love."

"Thank you," Jo murmured, tears of joy spilling from her eyes. "I love it so. And, yes, yes, I will marry you, I'll marry you tomorrow!"

She looked quickly at her father to see his reaction. She was relieved when she saw the shine of tears in his eyes, which meant that he was happy for her, for he never cried when he was sad. He cried only when he was happy about something.

Jo wanted to go to him and hug him, but stopped when Wolf turned to her father. "My gift to you is also a form of wampum," he said. He slid his hand inside the bag again and took out a wide, beaded belt, with many porcupine quills sewn amid the beads. "This is my bride price to you for your daughter."

Addison took the belt. Tears fell from his eyes as he studied it. Clutching it to his heart, he gazed at Jo, and then Wolf. "I am glad to welcome you into our family," he said thickly. "In a sense, I am not losing my daughter at all. You, you alone, had the power to bring her back to me after I had lost her to grief for so long after the death of her mother. After she met you, she became alive again inside her heart. For that, I will forever be grateful, Wolf."

Jo swallowed back a sob. Smiling, she went to her father. She took the belt gently from him and placed it around his waist, the beads in front, the thong ties in the back. He held his arms away from his sides as she tied the belt in place.

Jo stepped around in front of him again and gazed admiringly at the belt. Then she smiled at Wolf. "Your mother is so skilled at beading," she murmured. "What you brought today is beautiful."

Glad to bring sunshine into his woman's heart again after she had come so close to being violated by Max Schmidt, Wolf drew her into his arms and held her. "You said the beads are beautiful," he whispered into her ear. "My woman, *mee-kah-wah-diz-ee*."

"What did you just say to me?" she whispered back.

"My woman," Wolf said as he leaned away from her, his hands now on her waist. "I told you in my tongue that *you* are beautiful."

"That she is," Addison said, smiling from one to the other. "Yes, that she is."

Addison gazed down at his belt. "And tomorrow there *will* be a wedding," he murmured. He jerked his eyes up and looked questioningly at Jo. "Where will the wedding be? Will it be at Father Samuel's church?"

"I would prefer that it is done at my village," Wolf said softly. "But my friend Fast Horse, who is called Father Samuel by whites, will be the one sealing the bond between me and your daughter. I went to him before coming here and he said that he would be honored to perform the ceremony."

"Which kind?" Jo asked, wondering how she would speak her vows. Would they be spoken only in the Ottawa tradition? If so, would she feel that she was legitimately married?

"Fast Horse will perform a dual ceremony tomorrow," Wolf said. "It will be done in the

Ottawa's tradition and then in your own. That will make our vows binding to any who might question them."

Jo heard his words, yet none of this seemed real. It was as though she were living in some dream world. Surely someone would soon pinch her and she would wake up still crippled and lonely.

Yet she knew it was all true, and she could hardly wait until tomorrow, the day she would truly begin life anew!

Yes, she was immensely happy, yet deep inside where her fears lay smoldering like hot coals, she was remembering Max's warning. She knew what he was capable of and was afraid not only for herself, but for the Ottawa people. No one knew where Max or Sheriff Gowins had disappeared to. Together they could wreak much havoc!

Chapter Twenty-six

The vows had been spoken, and now Jo and Wolf sat side by side among the Ottawa people on the outskirts of the village where land had been cleared for games. Although Wolf was one of their most accomplished athletes, he did not play among his warriors today. It was a day set aside for him to be with his new bride.

Beaming, and attired in her new necklace and white doeskin dress that Blue Moth had loaned her, saying it was the very dress in which she had married Sleeping Bear, Jo felt special.

She felt as though she might even be glowing as the afternoon sun slid lower in the sky. Soon the celebration would be concluded and she and Wolf could retire to Wolf's cabin, which would be shared with Jo from now on.

She hadn't yet had the chance to bring all of her belongings to the cabin. She would spend the full night with Wolf and return to her father's house tomorrow to get her clothes and books.

She glanced over at her father, who was sitting with Fast Horse. The way her father continued to chat and smile with Fast Horse, Jo knew that he had accepted her marriage, as well as the fact that he would be alone in his house now.

Although the memories of Jo's mother were still vivid in her mind, as they were in her father's, Jo hoped that sometime in the near future her father would marry again so that his life would not be so empty.

Loud cheers and laughter brought Jo's eyes back to the young braves, who were playing a game in the center of the wide circle of observers. The braves were playing what she knew was their favorite sport, a game called *bat-a-way*, which to her was similar to soccer.

While the first game of the afternoon was being played, Wolf had told Jo that this sort of recreation was the Ottawa's forte. They were naturally athletic. In games, the competition was keen.

She had watched several wrestling matches already and another game that seemed similar to throwing a javelin.

"The games will be over very soon," Wolf said as he leaned closer to Jo.

She turned to him and smiled almost bashfully, for it wouldn't be long now until she and Wolf would be sharing their first full night of marriage.

She thrilled inside at the thought of how it would be spent. They would make love over and over again, the experience enhanced for Jo by knowing that this time she was lying with Wolf as a wife, not just as a lover.

She knew that although she had enjoyed their earlier lovemaking, being married would surely make her relax even more, for there would be no nagging guilt.

In a way, they were doubly joined in the eyes of God, for she had gone through two marriage ceremonies with the man she loved—in her Methodist tradition and in his Ottawa one.

Suddenly the excitement of the games and the thrill of being married to such a wonderful man was interrupted by the sound of horses' hooves as several horsemen appeared at the far edge of the village.

Jo moved quickly to her feet with Wolf, her eyebrows rising when she saw who was at the head of the riders. Judge Harper. And he looked so different! He wore leather pants and a loose-fitting shirt with no tie. And now that he was so close, Jo could also see that he wore boots and that his usually meticulously combed hair was windblown; his face was ruddy and slightly sunburned from his time on horseback today.

Her gaze went to the men who had arrived

with the judge. She recognized none of them, yet it appeared they were a posse out to search for Max and the others.

Jo had never thought Judge Harper stuffy and cold; still, she had to smile today, seeing him on horseback in such an unusual setting.

Then she wondered why Judge Harper was there at all. She doubted that he would come in such a way just to congratulate the newlyweds.

No. It must have something to do with Max.

She moved closer to Wolf as he gave her a quick glance, then waited for the judge to halt before them.

When the judge finally brought his horse to a stop, his eyes met Jo's.

The uneasiness in his gaze made Jo's heart skip a beat. Surely he had come with news that was not good.

She said nothing, just watched Judge Harper look past her at the Ottawa people, who were standing now and looking quietly at him.

Then Judge Harper slid out of his saddle and stepped up to Wolf and Jo. "I'm sorry that I had to interrupt your wedding celebration," he said. He reached a hand out to Wolf, who accepted the handshake.

He then took one of Jo's hands and held it. "And I'm sorry I couldn't attend your wedding," he said, releasing her hand when Addison came and stood next to her. "But after I discovered just how corrupt things were at the sheriff's office in Lone Branch, and how all of

246

those who were involved had disappeared, I decided to take charge."

Addison gave Judge Harper a quick handshake. "Everything you are doing is appreciated," he said, then dropped his hand to his side.

"You are so kind to get involved," Jo murmured. "What have you found out? Do you have any leads?"

"We've scoured the countryside today since dawn and there is no trace of any of the men," Judge Harper said. "Even Roy Bates. His office was cleaned out. It's as though he expected this to happen. His wife is distraught. Seems he has abandoned her and their two children."

Jo looked toward the high bluffs in the distance, then gazed into the dark shadows of the forest. "Where could they have gone?" she asked in a whisper.

"They'll do something that will break their cover," Judge Harper said. "I know they are still in these parts, perhaps well hidden in the forest somewhere. They couldn't have gotten organized quickly enough to leave on the train. In fact, I went into Detroit. I checked the train station. No tickets were bought for any of those men."

"They are somewhere in the forest," Wolf said, having stayed quiet only to listen. He had come to his own conclusions about where the missing men might have gone. "They can stay in hiding only so long. And I cannot see Max

Schmidt totally abandoning his lumber business. He is a greedy man who would give nothing up without a fight."

"If a man's life lies in the balance, he would give up the world to make sure he's safe," Judge Harper said, himself looking into the dark shadows of the forest. "Seems that in the end, Max's greed gained him nothing."

"I wouldn't place bets on anything that has to do with Max," Jo said tightly. "If he doesn't achieve what he wants in Michigan, he will somehow find a way to take his wealth elsewhere and make a fresh start at amassing wealth."

"I'll let you and Wolf get back to your celebration," Judge Harper said, slowly raking his fingers through his thick red hair to get it back from his face. He smiled at Jo and then Wolf. "I wish you the best."

"Thank you," Jo said, sliding her arm through Wolf's. "We're very happy."

Judge Harper shook Addison's hand again, then mounted his brown mare. He gave a salute, then swung his horse around and rode off, the throng of men following behind him.

"I'd best head for home myself," Addison said. He embraced Jo, shook Wolf's hand, then smiled at Blue Moth, who had come to stand beside her son. He placed a hand on his wampum belt. "Ma'am, thank you again for the belt. It means a lot to me that you made it with your own hands."

"Come and visit often with me and my husband," Blue Moth said, glancing over at her cabin where Sleeping Bear had stayed throughout the ceremony. He was the only one who seemed to have resented Wolf's marriage today.

Wolf had tried not to show how much this had hurt him, but in his eyes it was evident each time he had glanced at his father's lodge.

"Thank you, I shall," Addison said, sweeping his arms around Blue Moth and gently hugging her.

When he stepped away from her, Wolf embraced him, then stepped back and motioned toward a group of warriors. "*Gee-bah-bah*, you will be escorted home," he said. Tears filled Jo's eyes to hear Wolf refer to Addison as "father."

"Naw, that isn't necessary," Addison said, limping toward his horse and buggy.

"Father, please?" Jo said, following him to the buggy. "We've got to be more careful. Max. Remember Max. He won't stop at anything now."

Addison stopped and turned and placed gentle hands on Jo's shoulders. "Now listen here, daughter," he said flatly. "I'm not going to let a pipsqueak like Max alter one thing about how I come and go. Just let him come. I'll have my trusty shotgun on the seat next to me in the buggy. I'll fill someone's belly with lead if they try anything with me."

"Yes, I believe you would," Jo said, laughing. She flung herself into his arms and hugged him again. "But still keep a close watch. The sun is lowering. There will be shadows everywhere for men to hide among."

"I'll be just fine," Addison said, drawing himself away from her. He shook Wolf's hand, then climbed into his buggy. "Don't do anything I wouldn't do tonight, Jo," he joked, his eyes dancing.

Blushing, Jo waved at him as he rode off.

She giggled when Wolf grabbed her by a hand and led her toward their cabin. She looked over her shoulder at how everyone was watching.

Suddenly she felt timid, for she knew that everyone was very aware of what would transpire behind Wolf's door tonight.

She was relieved when she got inside and he closed the door.

She fell into his arms. His lips were hot and hungry as he kissed her.

Just as she was beginning to feel deliciously amorous, everything within her warm and ready for her new husband, Wolf drew away from her. He shoved a blanket into her arms, then grabbed up one for himself.

"What are you doing?" she said as he went to the door and opened it. "Where are you going?"

"Come with me and I will show you," Wolf said, his eyes gleaming as he gestured toward the open door. "Tonight you will meet some of my special friends."

Jo's eyebrows rose, for she had thought she had already met all of his friends today at the wedding. And she didn't want to meet anyone else. She just wanted Wolf all to herself on their wedding night.

Seeing how determined his pace was as he walked toward the horse corral at the back of the cabin, she followed him.

She mounted her horse, which had been readied for traveling, the saddle snugly in place. She slid the blanket inside the saddle-bag as she watched Wolf mount Midnight after sliding his blanket inside his bag.

When they rode off, she looked over her shoulder and waved at his people, who still stood watching.

She questioned Wolf with her eyes when he glanced her way. "Won't you please tell me where we're going?" she asked, riding out from the village.

She couldn't forget her warning to her father about Max and his friends.

She knew that everyone was in danger of an ambush as long as Max was out there filled with dark, searing vengeance.

"Wait and see," was all that Wolf would tell her.

She sighed.

She had no choice but to wait.

She rode onward, the evening breeze cool as it blew through her hair and lifted it from her shoulders.

She looked heavenward and saw her first star of the new evening in the northern sky.

An uncontrollable shiver rushed over her flesh, for soon it would be dark and all of the shadows could come to life!

Chapter Twenty-seven

Just as the autumn moon came up over the horizon, large and misty orange, Wolf took a sharp right toward a bluff that loomed high overhead.

Jo followed him, then caught up with him and rode at his side, battling her mounting fears.

She tried to push her fears from her mind when Wolf suddenly drew a tight rein and stopped.

Jo brought her horse to a quick halt and started to dismount as Wolf slid from his saddle. She stopped when she saw a sudden streak of white racing out of the darkest shadows.

Her mouth dropped open in utter surprise

when she saw several white wolves rushing toward Wolf, yelping, their tails wagging.

Too stunned to move, Jo sat quiet as Wolf knelt and gathered the wolves around him. First one and then another licked his face like friendly dogs.

Wolf looked up at Jo. "These are the friends I want to introduce you to tonight," he said, playfully running his hands over the wolves while they wriggled in enjoyment.

When one of them reached a paw out for him, Wolf looked away from Jo and shook the white paw. "Hello to *you*, my friend," he said, chuckling.

He glanced up at Jo. "Come," he murmured. "They are friends. I will tell you the story of how we met and sealed our friendship."

Never having been around a wild creature such as a wolf before and having heard horrendous tales of their viciousness, Jo hesitated. "I don't know," she said, gripping the pommel tightly with one of her hands. "I'm not sure . . ."

"Jo, they are even friendlier than most dogs I have known," Wolf said. He gave her a soft, pleading look. "It is all wrongful tales that make wolves out to be what they are not. Come and let them prove their friendly nature to you. Pet them. Hug them. You will become as entranced with them as I."

Her pulse racing, her eyes still wary, Jo dismounted.

Wolf lifted one of the smallest wolves into

his arms and took it to Jo. "Pet her," he encouraged. "Her name is Star. She is the mother of two brand-new pups. Make friends with her and she will then trust you with her pups."

"I was bitten by a dog when I was a child," Jo blurted out. "I still have a scar on the back of my right leg to prove it. I've never since gotten near dogs, much . . . less . . . wolves."

"You do not trust this man who is now your husband?" Wolf asked, his voice revealing a tinge of hurt.

Jo swallowed hard.

Her eyes wavered.

Then she forced a smile and held her hand out to the wolf.

When Star did not hesitate to lick Jo on the face, Jo was instantly taken with the animal.

"It tickled," Jo said.

"Do you see how she not only trusts you, but also likes you?" Wolf said, reaching to stroke Star's thick, white fur. "I will show you her new pups. They will steal your heart."

Jo followed Wolf to a cave in the side of the bluff.

After getting just inside the cave, Jo heard a soft whining sound.

She jumped in alarm when Star raced past her legs, then threw herself on her side only a few feet from where Jo still stood.

"Bend low," Wolf said, sliding an arm around Jo's waist to guide her downward. "The moon is casting enough light down here

255

along the cave's floor for you to see the pups. They are nursing. It is a sight that makes me hunger for my own children."

Jo sank to her knees.

Her insides melted when she saw the tiny black pups nestled against their white mother, their paws kneading Star's nipples as they suckled hungrily.

Jo badly wanted to reach out and touch the pups, but thought better of it because she'd read somewhere that it is best not to put a human smell on newborn animals. That caused some mothers to abandon their babies.

She looked quickly over at Wolf. "How did this happen?" she murmured. "That you and the wolves are bonded in such a way? And does this relationship have something to do with your being called Wolf?"

Wolf led her from the cave.

He took the blankets from their saddlebags, then spread them atop the colorful fallen leaves of a maple tree.

Wolf then took Jo's hand and led her down beside him on the blankets.

As he held her close and their eyes watched the stars multiply in the dark heavens, he told her about his relationship with the wolves and how he tried to protect them from evil hunters.

"That's so beautiful," Jo murmured when he was done. "It's so mystical."

"Now that they know you are a friend, they will bond with you as well," Wolf said, then

turned Jo to face him. Their eyes met and held
as he slowly undressed her.

Kneeling before him, her breasts soft round
globes in the moon's glow, Jo swept off his
doeskin shirt, then watched him as he stood
and finished undressing.

Aflame with desire, Jo reached her arms out
for him. Her breath caught when he came to
her and pressed her down onto the blankets
with his body.

A surge of ecstasy swept through Jo when
Wolf shoved his manhood deep inside her hot,
moist entrance and began his eager, rhythmic
thrusts.

Thrusting her hips toward him, she gasped
with pleasure when that brought him even
more deeply into her.

His lips came down upon hers, hungry and
urgent. He filled his hands with her aching
breasts and kneaded their soft fullness.

A hot, demanding pleasure knifed through
him as she pushed her breasts into his hands,
her nipples swollen, throbbing, and hot
against his palms.

Wanting to touch him, *all* of him, Jo swept
her hands down his back. As his tongue
brushed her lips lightly, she reached down and
spread her fingers around him as he momentarily withdrew his manhood from inside her.

Wolf moaned with pleasure and buried his
face in the hollow of her throat when her
hands moved on him in fast, sure movements.

She closed her eyes with intense pleasure as

one of his hands dove between her legs and caressed her smoldering woman's center.

The rhythmic pressure of his fingers between her legs was almost torture, the pleasure was so intense.

They pleasured each other in such a way for only a moment longer, and then again he was inside her, diving in and out, his mouth crushing hers with an intense kiss, his tongue surging over and over again through her parted lips.

When they reached the ultimate ecstasy together, Wolf held Jo tightly against him. He savored the joyous bliss of being able to call her his wife; of calling her his woman!

Afterward, as they lay side by side, a blanket thrown across their naked bodies, they gazed toward the sky again. When a star went plummeting across the vast heavens, one of the wolves somewhere in the distance began to howl.

Jo's body tensed.

She sat up quickly and gazed at the white wolf that had gone to the bluff overhead.

"It is reacting to many things tonight," Wolf said. He gently took Jo by a wrist and brought her down beside him again. "The wolves feel my joy . . . they feel *our* joy."

Jo twined her arms around his neck and drew his lips down to hers. "I'll love you *ah-pah-nay*," she whispered, then cuddled against him as he brought his mouth over hers and gave her a long, deep kiss.

Jo only vaguely recalled having been worried about something earlier. For the moment she forgot what, for there was only now, there was only Wolf, herself, and the wondrous wolves that were nestling around Jo and Wolf as their lovemaking began anew.

Chapter Twenty-eight

Still feeling as though everything were unreal, Jo continued packing her law books in boxes to take to her new home. Wolf had told her that he was going to build her a bookshelf in their living room for her books, and that when they began having children he would build a separate bedroom just for them.

She stopped and gazed at the grandeur of her library, the one room she had always loved above everything else in her father's grand house. She would miss it. If the library burned, along with all of her beloved books, that would have been a true tragedy. As it was, bedroom furniture had been easy to replace.

Books?

No.

Nothing could ever replace those that she

had collected since she was old enough to understand the pleasure one got in the pages of books.

Dressed in a fringed buckskin skirt and loose buckskin blouse, wearing the clothes of her husband's people, Jo proceeded to place not only her law books in the boxes, but also her books of fiction. She became lost in recollections of her wedding day, and then the first full night that she had spent with her husband. It had been paradise.

It made her smile to think of the future that lay ahead of her. She would forever be grateful to Fast Horse for bringing Wolf into her life.

"*Ah-pah-nay*, forever," she whispered, proud to know how to say some words in Chippewa.

She hoped to learn all of the language Wolf's people spoke. Surprisingly they used more Chippewa words than Ottawa. Very rarely did she hear the Ottawa people speak in any other way than English or Chippewa.

Her thoughts went to her career. She felt guilty for having taken so many days from her office after giving up her practice for a full year.

But since she had been gone for so long, there wasn't anyone breaking the door down for her services now.

She wasn't even sure if she would resume her career. She had Wolf's blessing if she chose to go back to it. He had told her that he would never hold her back or stifle her in any way.

She loved him even more for that, but deep

inside her, where contentment was built within one's soul, she wanted to be a one hundred percent wife, and, she hoped, a mother. Only special cases would draw her from her home, her *den*.

She laughed softly to herself when she thought of the white wolves and the two black pups. Yes, it seemed that the she-wolf had strayed a mite, for her pups' father had to be at least part black for her to have black pups.

Ah, but it was so wonderful to have made their acquaintance! They were so special. She hoped to be with them often now that they knew her and seemed to have accepted her among their pack.

Thinking she heard the faint sound of horses' hooves in the distance, perhaps her father returning home from town in his horse and buggy, she started to go to the window to see if it was him, but shrugged and instead continued packing.

Her father had gone to town with a list of provisions that she had asked him to get. There were so many things she needed to make Wolf's home more welcoming.

Especially kitchenware. She needed everything that would make the kitchen a true place to prepare meals for her husband. And she did love to cook. She would surprise him, that was for sure.

Jo's spine stiffened when she realized that it was not her father's horse and buggy that she had heard. Now that they were farther up the lane, she could tell there were several horses coming.

She feared that those approaching her house with such thunderous speed were not *her* friends. Surely they were Max's.

Her heart echoed the thundering of the horses' hooves, beating out an erratic tattoo inside her chest. Jo picked up the hem of her skirt and ran from her library.

Her face hot with a frightened flush, her fingers trembling, she ran down the corridor until she came to her father's private study at the very front of the house.

Breathing hard, even feeling somewhat lightheaded, Jo grabbed shotgun shells from the desk drawer, thrust them into the front pocket of her skirt, then went into the foyer and grabbed up her shotgun.

Just as she took a deep breath of courage, she heard the horses come to a stop outside her house.

She flinched as though shot when a man began shouting her name. This was followed by several men shouting obscenities at her through the closed door.

Jo lifted her eyes heavenward. "Please, God, give me strength to do what I must do," she prayed. "Please get me through this."

Her shotgun anchored beneath her right arm, the barrel aimed straight ahead, Jo yanked the door open with her left hand and stepped outside.

Immediately she raised and steadied the shotgun with both hands as her eyes darted from man to man. She recognized most of them. They were lumberjacks from Max's lumber company, and she knew them well enough to know they were rough and tough.

And if they were promised a big enough paycheck for doing it, who was to say to what lengths they would go to please the one handing out the money?

"Because of you we're out of a job!" one of the most burly men shouted as he waved a fist in the air. "Max has closed down his lumber company. That takes food from the mouths of our wives and children!"

"Yeah, because of your love for savages!" another man shouted, his fist waving at her. "We've heard about your marriage to a savage heathen. That's surely why your mind has become so warped you don't know what you're doing! How dare you tell tall tales about Max to Judge Harper!"

"I don't blame Max for trying to kill you!" another man shouted. "If a woman I had planned to marry slept with a redskin, I'd blow her away!"

Jo's head was swimming as threats and insults came like buckshot at her from one direction and then another. It was hard to believe that those men could hate her so much that they actually would harm her if they got the chance.

She knew that if she didn't have her shotgun, she wouldn't have had a chance against the angry men.

"Get on out of here!" she shouted, her finger

sliding onto the trigger. "And you can go and tell Max, wherever the coward is hiding, that nothing he does will scare me. Tell him that he can hide for only so long. Then, by damn, the law will find and arrest him. I'll never take back what I told Judge Harper about him. Max Schmidt deserves to be locked up, and you all know it. It's only because you're too lazy to go elsewhere to find jobs that you come to my doorstep whining like dogs."

"You'll eat them words," another man shouted at her. "Max'll get even. *We'll* get even."

"And, savage lover, you'd better never take any more cases into the white man's court!" another man warned. "You'll be boycotted because you are now an Indian *squaw*."

Anger taking the place of her fear, Jo aimed the shotgun heavenward and shot off a round.

She smiled when she saw the men's horses become frightened by the gunfire, some rearing, others shuffling their hooves nervously.

"Now get on out of here or my next round of gunfire will damn well not be shot at the sky," Jo shouted, aiming once again at the men. "And remember this! No one is going to scare me into leaving my law practice. I will only stop practicing law when I'm good and ready to stop, not when someone else tells me to."

Shouting obscenities, their fists waving, the men wheeled their horses around and rode off.

Jo wanted to feel as though she had won, but something deep inside her told her that she was truly in trouble this time.

Shaken, and not thinking straight, she ran

to the barn and saddled White Cloud. Thrusting the shotgun into her gun boot at the side of her horse, Jo rode off to go to Wolf. She couldn't help being afraid.

After leaving the outskirts of Lone Branch, she was suddenly surrounded by the same men who had brought the warning to her home. She realized that she had just played into their hands.

Grabbing her shotgun from the gun boot, she started to aim it at the men, then screamed when a gunshot rang out, and the shotgun flew from her hand.

Her hand stinging from the bullet grazing its flesh, Jo drew it up to her mouth and blew on it.

She had no choice but to wait and see what the men's next move would be.

She was at their mercy.

Her thoughts went to her father, who would surely realize that something was amiss when he found her gone and saw that the books were still only half boxed up. He knew that she would never leave anything only half done.

Surely . . . he . . . would go and seek Wolf's help to find her!

But then, if he did, that would draw both of them into danger.

"Move onward," one of the men growled, nudging Jo in the side with the butt end of his rifle. "Follow us."

"Where are you taking me?" she asked warily.

Their throaty, sarcastic laughter was their only response.

She lurched forward when someone grabbed her reins and yanked on them. White Cloud responded by taking off in a gallop along with the men.

Although she was frightened almost senseless, Jo kept her chin lifted proudly. She wasn't about to let these men know that she was afraid.

And if she could keep a clear mind, just perhaps she could find a way to best the men.

She watched guardedly as they passed a bottle of whiskey amongst themselves.

Yes, if they got drunk, they could get careless.

Yet there was another way to look at that. If they got drunk, they might not even wait to get her to wherever they had planned to take her. They might decide to defile her on the spot, for they now saw her as a squaw, as something less than human.

She swallowed hard.

Chapter Twenty-nine

Jo didn't have a timepiece with her, but she knew without checking that at least one hour had passed since the men had slowed their mounts to move through a denser timberland. Sometimes it was so thick in vegetation, there was barely enough room for a horse to pass between the trees.

Riding in single file, with Jo's horse penned in the middle, the men continued making their way beneath the trees where the sun was shining in velveteen streamers through branches whose leaves had given in to the relentless coming of autumn.

The stench of the rotting leaves strewn across the ground made Jo's nose twitch.

The sudden, shrill shriek of a bluejay from

somewhere overhead made her jump in her saddle.

The leap of a doe taking cover on one side of her made her head jerk in that direction.

The rat-a-tat sound of a woodpecker beating its beak against a tree echoed around Jo.

But the sound of water falling over cliffs through the trees at her right side made her finally realize where she was. Long ago, when she was on a full day's outing with her father on horseback, they had found a waterfall. They had stopped and had their picnic beside it while they watched magical rainbows being formed as the water plummeted over the cavernous rocks into the stream below.

Yes! She finally knew where she was! If she could ever find a way to escape these men, she would even know a shorter way to get home than the path these men had followed.

It was because the men had brought her by a different route that she had not figured out sooner where she was.

But even knowing her location gave her no reprieve from her building fears. She knew that Max was behind her abduction today. And once he had her this time, he would make certain that she did not walk away from him alive.

Her heart skipped a beat when she caught sight of a dingy, precariously leaning cabin through the trees a short distance ahead. She knew without being told that Max awaited her arrival in that cabin.

In flashes she remembered how Max had wrestled her to the ground inside his mansion and lifted her skirt, then held the knife so close she just knew that at any moment she was going to be assaulted, then left to die.

Over and over again she recalled how she had lifted her knee into his groin and how he had yelped and dropped the knife, then rolled away from her, his hands desperately clutching his injured private parts.

Because of that alone he would get, oh, so much pleasure doing whatever he wanted to do to her. And this time he would have many men around him to make sure Jo didn't get the best of him.

She glanced over her shoulder at the men who were lagging behind her. She recognized many of their faces, yet if she ever did get the chance to tell the authorities about who had abducted her today, she could provide no names.

And she doubted that they would stick around Lone Branch to be pointed out. She had to wonder about their families. Yes, because of Max's underhanded schemes, surely the women and children would be uprooted, as well.

Jo looked ahead again and tensed when they reached the cabin. She could see only two horses reined at the hitching rail. She recognized them both. One belonged to Max. The other belonged to that weasel Roy Bates.

Her heart sank to know that two of her most

ardent enemies had schemed against her. She truly doubted that she would get out of this mess alive.

Even if her father did arrive home and find her gone and went to Wolf or the judge for help, she doubted they would ever be able to find this place hidden so deeply within the forest, not in time to save her life.

As they stopped in front of the log cabin, Jo scarcely breathed when first Max and then Roy came out onto the small, creaking porch.

Her eyes met and held in a silent battle with Max. Then her breath was stolen away when one of the men yanked her from the horse so roughly she fell to the ground on her back.

Stunned for a moment, Jo just lay there. She slowly shook her head back and forth to clear it of the strange stars that had blossomed there when her head struck the ground.

When her vision did clear and she opened her eyes and saw spotless, shining boots beside her face, she was transported to the first time she had seen Max spit on his leather boots for the spit shine.

Her pulse racing, both from anger and fear, Jo scrambled to her feet and glared at Max. "You pig," she said. "If only your father could see you now. He'd lose all the pride that he had in you when you were a child. Max, when did it begin to change? When you realized the wealth that could be had by swindling others?"

"Shut up," Max said, grabbing her roughly by an arm. He forced her inside the cabin.

She was surprised to see how neat and clean

it was, whereas by the looks of the outside, it was ready to tumble sideways.

But she knew that Max wouldn't reside anywhere that was unkempt. It didn't matter how the outside looked as long as the inside was spotless and had the comforts of home.

A stately white iron bed stood on one side of the room with blankets arranged neatly on top and pillows fluffed at one end.

On another side of the cabin was the kitchen area, where a table and two chairs sat not far from a pot-bellied stove that glowed orange from the fire inside it. Coffee boiled on the top of the stove, and eggs had only recently been cooked in a skillet; the aroma still lingered in the small cabin.

Two plush overstuffed chairs sat before a grand stone fireplace where a soft fire leaped across logs on the grate. Pine cones lay smoldering at the edges of the coals, giving off a pleasant aroma.

"My second home," Max said, chuckling as he saw Jo looking slowly around the room. "But not for long. It's been my hideout from time to time, Jo, when I wanted to get away from this or that pestering creditor from Detroit or Lone Branch, but I'll soon be leaving it all behind and heading out for better pickings."

"Yes, I imagine so," Jo said sarcastically. "Now that you've ruined yourself in Lone Branch, what other town will be forced to tolerate you until you're seen for what you are?"

"You think I'd tell you or anyone where I'm

headed?" Max said, roughly shoving Jo onto a chair.

"Wherever you go, I pity those who will be suckered in by your good looks and cleverness," Jo said, eyeing the men as they came crowding into the small cabin, bringing the scent of whiskey with them as they idly passed a bottle among themselves.

"And what about them?" Jo dared, nodding toward the men. "What about their families? You know it will be all but impossible for them to find jobs elsewhere." She laughed sarcastically. "And just how soon do you think you'll be able to sell the lumber company without giving the authorities a way to trace you so they can come and arrest you?"

"Just shut up, Jo," Max snarled as he took a rope that one of the men brought to him. He knelt and tied Jo's hands together before her. "And none of my men blame me for losing their jobs and homes," he said stiffly. "It's *you*. We all blame our bad luck on *you*."

"Max, you know I'm not to blame for any of this. Everything you've done these past several years has led you to your downfall today," Jo said, her voice breaking. "Trying to kill me was the straw that broke the camel's back. You had to know you couldn't get away with that. It's a shame you had to take so many people down with you."

"You had to go and blab, didn't you?" Max hissed. He leaned into her face so close she could smell the alcohol on his breath. "Well, *friend*, I'm going to finish what I started, then

274

be on my way and never think about you again. You made your mistake when you made a fool outta me."

"Max, *you* are the one who broke it off with me, remember?" Jo said, trying to reason with him, but not for his benefit. She was trying to say things that would reach his men. She wanted them to see that she was the wrong one to blame for their unfortunate lack of employment. "Then when you saw me well and healthy again and thought you could come back into my life, you had to know that I wouldn't allow it. And, Max, when you threatened me with that knife, planning to actually mutilate me before you killed me. . . ."

Her voice broke so that she couldn't continue. And she knew that she wasn't getting across to the men, anyhow. They had consumed too much whiskey to reason out anything inside their alcohol-soaked brains.

"Enough of this!" Max shrieked. He stood away from Jo and motioned toward the door. "Men, get on out there. You know what you've been told to do. Time's a-wasting." He laughed throatily as he gazed at Jo again. "I'm eager for Miss Prissy J. T. Stanton to see what my plans are for her."

The men grinned at Jo, then left the cabin.

She soon heard the sound of hammers nailing something together.

She eyed Max questioningly, getting no response except a leering smile.

When Max left the cabin, Roy Bates came and stood directly over Jo.

275

Snickering, he began striking one match after another, holding each one until it almost burned his fingertips, then dropping it to light another one.

Trying to ignore Roy, Jo peered toward the open door, but couldn't see anything. She wanted to get up and try to run away, but knew she wouldn't get far. She was trapped with a bunch of lunatics.

"Want to see what they're doing?" Roy suddenly blurted out. He made Jo wince with pain when he grabbed her wrist and yanked her from the chair. He half-dragged her to the door. "Take a look, J. T. What do you see?"

Jo swallowed hard as instant terror grabbed her. She was looking at a cross being erected out in the middle of the yard. Surely Max wouldn't . . . !

"J. T., you're going to be a modern-day Joan of Arc," Roy said, laughing throatily. "You're going to burn at the stake."

He grabbed her hair and yanked her face around so that she was forced to look at him. She grew cold inside as she looked through his thick eyeglasses into the eyes of a madman.

"Yes, J. T., you're going to die. And I'm going to be the one who sets the fire," Roy said, his eyes taking on an even more crazed gleam. He leaned closer to her face. "Don't you know how much fun it is to set fires? I set 'em and watch 'em. J. T. I've set fire to many things."

The color drained from Jo's face. "It *was* you," she gasped out. "You are the one who set fire to my father's home, his trees and roses, and the Ottawa's corn crop. You . . . even . . . hit my father over the head and left him there to burn alive."

"Yep, the one and only," Roy bragged, then yanked her out of the way when he saw Max approaching the cabin.

Roy stepped aside when Max stood before Jo, his hands on his hips.

"Josephine Taylor Stanton, are you ready?" Max said mockingly, a slow smile quivering across his thick lips. "Sweet darlin', are you ready . . . to . . . die?"

Chapter Thirty

Something, a strange nagging feeling, had made Wolf leave a council with his warriors to go and check on Jo. It wasn't because he had expected her at the village yet. He knew it would take some time for her to get her things together to bring to her new home.

Although he had much to discuss in council with his warriors and the elders of his village, he had volunteered to help Jo. But she had wanted to do it alone . . . to be alone with her memories before beginning her new life with Wolf and his people.

Just as Wolf turned his horse onto the lane that led to Jo's house, he saw her father riding toward him in his horse and buggy.

Wolf drew a tight rein and waited, and as he did so he studied Addison's expression.

Cassie Edwards

Addison seemed troubled by something. It was evident in the way he only half waved at Wolf and in the way he frowned, when he usually offered Wolf a good-hearted, kind smile.

This confirmed Wolf's belief that something was wrong, and surely with Jo.

"Wolf, why are you here?" Addison asked as Wolf drew up beside him. "Has something . . . happened . . . to Jo?"

"Something seemed to tell me that things were not right with my wife," Wolf said somberly. "That is why I am here . . . to see if she is alright." He paused, frowned, and leaned down closer to Addison. "Why did seeing me make you ask if something happened to Jo?"

"It was the same for me, I . . . I . . . got the same feeling, a premonition of sorts," Addison said. He snapped his reins and guided his horse onto the lane, with Wolf riding in a slow lope beside him. "I was just completing my shopping for Jo when I got the strangest feeling inside my heart and at the same time saw Jo's face flash before my eyes. I couldn't get to my horse and buggy quickly enough. I . . . I . . . didn't even load up the supplies that I had already paid for. I had to see if Jo was alright."

"If we both had the same premonition, then surely things are not right with Jo," Wolf said, his heart sinking. "I will ride ahead. I will see."

"Yes, I will follow," Addison said, then reached a hand out for Wolf to stop him. "Wait! I have something else to tell you!"

Wolf was anxious to ride to the house, but he waited to see what Addison had to say, for he could tell that it was something that disturbed him.

"Wolf, while in town I heard the rumor that Jo is going to be boycotted," Addison said, his voice breaking. "I heard that because she married you, she wasn't going to be allowed to practice law in Lone Branch and Detroit, nor any of the surrounding communities."

"Who is to blame for this?" Wolf asked, his voice tight with emotion.

"I went to the courthouse and talked to Judge Harper," Addison said quickly. "He said that he hadn't heard anything about a boycott. He said that Jo can practice law in this community as long as she wishes to. He admires her spunk and her knowledge of the law."

"Those who spread the rumor only did so because they hold a deep grudge against my wife," Wolf said solemnly. "And if they realized that the judge would not allow this to happen to Jo, would they not come and threaten her in some way, personally?"

Addison hung his head, then looked slowly at Wolf again. "Yes, I'm afraid so," he said, his voice breaking.

Wolf rode away from Addison at a hard gallop.

Addison flicked his reins and shouted at his horse; the wagon careened back and forth dangerously on the loose rock as Old Tom took off in a faster lope behind Midnight. Addison gazed heavenward. "Please, God, let us be wrong," he whispered, then looked anxiously toward the house when Wolf reached it and slid out of the saddle. He held his breath as Wolf ran up the steps and hurried inside.

The minute Wolf went through the front door he became aware of the silence. He stopped and listened more intently for any sound that Jo might be making as she boxed up her belongings.

His spine stiffened when he heard nothing except the thunderous sound of Addison's horse's hooves outside the house and the crunch of gravel as the buggy's wheels rolled over it.

"Jo?" Wolf shouted, rushing down the long corridor, looking in one room and then another.

When he got to the library and saw Jo's books only half packed, he knew that things weren't right.

"Wolf!" Addison shouted as he came limping into the house. "Her horse is gone. I checked in the barn. White Cloud is gone. Surely she's gone to your village."

Wolf stepped out in the corridor and met Addison halfway. "She did not come to my village, and I did not come across her while I rode toward your home," he said, his jaw tight. "Our premonition was accurate. Something is wrong. Something has happened to my wife."

Addison walked past Wolf and checked his supply of firearms.

When Wolf stepped up behind him, Addison turned and gazed at him, his face pale and drawn. "A shotgun is missing," he said thickly. "Very rarely has Jo taken a firearm with her when she leaves, especially a shotgun. Something . . . someone . . . threatened her enough that she felt she needed a shotgun for protection."

"I will follow her horse's tracks," Wolf said, rushing past Addison.

When he found White Cloud's tracks leading away from the barn, he started to follow them, then stopped, his heart sinking when he saw many fresh hoof prints close to the porch of the house.

"Many were here," he said, stooping to study the prints more closely. He looked up at Addison as he came and stood over him. "I know fresh prints. These were made only a short while ago. Someone came and frightened Jo enough that she left on her horse with the firearm."

"Was she forced to go with them?" Addison asked, his voice quivering with fear. "Did *they* take the shotgun?"

"No, she did not leave with those who came today," Wolf said, slowly standing, his eyes again on the tracks that led from the barn. "As you can see, Jo did not bring her horse over to those who were here. They turn and ride from the house. Hers led directly from the barn toward the forest and she rides alone."

"Thank God," Addison said, wiping nervous

beads of sweat from his brow with his shirt sleeve. "Then maybe she'll be alright until you find her."

"And I *will* find her," Wolf said flatly.

"I'll go with you," Addison said, turning to scramble toward his horse and buggy.

A heavy hand on his shoulder stopped him.

Wolf slowly turned Addison to face him. "No, you stay," he said softly. "Stay and be here for her if she returns. And if she does return, go to Fast Horse. Send him to find me. He is an astute tracker. We learned the art of tracking together when we were young braves striving to be warriors."

"Whatever you say," Addison agreed, eagerly nodding. When Wolf dropped his hand away from him and started toward his horse, Addison hurried after him. "Please find her, Wolf. Bring her back to me so that I can see she is alright."

Wolf stopped and gazed with wavering eyes at Addison. "To busy yourself as you wait, you might finish packing Jo's things for her move to her new home," he said thickly. "I love her very much, Addison. More than anyone can ever know."

"I believe I know," Addison said, wiping tears from his eyes as they crept down his cheeks. "And God be with you as you search for my daughter. I shall pray for you both."

Wolf nodded, then turned and ran to his horse and swung himself into the saddle in one leap. He guided Midnight over to the tracks made by White Cloud, then began following them until he found himself deep in the shadowy forest.

He now followed the trail of crushed leaves where Jo's horse had gone. Then his heart seemed to stop still when he saw where her horse had stopped and there were many more crushed leaves than only one horse could make. Soon he found signs of several horses' hooves all around Jo and White Cloud.

When he saw how White Cloud seemed to have been led away by those who had come upon Jo in the forest, he realized that she had been abducted.

A raging, hot anger swept over Wolf to think that his woman was helpless among men who surely hated her. He felt guilty for not going with her today to help her pack her belongings, for he had known even then that there were those who wished to harm her.

Yet when he offered, she had said she wanted to go alone. She had urged him to stay for his council.

Had he known that Addison would be leaving her alone in the house, nothing would have kept Wolf from going with Jo. He had thought that Addison would be there to protect her until she was under Wolf's tender care.

"If she is harmed . . . !" he cried, lifting his eyes and fist heavenward.

Knowing that he had wasted too much time in speculation, while she was being taken farther and farther from him, Wolf started to follow the path left by those who had abducted

Jo. Then he stopped suddenly when he saw something shining back at him from the weeds as the sun coming through the autumn leaves reflected onto it.

In one leap Wolf was out of his saddle.

He bent low and reached into the weeds, pulling out Jo's shotgun. "She no longer has any defense against those who have her," he whispered angrily to himself. "I must find her. I must find her quickly!"

He secured her shotgun at the side of his horse, then mounted his steed and continued to follow the track of crushed leaves.

His heart sank when the tracks led him to a dead end at the river.

He looked up one side of the river and down the other and saw no traces of where Jo was traveling.

Feeling a stab of pain in his heart to know that he might never find Jo, Wolf continued the search, but this time blindly.

He rode and rode.

He didn't take the time to eat or rest as he headed into the depths of the forest, where the land rose slowly toward the distant cliffs, to a place where anyone could be hidden . . . and never found.

Chapter Thirty-one

Now tied to the cross out in a clearing away from Max's cabin, Jo tried to look courageous. But nothing could control her feverish heartbeat. As she strained at the ropes at her wrists and ankles, Roy Bates stood watching her, his lips twisted into a cruel, evil smile. He struck one match after another, letting them burn down to his fingers before dropping them to the ground.

Not wanting him to read the fear in her eyes, and not wanting to know the exact moment he set fire to the pile of logs at her feet, Jo looked away from Roy.

Her gaze locked with Max's.

She could see that he was torn about what he was doing.

She didn't see how he could hate her this

much, for they had meant so much to each other as children.

But now that she had refused to allow him into her life again, he was a man scorned, especially since Jo had chosen an Indian over him. And Wolf was not just any Indian . . . but the man who had stood in the way of Max taking lumber that he wanted.

Jo's lips parted, then closed. She fought against the urge to plead with Max. She tightened her lips and looked away from him.

No. She would never belittle herself to ask this man for anything . . . not even her life.

He was someone she no longer understood. He was a man who could not be reasoned with, not now, when he had lost everything and blamed her.

"Quit playing with those damn matches and set the fire, Roy!" Max shouted, his fists doubled at his sides.

Roy chuckled beneath his breath as he gave Max a nod.

Jo closed her eyes and stiffened as she waited for the inevitable.

Inside her heart she spoke to her beloved mother, whom she would meet soon in the heavens above.

In her heart she said a sad farewell to her father, and then to the man she would love even after she was walking amid the heavens above him.

Everything was quiet, so quiet that Jo could hear when Roy struck the match that would ultimately take her life.

Her pulse raced.

She felt sick to her stomach.

Her throat constricted with a sob she did not want Max to hear.

She fought back tears that were burning in the corners of her eyes.

Courage! she told herself. *Stay courageous!*

She didn't want Max to see her as a whimpering idiot before she died.

She wanted to prove that she was far stronger than he!

"God almighty, what's that?" Jo heard Roy scream out.

Her eyes sprang open when she heard a scurry of feet and a blast of gunfire.

When she saw what was causing the uproar, she gasped and stared disbelievingly at the white wolves as they leaped on one man and then another, snarling and gnashing at them with their sharp teeth.

When the man who had gotten one blast of gunfire off at the wolves started to take aim again, a flock of buzzards swept down from the sky. One of them attacked the man with the firearm, biting at his scalp.

As he tried to fight the birds off, he dropped the firearm, then went yelping toward the cabin.

Screaming and hollering, the other men followed him inside the cabin and slammed the door closed.

When the buzzards started sweeping back and forth in front of the windows, the men drew the shutters closed.

Stunned, her lips agape, Jo watched the wolves come up around her, their bluish-gray eyes gazing warmly at her. What they had done was so unbelievable she wondered if she was imagining it.

And the buzzards!

As Jo looked up at them where they were perched along the edge of the cabin's roof, they gazed back at her as though trying to speak to her. She recalled the first time she had seen them. They, as well as the wolves, were Wolf's friends. And since she was his wife, they were her protectors!

But how did they know? she wondered. Had they been watching from the dark-shadowed forest all along?

"Thank you," she blurted out, her tears warm as they rolled down her cheeks. "Oh, Lord, thank you, precious wolves and wonderful buzzards. Without you, I'd . . . I'd . . . be . . ."

She stopped short of saying the word "dead." For now she was saved.

But for how long? she wondered despairingly. The men would surely find a way to best the animals.

Just as she was thinking this, the shutters of one of the cabin windows was thrown open.

Jo screamed when she saw the barrel of a rifle sliding through the window. It was aimed directly at her.

One gunshot was all that was required to finish what the fire had not been able to do.

When the gun coughed out its bullet, Jo looked away and pinched her eyes closed. She waited for the pain as the bullet entered her flesh.

When it didn't, she slowly opened her eyes and looked toward the window. Again she saw the man pull the trigger, but this time she didn't have the chance to look away.

What happened then made her heart skip a beat. She stared in wonder at where the bullet had gone. Something unseen had guided it away from her.

She gasped as it hit a tree on the far right side of her and became lodged in the trunk beside the other bullet.

"Damn, damn!" she heard Max shout as he showed himself at the window.

He stared at the tree where the two bullets were lodged, then gazed in amazement at Jo.

Jo swallowed hard when he raised his rifle again and aimed.

She couldn't believe that this was the same Max that she had loved as a child. He was trying relentlessly to kill her! How could he hate her so much? How?

Again the bullet was fired. Again it was guided away from Jo. Again it became lodged in the same tree.

Jo gazed at the white wolves rising to their feet, snarling as they peered toward the cabin.

Jo's breath caught inside her throat when she saw Max raise his rifle again and aim, but this time at one of the wolves.

Jo flinched and closed her eyes when the gunfire rang out, echoing all around her.

She waited to hear the yelp of the wolf that Max had shot at.

Again, mystically, the bullet missed.

Again it became lodged in the same tree.

Jo's heart skipped a wild beat when the buzzards that had been sitting on the roof of the house took flight. They began flying back and forth in front of the window where Max stood watching, his eyes wild, his lips parted.

When one of the buzzards started to fly directly toward him, Max scrambled to get the shutters closed, succeeding only moments before the buzzard could attack him.

The buzzard made a sharp turn and flew off with the others. Again they roosted, but this time in a tree whose leaves were a brilliant crimson.

Jo watched the wolves. Seemingly content, even somewhat lethargic, they once again spread themselves at her feet. Their eyes closed, they seemed to drift asleep.

But Jo was still in a state of shock over what had happened. Everything was so hard to believe . . . the unseen force that had kept the bullets from hitting her or the wolves . . . the wolves and the buzzards mysteriously appearing to protect her.

She could only believe that Wolf was somehow the reason for it all. Somehow Wolf knew of her abduction and had transferred his fears to his woodland creatures. They had come at Wolf's silent bidding to protect Jo.

"Thank you, my love," she whispered, her voice trembling.

She looked toward the cabin as one of the shutters inched open again. She saw someone peek through the tiny slit and then step away.

She winced and shuddered uncontrollably when someone struck a match for her to see, as a silent warning of what was yet to come.

She gazed down at the logs at her feet, then at the window again.

She felt her face drain of color when she saw that the window was fully open, and standing before it was Roy Bates, a lighted torch in his hands.

She glanced down at the wood, and then at the burning torch.

Could Roy throw the torch that far?

If so, would the unseen force be there again and guide it away from her?

Suddenly the buzzards took flight and flew high into the sky, and were soon gone from Jo's view.

When the wolves rose to their feet and snarled at Roy, his fright was evident as he clumsily dropped the torch.

Jo laughed to herself as she heard the men shouting and scampering around as they tried to put out the fire that the torch had set inside the cabin.

When she knew that the fire was out, Jo stiffened and wondered what the men's next move would be. Surely they would not allow the wolves to keep them from what they had planned for her for long.

Jo sighed with relief when someone closed the shutters.

She watched the wolves settle down again around her feet, seemingly waiting for something . . . or someone.

Jo gazed up at the sun, thankful that it was an autumn sun, its heat no longer as blistering as it had been during the summer months.

She then gazed over her shoulder in the direction of the forest. She just knew that Wolf was out there somewhere searching for her.

She hoped that he would get to her in time. . . .

Chapter Thirty-two

Just as Wolf rode into a clearing before starting his steep climb to the bluffs overhead, his buzzard friends swept down from the sky and began flying frantically around his head.

"*Bee-nay-shee*, bird friends, what are you trying to tell me?" he said, drawing his horse to a halt.

He watched as they flew a short distance away, then returned to sweep around his head. "You have never behaved in such an erratic, desperate way before," Wolf said, reaching a hand out toward the buzzards. "Why now?"

His spine stiffened when they flew away.

"Where are you going, friends?" he shouted.

He sank his heels into the flanks of his horse and rode after them. "*Weh-go-nen-dush-wi-szhis-chee-gay-yen*," he cried. "What are you doing? Are you purposely leading me somewhere?"

Then it came to him like a flash of lightning that the buzzards *were* leading him somewhere. He could only believe that it was to his wife. Somehow they knew of his desperate search for her.

Somehow it had been communicated to them from his heavy, aching heart, for they were as one with him, as were his precious white wolves.

"My wolves," he whispered. "Where are my wolves?"

He would have expected the wolves to be more attentive to his feelings and thoughts than his bird friends, and perhaps they were. Something told him that he would find them when he found Jo.

He smiled when he thought of his animal friends' skills at frightening their enemies. If things were as he now thought them to be, he even believed that the wolves were somehow, this very moment, protecting his woman!

"*Ae*, I feel deeply inside my soul that she is safe," he whispered. He looked heavenward. "*Gitchi Manitou*, let it be so!"

He continued following the buzzards.

They took him across wide, dipping valleys, up steep inclines, through streams, and then into a shadowy forest.

Wolf wound his way through the trees as the buzzards swept around them, and then suddenly he saw sunshine up ahead where the trees thinned out into a clearing.

Wolf rode onward until the buzzards were lost from sight as they flew from the forest and swept high into the sky.

Then Wolf's eyebrows rose when he saw a cross standing in the clearing.

He rode onward, then drew a tight rein and stopped when he saw who was tied to the cross.

"Jo!" he whispered, her name catching in the depths of his throat. The sun was setting behind the trees, yet still cast a golden glow on Jo as she helplessly hung there, her head dipped low, her eyes closed.

A fierce, hot rage grabbed Wolf. He clenched his fists at his sides as he gazed with narrowed eyes at the cabin on the other side of the clearing. Smoke was spiraling from the chimney.

But what seemed strange was how the shutters at the windows were closed. Surely whoever had placed Jo on the cross was there in the cabin.

Why had her tormentors closed the shutters so they could not see their captive?

Wolf edged his horse closer to the edge of the clearing, then smiled when he saw the white wolves lying around the cross. As he had thought, the wolves were protecting his woman!

Then his eyebrows lifted again as he wondered how the wolves could be out there in the open where the men could so easily shoot them? The cabin was some distance from the cross, yet should the men open a shutter and shoot at the wolves, there was no way they could miss.

Again he gazed at Jo.

His heart went out to her.

He wanted to go and get her, yet he knew that if the abductors heard him, he would die before carrying Jo to freedom.

He looked heavenward. Slowly the sun's colors were fading. The North Star was shining brightly against the darkening sky.

Again he looked at the cabin. He stiffened when he saw one of the shutters creep open. The barrel of a rifle slid into view.

His heart thundered wildly when he heard the gun blast. He wasn't sure whether the bullet was meant for his wife, or the white wolves.

He was astounded when he saw that the bullet hit the trunk of a tree some distance from where the abductor had surely aimed.

"How can that be?" Wolf whispered, thrilled that something had directed the bullet away from those he loved.

The gunshot had aroused the wolves, who were now standing. But instead of looking toward the cabin, where the shot had come from, they were looking in the direction of Wolf! It was as though they sensed his nearness.

If they came to him, it would alert the men in the cabin that he was there. Concentrating hard, he silently willed his friends to lie down again and to stop looking in his direction.

As the wolves lay around Jo's feet, gazing up

at her, the buzzards fluttered to the ground close to them and strutted around as though tempting the men to shoot at them.

"Fly away!" Wolf whispered, hoping that he could will the birds to obey his bidding. "Leave! Do not tempt fate!"

But the birds remained.

The wolves still lay at Jo's feet.

And when both of the shutters at one of the windows opened and revealed Max standing there, aiming at the wolves again, Wolf felt helpless to save them. He had to keep himself hidden so that when it turned dark he could rescue his wife.

He looked heavenward and thanked *Gitchi Manitou* for bringing darkness more quickly this evening than seemed usual.

Soon he would have his wife in his arms. Then her kidnappers would pay.

His body lurched at the sound of gunfire.

He gazed in disbelief when again the bullets veered away from the wolves and Jo as though some unseen force were directing them.

It seemed as though *Gitchi Manitou* was standing between the men and his loved ones, holding up a great shield to ward off the bullets, one by one.

"Thank you," Wolf whispered. "Thank you."

The gunfire ceased. Max stepped from the window and half closed the shutters, yet they remained open enough for Wolf to see the glow of a kerosene lamp as someone lit it inside the cabin.

Wolf could hear the muffled sound of voices. He could smell food as it was being cooked over the fire. For the moment the men had forgotten about their captive.

He doubted they would worry about Jo until morning. By then surely they would have devised a way to best the wolves so they could get to Jo.

He looked with a troubled heart at the logs placed around the foot of the cross at Jo's feet. A shiver raced up and down his spine when he realized why the wood was there. They had planned to burn Jo on the cross!

"Never!" he hissed, sliding slowly from his saddle.

He reached inside his saddlebag and drew out a sheathed knife. He slapped the sheath against his thigh and tied it securely in place.

He gazed at the rifle in the gun boot at the side of his horse, and then at Jo's shotgun. He doubted that he would need them. He wanted to do everything as silently as possible.

His jaw tight, he reached again inside his saddlebag and took from it a small buckskin vial of black paint.

He sat down at the foot of a tree and opened the vial. Slowly and methodically, he reached his fingers inside and covered his fingers with black paint.

Smiling, his eyes glinting, he spread the paint across his face with his fingers.

He removed his shirt and laid it aside, then blackened his chest and arms with the paint so that he would blend into the night. It was hard not to race right out to Jo and free her from the cross, but he knew that patience now would benefit them both later. Once the men were asleep and the sky was fully dark, then, and only then, would he chance going for his wife.

Chapter Thirty-three

Jo kept drifting to sleep, then jerking awake again when Max would laugh suddenly from inside the cabin.

She was weak not only from being tied to the cross for so long, but also from not eating for many hours. And her head and body ached unmercifully. Her hands were numb from being tied in one position for so long.

She gazed down at the wolves, which lay asleep close to the cross. Their white fur seemed almost to glow in the moonlight.

And a knot formed in her throat when she thought of how they had protected her from harm. She was still amazed at how the bullets seemed to be guided by some magical force away from both her and the wolves.

But the men inside the cabin were drinking

heavily—she could tell by the loud way they were talking and laughing—and she doubted they would stay inside the cabin for much longer. They would be so drunk they wouldn't even care about the danger of being attacked by the wolves in their eagerness to get at Jo.

Surely they would not allow themselves to be bested by a pack of wolves for long.

And even if they didn't come out of the cabin tonight to finish her off, they certainly would at the crack of dawn after sleeping off the whiskey.

"Please, Lord, oh, please let Wolf find me and save me," Jo whispered, her throat so scratchy dry she could scarcely hear the words as she spoke them.

Sleep.

She must sleep.

But if she did, she wouldn't be aware of the men if they came out in the middle of the night to kill her.

"No, I must stay awake," Jo whispered. She shook her head back and forth as she fought off lethargy.

She looked heavenward when clouds suddenly scudded across the moon, leaving everything around her in total blackness.

Then she became aware that she no longer heard sounds inside the cabin. The men must have fallen asleep in their drunken stupor.

Thank the Lord, she had until morning. Surely by then Wolf could find her. She knew that he was out there at this very moment searching for her.

A sound behind her made Jo's spine stiffen.

She jumped with alarm when the wolves leaped quickly to their feet, their eyes watching something approaching her from behind.

She was surprised when they didn't snarl. Instead, from the way their eyes lit up and their tails wagged, she could tell they welcomed this sudden visitor.

Suddenly it came to her that they would only be happy to see one person. It must be Wolf!

She watched them run friskily past her, yet they made no sound that might alert the men inside the cabin that someone was there.

Her heart raced when Wolf stepped around in front of her, not stopping to greet her, but instead eagerly slicing through the ropes at her wrists with his knife.

"Wolf, oh, Wolf, it's been so horrible," she whispered as one of her hands fell free.

She instantly began to feel the blood rushing to her fingers, making them tingle painfully.

When her other hand fell free, she wanted to fling herself into Wolf's arms, but waited patiently as he worked at the ropes at her ankles.

When she was free, he took her into his arms. Sobbing, Jo clung to him, then gasped with joy when he lifted her into his arms and began carrying her away from the cross.

"Thank you for finding me," she whispered, nestling closer to his chest, not caring that his skin was painted black. "Wolf, oh, Wolf, how did you know where to find me?"

"The buzzards," he whispered back. "My

bird friends. They came for me. They brought me to you."

The wolves romped and played all around Wolf as he ran into the forest toward his horse.

"The wolves protected me," Jo said, no longer feeling it necessary to whisper. "It's the strangest thing. Something kept the bullets that were shot at me and the wolves from reaching us. They were guided mysteriously away from us."

"*Gitchi Manitou* works in mysterious ways," Wolf said softly, then stopped beside his horse and slid Jo from his arms. He placed his hands at her waist and drew her close and held her. "And those who have done this thing to you will pay."

His lips came down upon hers in a crushing kiss.

Suddenly Jo forgot her thirst, her hunger, and her fear.

She was with her beloved.

And, yes, Max *would* pay!

She could hardly wait for him to get his comeuppance!

Chapter Thirty-four

As Wolf rode up the lane to Jo's house with Jo asleep in his arms, he saw many horses tied outside the house. Among them he recognized Fast Horse's steed.

Then he saw the glow from many lamps at the windows.

And as Wolf reached the house, several men came out on the porch.

Morning was just breaking along the horizon, giving Wolf enough light to see who was there. He now realized this was a posse formed to search for Jo, and perhaps even himself, since he had not found Jo as quickly as he had hoped.

His gaze swept over the men and saw that his loyal friend Fast Horse stood among them. Wolf nodded and smiled at his friend, who

Caseta EdwardsCassie Edwards

was dressed in buckskins instead of the usual robe he wore in his church.

Wolf recognized several men from his dealings with them at their business establishments in Lone Branch.

His gaze stopped on one man in particular—Judge Harper. This man, with his wild shock of red hair and blotches of freckles across his nose, had always spoken in behalf of the Ottawa people. And this morning it was obvious that he was going to join the posse, for he wore denim breeches, shirt, scuffed leather boots, and even had a heavy belt of guns strapped around his waist.

When Judge Harper smiled and gave Wolf a half salute, Wolf smiled back. Then his gaze went to Addison as he stepped away from the men and limped down the steps, tears streaming from his tired eyes as he looked at Jo.

"You found her," Addison said, already reaching his hands out for Jo, who was just stirring. "Oh, Lord, Wolf, you found her."

When Jo heard her father's voice, she opened her eyes and felt a sob lodge in her throat as her father stepped up to the horse, his arms outstretched for her. "Daddy," she murmured, feeling as though she were a child again who had always depended on her daddy to fix the wrongs in her life.

"Oh, Daddy, I'm alright," she said, her voice breaking when she saw the tears streaming from his eyes.

Wolf eased her from his lap and to the ground.

He watched with much emotion as father and daughter were reunited. Embracing, they cried in one another's arms.

Then Judge Harper and Fast Horse came up to him on his horse, questioning him with their eyes.

Wolf slid from the saddle. He placed gentle hands first on Fast Horse's shoulders and then on Judge Harper's. Then he stepped away from them and looked from one to the other as he began explaining what had happened, especially how and where he had found Jo.

"They were going to burn her alive?" Judge Harper gasped out, not realizing that his voice was loud enough for Addison to hear the horrible truth.

Jo felt her father stiffening in her arms. And she knew why. She had also heard Judge Harper repeat what Wolf had told him.

She withdrew from her father and gazed at his face. It had lost its color and his eyes were horrified as he reached a hand to her cheek.

"They . . . were . . . going to . . . ?" he began, but couldn't actually say the words that were like knives being thrust into his heart.

"Yes, Father, and *Max* gave the orders," Jo said, her voice breaking.

She turned on a heel and went to Judge Harper. "Judge, Max is behind most everything bad that's happened in the community of late," she said. "He gave the orders, and his men and Roy Bates were more than glad to obey."

As the men came down from the porch and

circled around her, while her father and Wolf stood on each side of her, Jo told them everything. She knew her words would condemn those who had wronged not only her, but the city as a whole, as well as the Ottawa.

"Roy Bates is the madman who has been setting fires not only in Lone Branch, but also Detroit and the surrounding area," Jo accused. "He admitted it all to me, but only because he didn't think I would live to tell it."

Even now she could see his eyes wickedly leering at her through the thick lenses of his eyeglasses.

She shivered inwardly as, in her mind's eye, she saw the reflection of fire in his eyeglasses.

She would never forget how he had struck one match after another just before he was supposed to set the logs afire at her feet.

She would never forget Max shouting at him to set the fire!

If not for the wolves and buzzards. . . .

No, she thought quickly to herself. She would not tell that part of what had occurred to her father, or the other men. The way the wolves and buzzards had saved her life was too mystical to explain. Others might think her a raving lunatic if she tried.

"Let's go and get 'em!" one of the men shouted as he raised a rifle in the air. "Wolf, lead us to them! Take us to their hideout. We'll blast 'em outta there! We'll have us a good old-fashioned lynching!"

"By now they have discovered that Jo has

310

been rescued," Wolf said solemnly. "I doubt they will stick around to be arrested."

"Max had many servants who were devoted to him," Jo said. "Surely he left instructions about where he was going so they can soon follow. Let's go and question them."

"Let's ride!" one of the posse shouted. "What's been done to Jo must be avenged. Yes! Those men must hang for their wrongful deeds."

Everyone ran to his horse.

Jo stood with her father and Wolf for a moment, then she ran with her father to get his horse and buggy.

With Fast Horse and Wolf on their horses flanking the horse and buggy, Jo and her father rode off behind the throng of men in pursuit of justice. Because of her long nap on Wolf's horse, and a long, delicious drink of water from a creek as Wolf had stopped to wash the black paint from his face and body, Jo felt revived and ready to tackle the world.

She only wished that the posse could go and arrest the scoundrels at Max's cabin. But she knew that once they saw she was gone from the cross they would hightail it out of there. She expected them to have a backup plan of where to go if things went awry.

But she also doubted that Max would leave all of his personal belongings behind, especially those that had been handed down from generation to generation of Schmidts.

Surely the expensive paintings that hung on

his walls would not be sacrificed. And then there were the stacks of money he kept in his safe. He loved having it on hand where he could count it whenever he chose.

The sun was a bright orange disc on the horizon when they reached the long, white-graveled lane that led to Max's house. As everyone turned into the lane, dust flew up from the horses' hooves like white fog.

When Max's house came into view at the far end, with its tall, white pillars gracing the front, Jo felt a pang of regret at the way things had turned out for Max. He was an intelligent man, who could have had anything he pleased because of the wealth his father had accumulated before him, but his desire to have what was not his had made everything slip between his fingers. He had turned out to be a monster, someone who actually turned Jo's stomach.

She glanced over at Wolf, who was the epitome of everything good a man could stand for. She felt so lucky to be loved by him and to have the chance to give him back that love twofold.

Her thoughts were brought back to the present when her father drew the horse to a halt before the steep stone steps that led up to Max's massive front porch.

"Jo, I think it's best if you stay here," Addison said. "As you can see, Judge Harper, Fast Horse, and Wolf are already going up the steps. Let them do the questioning."

"Father, you know I can't just sit here and

wait to be told what they find out," Jo said, already climbing from the buggy. She gave him a "please understand" look, then rushed up the steps to the porch and got to the door just as Judge Harper banged the brass knocker against it.

When the door opened, not only was the butler standing in the foyer, but also all of Max's other servants, their eyes wide.

"We're here to question all of you about your employer," Judge Harper said, taking it upon himself to be the spokesperson of the group.

Jo clasped her fingers around Wolf's when the servants and butler remained silent, their eyes widening even more when Judge Harper stepped inside the house with Jo, Wolf, and Fast Horse following behind him.

Knowing most of the servants, who had been in Max's employ for many years, Jo stepped past the butler, who was new to her.

She took the frail hands of Max's personal maid, a woman in her late fifties who was dressed in a crisp black dress with a white collar that contrasted against her dark neck. Jo felt the trembling and the coldness of Maria's hands. She could see confusion in her dark eyes and knew what the reality of Max no longer being there meant to this woman.

Max had brought her directly from Mexico years ago. Maria knew nothing but this house; she hardly knew anyone but Max and those others who worked with her at Max's mansion.

e home in a

several trips back and

. Will he be

's wanted by the

ax or where he

r eyes, for he could

telling a lie just by

none of us know anything,"

ng for them all.

at Jo's arm. "What

He looked at them

314

all. "All of you will be seen to. I won't let the likes of Max Schmidt destroy your lives."

Jo walked past them all and gazed down the long corridor, her eyes stopping on the closed door of Max's office.

She turned to Wolf as he stepped up to her, then her father who had followed her into the house. "I'm going to his office," she said. "I'm going to check his safe. Maria said he carried several bags to his horse. I imagine that was his money."

Judge Harper stepped away from Maria and looked up the massive spiral staircase. Then he nodded to the men who were awaiting his orders. "Go upstairs," he said. "Spread out. Search everywhere. See what he managed to take. See if there are any clues as to where he might be headed."

Addison went into the parlor alone to look around, while Jo and Wolf went to Max's office. When they saw the safe, they didn't need the combination to get inside it. The door was wide open. There was nothing left inside except for some files and a journal.

"I knew he wouldn't leave without taking his money," Jo said, sighing heavily. She looked up at Wolf. "Wherever he goes, he has made sure that he has enough money for a fresh start."

"He had it all planned from the beginning," Wolf said. "And long before he made his first move against you and your father. He had to know that his time was up in this area. He had to know that in the end he would be the big loser."

"People whose prejudices rule their lives usually are," Jo said, sighing again as she walked slowly around the office, touching things that were familiar to her. "Max had so much. I can't believe he gave it all up." She turned to Wolf. "His father would roll over in his grave if he knew how Max turned out." She swallowed hard. "If he knew what Max had done to me . . ."

Wolf took her into his arms. "Do not think about it," he said softly, holding her close. "You are safe. No one will ever get the chance to threaten you again."

"Take me home, Wolf," Jo murmured, so glad to be with him, to have him hold her. "Please . . . take . . . me home."

"You mean to your father's house to get your things?" Wolf asked, placing a finger beneath her chin and lifting her eyes to his.

"Yes, that also," Jo said, slowly smiling. "But when I speak of home, Wolf, I mean mine and yours."

"It was never truly a home until you became a part of it," Wolf said, then kissed her softly.

But even though Jo felt safe and loved, deep inside she still feared Max!

She prayed that he had given up on getting his vengeance against her.

But she was afraid that as long as Max had breath in his lungs he would not forget her, or what he blamed her for . . . his having lost everything that was dear to him!

Chapter Thirty-five

It was Halloween, one of Jo's favorite holidays. It was wonderful to have Wolf with her this year to enjoy the special occasion. Today it would be spent in the same way she had celebrated it for the past ten years, at the orphanage in Lone Branch.

Later in the evening she would honor Wolf's traditions, celebrating "The Feast of the Dead," which was also known to the Ottawa as a "Ghost Supper."

Jo sat in the buggy with her father, while Wolf rode beside them on Midnight. When the orphanage came into view, she looked over her shoulder at the two bushel baskets of bright red apples and several pumpkins that she had carved yesterday with Wolf's assistance. He had never seen pumpkins carved before. It had warmed Jo's heart to see his eyes shine as she showed him how to do it.

And he had been a quick learner, for his carved pumpkins were more creative than Jo's. She especially loved their jagged-toothed smiles.

And how she loved *him*. She glanced over at him as he looked toward the orphanage. He had never been there before. But she had explained about the children's situations and how it was that so many were there.

She knew that thus far no Ottawa children were housed there. If misfortune befell an Indian family, others took in the children that were orphaned. Thus, there were never any true orphans in the Ottawa community.

She knew for certain now that she was carrying Wolf's child within her womb. She gazed down at her stomach and gently rested a hand across it.

She could hardly wait to have the child.

She could hardly wait to tell Wolf.

But she had decided to keep the news to herself until Christmas. Telling him her little secret was going to be her Christmas present to Wolf. She only hoped that he would be too involved in his affairs to notice that she did not have a monthly flow between now and Christmas.

"Here we are," Addison said, smiling over at Jo as he pulled the horse and buggy up before the wide porch of the orphanage. "Let's make some children happy, Jo."

"Yes, let's," Jo said, then smiled over at Wolf as he dismounted and gently assisted her from the buggy.

"Halloween is such a fun time for the children in the orphanage," Jo said, reaching for Wolf's hands and squeezing them excitedly. She giggled. "It is as much fun for us adults."

Wolf didn't get the chance to respond. The children had been watching from the windows of the two-storey brick building and were now squealing and running out the door, soon taking turns hugging Jo and Addison.

When that was done, and they became quiet as they stood back and gazed questioningly at Wolf, Jo took his hand and smiled at the young ones. "Children, this is my husband," she said, looking adoringly up at him. "His name is Wolf."

For a moment the children stood silently studying Wolf, then they inched closer. "Why are you called Wolf?" one of the boys finally asked.

"It is a story I will gladly tell you," Wolf said, relieved that they were beginning to accept his presence.

"But not until later," Jo said. "Not until we are inside and enjoying stories and games."

The children suddenly parted as one of the orphanage attendants pushed little Judith Lynn toward Jo and Wolf in the wheelchair Jo had given to the child.

Seeing Judith Lynn smiling so broadly brought tears to Jo's eyes. The small child with her golden ringlets hanging across her shoulders and her rosy cheeks was so adorable Jo wished that she was hers.

She glanced up at Wolf as a thought struck her.

They could adopt the child!

Jo was married and had a home of her own and a husband who adored children.

Being the compassionate person that he was, surely Wolf could find it in his heart to accept this child into their lives.

Hadn't he already promised to add a room to their home for their own children? Surely one more child in that room wouldn't matter.

"Jo, Jo!" Judith Lynn cried. "I love the wheelchair, Jo. It's much better than any I've ever had before. I can wheel myself around now. Watch me, Jo. Watch!"

Judith Lynn turned her head and gave the attendant a nod. When the attendant smiled down at her and then stepped back from the wheelchair, lowering her hands to her sides, Judith Lynn placed her tiny hands on the wheels.

A smile as wide as one of those Jo had carved on the pumpkins spread across the child's face as she wheeled herself toward Jo.

"See?" Judith Lynn squealed. "See, Jo? I can do it. Isn't it wonderful?"

Jo wiped tears from her eyes, then went and knelt down before Judith Lynn. "Yes, it is wonderful," she said, a sob lodging in her throat. "I am so proud of you."

They shared a long, affectionate hug; then, afraid the other children were feeling left out, Jo rushed to her feet and ran to the back of the buggy.

With the help of Wolf and her father, the jack-o-lanterns were taken from the buggy and handed out to the delighted children.

When the huge baskets of apples were taken from the buggy and set in the midst of the children, it was only a matter of moments before each child had an apple thrust inside a pants or skirt pocket.

"All we need now are candles for the jack-o-lanterns," Jo said, a mischievous glint in her eyes.

"But we have no candles," Judith Lynn said, her lips curving into a pout.

"Oh, yes but we *do*," Jo laughed, reaching inside the buggy and bringing out a huge sack full of candles cut down to fit the pumpkins. "Let's take everything inside to the parlor. Then we can make the faces on the jack-o-lanterns light up like all of your own smiling faces!"

There was a scurry of feet as the children ran into the orphanage building with their pumpkins while Wolf and Jo stood outside, watching.

Addison had gone in before the children and awaited their arrival with matches for the candles.

"Wolf, aren't they all so dear?" Jo said, twining an arm around his neck and gazing into his midnight dark eyes.

"All children are special in the eyes of *Gitchi Manitou* . . . and your God," Wolf said softly, reaching a hand to smooth a lock of her hair back from her eyes. "But I can tell that one child holds a special place in your heart."

"Yes, Judith Lynn has always been my favorite," Jo murmured. "It's such a shame how her family abandoned her because . . . because . . . she couldn't walk. While I was confined to the wheelchair, I discovered many things about myself. Life is precious, even when one cannot walk."

She paused, then blurted out. "Wolf, can we adopt Judith Lynn? Can we take her home and be her family? I love her so much, Wolf. It is already the same as if she were mine."

Wolf gazed intently into her eyes as he considered this special gift his wife wanted to give the child.

He was touched deeply by her compassion.

He could never love her as much as he loved her at this moment.

"She will make a wonderful sister to the child we bring into the world," he said, his eyes dancing. "*Ae*, if you wish, we can adopt Little Judith Lynn."

Touched by his kindness, and by the fact that he didn't pause to question her about her sudden wish to have Judith Lynn in their lives, Jo flung herself into his arms and hugged him. "Thank you," she said, sobbing. "Thank you for being you. I love you so, Wolf. Oh, how I love you."

"Jo!"

Judith Lynn's voice shouting from the open door of the orphanage caught Jo's attention. She wished that she could tell the child right away that she would soon no longer be a part of the orphanage. But Jo always did things by the book, and she knew she would have to meet with Judge Harper to legalize the adoption.

Until then she would keep the secret from Judith Lynn, for if there were any hitches that would prevent the adoption, she felt it was unfair to raise the child's hopes.

Jo knew who Judith Lynn's parents were: Jerome and Alice Schmidt, Max's very own cousins. If Max could discover what Jo wanted to do, surely he would put a stop to it. Even Jerome himself might try to stop it.

Putting her fears out of her mind, Jo went inside the orphanage with Wolf and joined in the fun and laughter.

After several games were played and refreshments were shared with the children, Jo and Wolf left to go to their own Halloween celebration at his village. Addison had been invited, but he had chosen to go on home, complaining of a headache.

When they arrived at the Ottawa village, the women were busy cooking Indian corn soup and bread. It would be consumed during the Ghost Supper tonight when the moon would rise slowly and mystically white in the dark heavens above . . . when the Ottawa would gather to eat for the dead.

But Wolf and Jo had other plans, something that would keep them busy before the excite-

ment of the evening. So much had gotten in
the way of their sweet, private moments together that they had set aside the whole afternoon to make up for those moments denied
them these past several days.

As soon as the door was closed between
them and the world, Jo leaned into Wolf's embrace. "I love you," she murmured, gazing lovingly into his eyes. "I want you."

Wolf framed her face between his hands
and brought his lips closer to hers. "*Gee-ah-
bee-nah-ah-bee-ding-gay-di-kid*?" he said, his
voice husky.

"What did you just say to me?" Jo asked, her
heart racing as his hands slid down and
cupped her breasts through the cotton fabric
of her dress.

"I said will you please say it again . . . that
you love and want me," Wolf said, his face a
mask of naked desire. He brushed kisses
across her lips.

"I . . . love . . . you . . ." Jo whispered, coming
alive beneath his touch. Her face felt feverish
with want. "I . . . need . . . you. I want you."

Then she surprised him when she proved
her own knowledge of his language. "*Gee-zah-
gi-ee-nah*?" she whispered, her eyes glittering
mischievously as she saw his surprise that she
knew a full phrase of his language.

"*Ae*, yes I love you," he responded to her
question, then wove his fingers through her
thick, golden hair and brought her lips to his
in a powerful kiss.

Ecstasy moved through Jo with bone-weakening intensity. She slid her hands between them and found the waistband of his buckskin breeches.

Her pulse racing, eager to touch him, to have him inside her, she untied the thongs at his waist and began shoving his breeches down past his hips.

When they were lying at his feet, and his manhood was free to be touched and caressed, Jo twined her fingers around him and began moving them on him.

She thrilled at the way he moaned and stiffened. Then he jerked his lips away from her and threw his head back in a cry of sweet agony.

She moved her hand on him for a moment longer, then stepped away from him and hurriedly undressed.

When she was standing silkenly nude before him, the knowledge that their growing child lay within her made Jo want to shout that she was pregnant. But she wanted even more badly to wait and give him the special Christmas present by telling him then, so she held the secret inside her heart, and reached her hands out for him.

"Let's go to bed," she murmured, her eyes aflame with passion as he stepped completely out of his breeches, yanked his shirt over his head, and tossed it aside.

When he swept her up into his arms and began carrying her toward their bedroom, Jo feathered soft kisses across his muscled chest, her tongue flicking his nipples.

Jo sucked in a breath of rapture as he stopped long enough to flick his tongue over the nipples of her breasts; then she sighed wondrously as he stretched himself against her while pressing her down to the bed.

Their bodies became quickly entangled, their lips frenzied as they worshiped each other's bodies.

His mouth covered hers, his tongue seeking, searching, probing, and at the same time he thrust his manhood deeply inside her where she ached unmercifully for him. Jo felt herself floating away on clouds of ecstasy, shuddering with each long, deep stroke.

Their hunger was tempered by their love, by their needs, as their bodies strained together, their lips joining in fierce, fevered kisses.

Her body pliant in his arms, her head rolling as his lips moved to her breasts, worshiping them with his tongue and teeth, Jo felt herself climbing quickly to that place where ecstasy would totally claim her.

She clung to Wolf and moaned as his thrusts became more demanding. His arms locked around her now, holding her close, his lips forcing hers apart, their tongues meeting.

Wolf felt the pleasure building, like the deep rumbling of a volcano roaring through him.

He slid his lips down Jo's neck, then again sucked one of her nipples between his teeth.

His hands moved over the smooth skin of

her breasts, and then down to that moist place where he found her swollen womanhood. One touch and he knew that she had found paradise.

He gave himself to the same wild ecstasy and sensual abandonment as he thrust even more deeply into her and released his seeds.

Afterward, as they lay breathlessly together, Wolf ran a hand over her flat tummy. "Soon a child will be growing inside you," he said thickly. He chuckled. "Today I planted enough seeds to make *many* babies."

Jo suddenly felt guilty for not telling him about the pregnancy, yet she still wanted to wait. It wouldn't be that long until Christmas. Ah, what a wonderful Christmas present it would be!

And she hoped by then Judith Lynn would be a part of that special Christmas! She planned to go into Lone Branch tomorrow and begin the adoption proceedings. She only hoped that Max was far, far away so that he could not interrupt her plans to bring Judith Lynn a life of love and happiness. The child had been denied such love for too long.

"I smell corn soup," Wolf said, leaning on an elbow. "I hear laughter. It is time, my wife, to join the celebration of Ghost Supper."

"I think I'm too weak to get up," Jo teased. "You've exhausted me, husband. Totally exhausted me."

"That is not good to hear," Wolf teased back, reaching to cup one of her breasts within a hand. "For I had planned to make love again after the Ghost Supper. Now I guess I must find entertainment elsewhere."

"No, you don't," Jo said, laughing as she playfully hit him on an arm with a fist. "I am the only 'entertainment,' as you call it, that you will ever need. And I am never too exhausted to make love, my darling. Never."

He swept his arms around her and drew her close. "I did not think so," he said, then gave her a long, deep kiss that truly left her weak, yet wanting.

Chapter Thirty-six

Fires burned high and warm in the fireplaces at both ends of the council house as the winds blew cold outside and snow made a blanket of white over the ground.

Fast Horse, in his capacity as Father Samuel today, stood before everyone in his black robe and sparkling white collar. He smiled radiantly as he led the Ottawa people in singing Christmas songs, the children's voices the loudest and sweetest of them all.

The weeks had gone by quickly and it was now Christmas morning. Jo sat among Wolf's people in the council house celebrating the Ottawa's "Three Kings Feast" which was held in honor of the three kings who followed the light of the star and found the baby Jesus.

Long tables had been pushed together to

hold a delicious-smelling assortment of food and hot, sweet drinks.

But the most eagerly anticipated food today was fry bread that the women had made for the feast. A coin had been placed in three loaves. Whoever found the coins while eating the bread became one of the three kings who would each host a dinner in the council house during the upcoming coldest months of the year. There were three dinners to represent the three kings.

Jo had been told that many years ago, when things were not as good for the Ottawa, when it was hard for all families to find food, there had been another practice at Christmas time. Some pieces of fry bread would have beans in them. Some loaves would hold one bean, some two, some three, while others had none at all.

A basket would be placed in the center of the feast table. Whoever found beans in his bread would put the same number of gifts in the basket as there were beans in the bread.

After their feast on Christmas day, the people would decide on some family that was in need. The next day the host would take the basket of gifts to that family. This was a custom where the Christianity they had learned came in, as a living interpretation of the story of the three kings who presented gifts to the baby Jesus.

Now, at the Ottawa village, everyone prospered, for things were shared equally among the people. When one family was struck by some misfortune, the other families of the village gave of their own wealth so that those who were suffering could rise again above their personal tragedy.

Today everyone, the elderly and the young, sat along the tables. Blue Moth sat with Sleeping Bear on Wolf's left side, Jo on his right.

Even though Sleeping Bear had not warmed up to Jo yet, Blue Moth treated her like a daughter, which pleased Jo since her own mother was no longer with her.

Jo was surprised to discover that the Ottawa put up Christmas trees in their personal lodges. Today there was also a huge Christmas tree in their council house. Wrapped gifts that would be exchanged after the dinner were beneath the tree. Names had been drawn among them all to choose who would be the recipient of each gift.

But even though the tree stood tall at the far side of the council house, with candles burning on its limbs, and with bright and glistening balls hanging on it, Jo's spirits were too low to join in the merriment of the day. For Wolf's sake she sat beside him, forcing herself to smile and look as jolly as the others, but deep inside herself she felt sad.

No matter how hard she had struggled to adopt Judith Lynn, Max's family had found ways to stop it. The child's parents were even now trying to get her back, but for the wrong reasons. They were doing so only to make sure that Jo did not have her.

331

Even Jo's wonderful gift to her husband, the news about their baby that she had planned to tell Wolf tonight after the celebration, had been clouded by her trouble with Max's cousins, aunts, and uncles. None of them wanted to cooperate with Jo. They all resented her for driving Max out of town.

Their behavior when she was face to face with them had become frightening. They had made threats she had not told Wolf about. She didn't even like to think about them herself.

But there was one person she had told. Judge Harper. He had promised that he would take care of this . . . that the threats warranted the attention of the authorities.

Therein lay Jo's only hope, for those threats might enable Jo to adopt Judith Lynn.

Yet it had been a full week since Judge Harper had told her that to encourage her. As each day had passed, her hopes had waned.

She now even doubted that Judith Lynn would ever visit her, much less live with her. The Schmidt family hated Jo with a vengeance unlike anything she had ever experienced before.

Jo's troubled thoughts were brought back to the present by the jangle of bells outside as a horse and sleigh came into the village.

Jo and Wolf exchanged quick, questioning glances, both wondering if the one who was arriving late was Judge Harper. Judge Harper had been invited to attend the celebration but had declined, saying business kept him in his Lone Branch office.

He had not even returned to his home in Springfield to join his wife for Christmas.

Jo believed that Judith Lynn's case was the cause, for he wanted the child to be with Jo and Wolf, not with people who did not truly love her.

Jo leaned closer to Wolf as Fast Horse continued to lead everyone in song.

"That *must* be Judge Harper," Jo whispered to Wolf. "Do you think he changed his mind about joining us? Or do you think he . . . has . . . news about Judith Lynn?"

She swallowed hard. "Oh, Lord, Wolf, if it *is* Judge Harper, and he has brought news to us, is it bad . . . or good?" she said, her voice breaking.

"You must accept whichever it is and move onward with your life," Wolf whispered back. "I have seen how withdrawn you are. My wife, it is time for rejoicing. Do we not have each other? Do we not plan to have children of our own? Is that not enough for you?"

Hearing what he said, and now feeling guilty for having acted in this way, Jo flung herself into his arms.

"I'm sorry," she whispered, reveling in the warmth and gentleness of his arms as he swept them around her. "I'll stop fretting so over things I have no control over. I went to court. I presented my case. That is all anyone can do."

"*Ae*, and now let us go quietly from the lodge and see who has come to our village on this cold, blustery day," Wolf said, easing Jo from his arms.

He took her by one hand, smiled at those who turned to see him and Jo leave, then walked with Jo to the council house door and opened it just as Judge Harper stepped up to the door. He was dressed in a heavy wool coat that reached down to his ankles. On his head he wore a fur hat. And on his hands were leather gloves.

"Judge Harper, come on inside," Jo said, gently taking his elbow.

He didn't step forward. "Can we go to your cabin?" he said, looking from Jo to Wolf. "What I have to say is something I feel should be said in privacy."

"*Ae*, we will go to our lodge," Wolf said, going inside to grab his and Jo's long, thick bear robes. After placing Jo's robe snugly around her shoulders, he put his own on and quietly closed the council door behind him.

Her pulse racing, Jo gazed questioningly at the judge and tried to read his expression as they trudged through the ankle-deep snow. She was dying to know whether the news he brought was good or bad.

But with his hat drawn down so low on his brow, and with the snow coming down in white sheets between her and the judge, there was no way she could decipher his mood.

But she was almost certain that what he had to say wasn't good. Surely she had lost the most important courtroom battle of her life!

Shivering from the cold, Jo stepped eagerly inside her lodge as Wolf held the door open for her and Judge Harper.

"Come on over by the fire," Jo said, shaking out her robe and hanging it on a wooden peg on the wall. She reached a hand out for Judge Harper's wrap. "Here. Let me have your coat. Give me your hat and gloves also. I shall place them on the hearth to dry."

"First let me slip out of these boots," Judge Harper said, reaching to slide them from his feet.

Jo took them and sat them on the hearth, then took his coat and hat and placed them over the back of a kitchen chair to dry.

"Jo, you'd best change out of your wet moccasins, don't you think?" Judge Harper said, backing up to the hearth and rubbing his hands together behind him as the warmth from the fire penetrated his flesh.

"I will go for dry moccasins for both of us," Wolf said as he went to their bedroom.

Jo nodded at the judge and gestured toward an overstuffed chair before the hearth. "Please sit down and be comfortable," she said, then walked to the kitchen area and stopped before a pot-bellied stove whose sides glowed orange from the fire inside. "I've left coffee warming on the stove for our return home. Let me get us all a cup."

"Sounds good to me," Judge Harper said, easing down onto one of the three plush chairs arranged before the fireplace.

Wolf came from the bedroom. He set dry moccasins before the chair Jo would sit in and sat down on the chair to Judge Harper's left, where he exchanged his own wet moccasins with dry.

"And so you were enjoying your Christmas celebration, were you?" Judge Harper asked, nodding a silent thank you to Jo as she handed him a cup of coffee.

"Yes, did you hear the singing as you arrived?" Jo asked, giving Wolf a cup, then going for her own and taking it back to a table beside the chair where she sat down next to the judge.

She quickly changed into dry moccasins, then picked up the cup.

But drinking coffee was the last thing on her mind. She wanted to know why Judge Harper was there!

His hesitancy made her think the worst. Judith Lynn was going to be denied a home filled with love and warmth. Jo and Wolf were going to be denied the child!

Yes, for certain she had lost, as had the little girl, for Jo and Wolf could have given her the sort of life that Judith Lynn deserved. If the child had been forced to go back to parents who had no feelings but silent loathing for her, the sin would lie on Max's shoulders, for Jo knew that he was behind the battle that had ensued over the rights of the child.

"Yes, I heard the singing, but, Jo, one voice was missing," Judge Harper said, a smile on his lips. He set his half-drunk cup of coffee aside on the table and leaned toward Jo. "I didn't hear one voice in particular."

"Oh, you mean mine?" Jo said, laughing awkwardly. Judge Harper had heard her singing a solo one day when he and his wife had attended services at Fast Horse's church.

She lowered her eyes. "No, you didn't hear me singing today, Judge Harper," she murmured. "I . . . I . . . wasn't in the mood."

Then recalling Wolf's words of encouragement, and knowing she was letting him down by her solemn behavior, she quickly lifted her chin and forced a smile. "But that is going to change," she blurted out. "I'm going to forget—"

"Jo, *your* voice wasn't what I was referring to," Judge Harper said, interrupting her. He reached over and took her by the hand. "Jo, I was speaking of Judith Lynn. *Her* voice would sound beautiful among the other children's, wouldn't it?"

"Judge Harper, let's not talk about Judith Lynn," Jo said, her voice breaking. "I've got to accept what's happened and go on with my life."

She smiled over at Wolf, anxious now to reveal her secret to him.

Oh, what joy she would see in her husband's eyes when she told him! Oh, how she wished now that she had not waited. But she would make it up to him.

Never would she keep secrets from him again about anything!

"But, Jo, *listen*. You don't seem to understand," Judge Harper said. He looked toward the door when the faint jingling sound of bells could be heard in the distance.

Jo also now heard the bells.

When Judge Harper turned toward her and their eyes met, she silently questioned him.

"Seems someone else is coming today for your Christmas celebration," Judge Harper said, a mischievous glint in his eyes. He reached a hand out for Jo. He smiled at Wolf. "Both of you. Come to the door with me. Let's see who is arriving in that second sleigh."

Jo's eyes widened. And as she took the judge's hand and felt him squeeze it affectionately, she looked at him again.

"Come on," Judge Harper said, tugging on Jo's hand. He nodded toward Wolf. "Whoever it is should be just arriving outside the door."

Wolf shoved the latch down, then pulled the door open. The snow had stopped falling. He could see perfectly clearly who sat with warm blankets around her shoulders and spread across her lap. He also saw the wheelchair behind her in the sleigh.

Jo stepped past Wolf. Her hands flew to her mouth and tears fell from her eyes when she saw little Judith Lynn sitting there, her golden curls spilling out from beneath her knit hat, her eyes shining with happiness as they met Jo's.

"Jo!" Judith Lynn cried, reaching her arms out for Jo. "I can live with you!" She looked toward Wolf. "Wolf! You can be my daddy!"

Jo stumbled all over herself and almost slid

on the snow as she ran to the sleigh and grabbed the child into her arms. "Darling, darling child," she murmured. The little girl's tears mingled with Jo's as they cried and clung and laughed.

"Let me take her inside," Wolf said, his own eyes misting as Jo stood up and smiled at him.

"She's ours," she said, sobbing. "She is actually our child, Wolf."

The blankets fell away from Judith Lynn as Wolf swept her up and into his arms.

Jo gathered the blankets as Judge Harper came and got the wheelchair.

When they were all inside, the warmth of the fireplace filling their cheeks with rosy color, Jo knelt before Judith Lynn in the wheelchair, their hands clutching.

"It wasn't easy," Judge Harper said, settling down again in the thickly upholstered chair. "But, by God, I made those cold-hearted bastards see who was boss. No way in hell would I allow the child to live under the same roof as her true parents."

"Thank you, oh, Lord, thank you," Jo said, unable to take her eyes off Judith Lynn.

Wolf came and knelt beside Jo. He reached a gentle hand to Judith Lynn's cheek. "Welcome to our home," he said thickly. "Welcome into our lives."

"Thank you," Judith Lynn said as she leaned her cheek into his hand. "I love you, Wolf . . . I mean . . . Daddy."

"I am proud to be your father," Wolf said softly. "And one day you will be a big *sister*."

Jo gave Wolf a smile that he wondered about, but did not question. They joined the others at the council house. It gave Jo such a joyous, blissful feeling to see how the Ottawa people accepted the child among them so quickly.

Except for one. Jo saw the resentment in Wolf's father's eyes and doubted that he would ever accept either her or Judith Lynn.

Jo forced the concern from her mind. There were too many other things to be happy about to worry about just one thorn in her side.

Food, song, drink, and gifts were shared by everyone.

Even Judith Lynn had a gift beneath the tree. Judge Harper had seen to that. When no one had noticed, he had slipped a package under the tree for Judith Lynn . . . a porcelain doll with eyes that opened and closed!

Then night came and with it more snow. It was too dangerous for Judge Harper to travel, so he accepted Jo and Wolf's invitation to spend the night.

Although he protested loudly, Judge Harper was given Jo and Wolf's bed.

Jo and Wolf now lay on a pallet of blankets and furs beside their lodge fire, while sweet Judith Lynn slept peacefully on her own pallet at their side.

Chapter Thirty-seven

Jo snuggled against Wolf. "I am so content," she whispered as the glow of the fire danced in her husband's eyes.

The moment of truth had arrived. Jo was ready to give Wolf his very special Christmas present, one that he would remember for the rest of his life.

Jo sighed, for now she was glad that she had waited to give him the special news tonight after everything else had turned out to be so wonderful.

Her news would just be more icing to add to the cake.

Just as she opened her lips to tell Wolf, she gasped. On the ceiling of the cabin huge flames were reflected, and someone began screaming in panic.

"Fire!" Jo cried, bolting upright just as Wolf noticed the reflection. Even now, smoke was wafting beneath their door.

Along with Wolf, Jo rushed to her feet.

As Wolf scrambled into his buckskin breeches, Jo ran to the window and looked for the source of the fire.

She went cold when she saw that Sleeping Bear and Blue Moth's cabin was completely engulfed in flames. The fire and smoke rolled from the windows and through large holes in the roof that had been made by the lapping flames.

"Wolf!" Jo screamed, awakening everyone in the cabin. "Your parents! Wolf, your mother and father's cabin is on fire!"

Not stopping to put on moccasins or to get a blanket to wrap around himself, Wolf ran from the cabin.

His bare feet sank into the snow as he came to a halt and stared blankly at his parents' cabin.

Horror filled him when he saw that there was no way for him to go inside to save his parents, for the entire cabin was ablaze.

Grief stabbed at his heart, for he knew that no one could have survived the raging fire.

He lifted his eyes and hands heavenward. "Why?" he cried. "Why?"

Torturous screams came from another burning cabin.

Wolf turned his head and saw Red Hawk's wife screaming.

His friend's cabin was aflame. His wife and children were standing, clinging, crying as they watched the fire eat away at their home.

If Red Hawk wasn't with them, that had to mean he was still inside his lodge.

"Red Hawk!" Wolf cried, breaking into a mad run when he saw that the cabin was not yet totally consumed by flames. He hadn't been able to save his parents, but perhaps he could save his friend.

Someone, he did not even look to see who, threw a blanket around Wolf's shoulders.

Lifting it over his head even as Jo begged him not to, he rushed inside the burning cabin.

Heat and flames ate at his flesh. His throat and eyes burned as he felt around for his friend.

Finally Wolf saw Red Hawk's body. He was lying on the floor not far from his bedroom. But Wolf couldn't tell if he was alive or dead. The smoke was too thick.

But when Wolf bent low to pick Red Hawk up, his friend's skin peeled off in black masses onto Wolf's fingertips. Wolf felt sick to his stomach.

His friend . . . was dead!

Tears rushing from his eyes, Wolf swept the blanket from around himself and wrapped Red Hawk's body in it.

Then, dashing through the greedy fingers of fire and the great bursts of choking smoke, Wolf carried what remained of Red Hawk outside to his waiting family. All his people were now standing outside, shock on their faces and in their eyes.

"He did not make it," Wolf said, gently laying Red Hawk in the snow.

"Red Hawk saved us, then went back inside for his prized bow and quiver of arrows," Red Hawk's wife cried as she fell to her knees beside her husband. Wailing, she hung her head and began rocking back and forth on her knees as her three-year-old daughter and four-year-old son clung to her.

"Wolf?" Jo said, tears rushing from her eyes. "I'm so so sorry about Red Hawk . . . about your parents."

Wolf drew her into his arms. He turned and gazed at his parents' cabin as the roof fell into the flames.

"Why must there always be bad with the good moments of life?" he said, his voice breaking. Tears rolled down his ash-blackened cheeks, leaving streaks in their wake. "These fires must have been deliberately set for two homes to have burned at the same time. But who would do this thing? Who could hate so much?"

Jo grew cold when the obvious came to her mind.

Roy.

Roy Bates!

Perhaps he had not fled the area after all, or he had fled, and then returned to do Max's dirty work again.

Suddenly Jo saw something in the forest

just behind Wolf's cabin . . . a reflection of fire in eyeglasses.

It *was* Roy!

He *had* returned!

He *had* set the fires!

He had coldly and calculatedly murdered tonight.

But he had miscalculated by not having murdered the one he had surely been paid to do away with. He had chosen the wrong cabins to burn. *Jo* was *alive!*

Then, before Jo's very eyes, she saw Roy strike another match. But this time the fire accidentally caught on his coat sleeve.

Jo screamed as she watched the coat go up in flames so quickly he had no chance to remove it.

"It's Roy Bates!" Jo cried as everyone's eyes shifted. They saw him scream and run around in the snow, then fall to the ground in a burning heap of flames.

Even Red Hawk's wife's wailing stopped when everyone went to stare down at the dead, blackened man.

"Here is why he died so quickly," Wolf said, coming toward Jo carrying a can of kerosene that Roy had obviously set aside to use later. "He used this to start the fires and while dousing the cabins with the lethal liquid spilled some on himself. One spark of fire would have sent flames all over his body."

"I saw him strike a match," Jo said, staring down at the can. She then looked up at Wolf. "He was going to burn our house, Wolf." The color rushed from her face as she looked quickly at their cabin. "Oh, Lord, surely he already splashed kerosene on it. Judith Lynn! We must get Judith Lynn out of the cabin."

"I already have her, Jo," Judge Harper said as he stepped up next to Jo with Judith Lynn in his arms wrapped in warm blankets.

"Give her to me," Jo said, tears flooding her eyes.

"Sweetie, sweetie," Jo murmured as Judge Harper slid Judith Lynn into her arms. "I'm so sorry you had to witness this terrible thing tonight."

Her eyes hidden against Jo's chest, Judith Lynn clung to her.

Jo's attention was drawn into the forest again, where snow had drifted high around some bushes. "Wolf, I think I see . . ." she began, her heart thundering.

She gasped with happiness when Wolf's mother came into view, and then the wheelchair as Blue Moth wheeled her husband through the snow. Both Blue Moth and Sleeping Bear were blackened with smoke, but unharmed.

"Gee-mah-mah!" Wolf cried, rushing through the snow toward them. *"Gee-bah-bah!"*

When he reached them he grabbed his mother in his arms and hugged her, then fell to his knees before his father in the wheelchair and embraced him.

"Wolf, your father saved our lives," Blue Moth said as she fell to her knees beside her son. "When I became aware of the flames, I refused to leave the cabin without him, but he was too heavy for me to carry. He crawled to the wheelchair. He managed to get in it. By then I was so weak from the smoke, I could barely walk. He . . . wheeled . . . us both outside, and then this man . . . this evil, ugly man with strange glasses on his nose, grabbed hold of the wheelchair and pushed us into the forest and left us. I . . . I . . . was so afraid. But your father insisted that together we could get the wheelchair through the snow to return to the village. The snow was so deep. It was so slick. But he wanted to come and warn everyone about the evil man and what he was doing."

She shuddered visibly. "When I saw the man go up in flames I almost fainted from such a sight, but kept my senses so that I could wheel your father back to the village," she said. "He could not do it alone. He was too weak from having already done so much." She reached over and gently touched Wolf's face. "But he saved me, Wolf. Your father saved me in the wheelchair."

"I no longer resent it," Sleeping Bear said, stroking the arm of the wheelchair. "It is a blessing to me and your mother. Because of it . . . we . . . are alive."

Jo came and stood over them, Judith Lynn still clinging to her. "I'm so glad that both of you are alright," she said, tears again flooding her eyes. "I'm so glad that you . . . you . . . found a use for the chair."

"It will be my legs forevermore," Sleeping

Bear said, proudly lifting his chin. "Thank you, my son's wife, for the gift of legs."

Sleeping Bear turned to Wolf. "Did anyone lose his life tonight?" he asked thickly, slowly shifting his gaze to what remained of Red Hawk's lodge, now a flaming, smoking heap.

"One of our most valued warriors died," Wolf said, finding the words hard to speak.

"Red . . . Hawk . . . ?" Sleeping Bear gasped out, blanching.

"*Ae*, Red Hawk," Wolf said, swallowing back a lump in his throat.

Jo felt that she was partly responsible for Red Hawk's death. Because she had become part of the Ottawa's lives, and had been stubborn about things that enraged Max, tragedy had come into the Ottawa's lives tonight.

But she couldn't allow herself to continue feeling this way. If she did, Max would have succeeded in his vengeance against her, after all.

No, she would not let this tragedy drag her down into despair. Her sorrow would bring the same despair to Wolf and their children.

Children! she thought to herself, remembering that she had not yet had the chance to tell Wolf about the baby.

Now, with Red Hawk's death and burial heavy on her husband's heart, it did not seem appropriate to tell him about the child. For no matter how happy the news would make him, he would not be able to truly, fully enjoy it.

And she did not want his first knowledge of their child to be tainted by the loss of his best friend.

After the funeral she would tell him. After his mourning was behind him. And this would give him a fresh hope for the future . . . *their* future.

Deep inside herself Jo hoped that what had happened tonight was the final assault on their happiness. With Roy no longer there to do Max's dirty work, surely Max would forget vengeance and go on with his life.

But where *was* Max? *Could* he put his need for vengeance to rest once and for all?

She truly doubted it. There was a dark, twisted, sinister method to his madness. She knew that it would be so, until he, too, was dead!

Chapter Thirty-eight

Jo couldn't believe how suddenly the weather had changed. It was as though it were spring instead of the dead of winter. The sun had melted the snow and was shining brightly in the blue heavens. Soft breezes blew through the bare limbs of the trees.

And as it was wont to do, a thunderstorm seemed to be brewing in the far distance along the horizon. Every once in a while there was a low rumbling of thunder.

Jo had caught sight of some flashes of lightning zigzagging down from the gray thunderclouds. She only hoped that it wouldn't materialize into a full-fledged storm, because it was Red Hawk's day . . . the last day of his four-day wake.

Jo sat on a bench before a great, roaring fire

in the middle of the Ottawa village. Little Judith Lynn was in her wheelchair on Jo's left side. Blue Moth was sitting on the bench on Jo's right side, while Wolf and his father, in his wheelchair, had joined Rose Sunshine, Red Hawk's wife, and his children as they mourned openly beside the pine coffin that sat on a platform a short distance from the fire.

As was customary for the Ottawa, the coffin had been painted black and a black cloth was spread out over it. And it was closed. The stench from Red Hawk's burned body was too unbearable for people to view his remains. Besides, he was hardly recognizable.

A lithograph sat on the black cloth. Red Hawk had taken time to have the lithograph made for Rose Sunshine one day while in Detroit getting supplies that could not be found in the small town of Lone Branch.

Although Red Hawk had known it was an extravagance, he had posed for the lithograph anyhow for his wife's twenty-fifth birthday.

And Rose Sunshine was so glad, for now that was all that was left of her beloved husband. As she knelt beside the coffin shrouded in a black shawl, her children clinging, she did not do what wives had done in the past when they mourned the loss of a husband. She had not lacerated her arms, nor had she cut her beautiful long hair.

And her wailing had ceased. Not wishing to frighten her children any more than they already were, Rose Sunshine mourned in silence, the songs of her people as they now sang the funeral rituals soothing her loneliness.

Earlier, Jo had watched the Ottawa people dance round and round the huge fire as they sang songs and the drummer beat the drums. Blue Moth had leaned over to Jo and whispered to her that every beat of the drum had a special meaning.

The songs they were singing had been handed down for centuries, since even before the white man came to America.

Blue Moth had told her that the songs had a lot of meaning that no white man could understand, and had promised Jo that she would teach her these things, as well as other things while Wolf was performing his duties as chief, or was on the hunt with his warriors.

Jo had been in awe of the little handmade flutes that several men had played during the singing and dancing. The wooden flutes had made better music than the most expensive instruments played in concerts at the Detroit Music Hall.

And the food. Jo had never seen the likes of the food that the women had brought for the wake.

She had made dishes for the occasion that she remembered her mother making for the families of those who had lost loved ones in Lone Branch. Her prepared dishes had been stared at, as though she had brought something alien among the Ottawa, but they had eaten the food just the same so that she would not be humiliated.

For four days now food had been consumed, stories had been told, songs for the dead had been sung, and dancing had been performed.

But today was the culmination of the wake. Today was the day of Red Hawk's burial. The ground, which had been frozen a foot deep, had miraculously thawed as if to allow the burial of a beloved fallen warrior.

Absorbed in remembering things that had occurred during the past four days of the wake, Jo was not aware that Wolf had left the ceremony momentarily. Now he stood before the fire, while everyone was quiet watching him.

Even Rose Sunshine and her children had turned away from the coffin to watch and listen to their chief play his musical instrument, which had been handed down from his great-grandfather before him, who had been a gifted student of . . . the violin.

When Wolf began playing softly and beautifully, the strings sent out the sweetest of melodies as he drew the bow across them. Jo's breath caught in her throat when she realized that it was her husband playing the instrument.

In awe of her husband's ability to play the violin so masterfully, Jo parted her lips in a low gasp of wonder. She gazed rapturously at Wolf as his fingers moved skillfully over the strings while he continued to draw the bow back and forth.

"My son plays the ancient wake song on his

violin," Blue Moth whispered as she leaned closer to Jo.

When Jo glanced at Blue Moth, she saw tears streaming from Wolf's mother's eyes.

"Do you know why I am shedding tears?" Blue Moth asked softly, reaching to clasp one of Jo's hands.

"Because of Red Hawk," Jo whispered back.

"*Ae*, I cry over Red Hawk," Blue Moth said, gently patting Jo's hand. "But also I cry because while my son plays the instrument that belonged to my grandfather, I can see my grandfather and old uncle and aunt and the other ones who are gone. I see them lie in their coffins again while music is being played at their wakes."

Blue Moth removed her hand from Jo and wiped the tears from her cheeks as she turned her eyes toward her husband, who was slumped over in the wheelchair, his old eyes sunk in and sad. "I . . . I . . . see Sleeping Bear in his coffin," Blue Moth choked out. "He does not look well. I am not sure how much longer he will be with us."

Jo reached over and wrapped her arms around Blue Moth. "After the mourning is past, and the sadness is gone from Sleeping Bear's eyes, he will look stronger to you," she said, trying to reassure her. She looked over at Wolf, who still played the violin so wonderfully. "Look at Wolf. Does he not look old today, himself? Sadness does that to a person. I myself feel so old today."

Cassie Edwards

"*Ae*, as do I," Blue Moth said, easing from Jo's arms. She sat straight and lifted her chin. "I must look stronger, not only for my husband, but for my son."

"*Ae*, as must I," Jo murmured, then felt a small hand on her arm. She turned and smiled at Judith Lynn and took the child's hand.

"Wolf plays so beautifully," Judith Lynn whispered to Jo.

"Yes, doesn't he?" Jo whispered back, her eyes sliding back to her husband. She was absolutely astounded over this new thing she had discovered about him. She wondered what else she would discover about him in the years ahead.

Tonight, though, *she* would be the one to spring a surprise on *him*. After the burial, when Wolf was ready to leave his mourning behind him, Jo would give him the best reason in the world to do so.

Yes, she would tell him about the baby tonight. After Judith Lynn was asleep on her pallet beside the warm fire, Jo would reveal to her husband such a wonderful thing, he could not help smiling again.

Lightning flashed overhead.

Thunder quickly ensued, causing the ground to shake beneath the bench on which Jo sat. Startled, she looked heavenward.

The clouds had rolled threateningly closer, and suddenly Red Hawk's burial came to a standstill.

Lightning was flashing all over the heavens now, and Jo knew the danger of being out in

356

the open. Lightning had struck a man on horseback this past spring.

Seeing the lightning, and feeling the quivering of the earth beneath his feet as thunder boomed all around the Ottawa village, Wolf lowered his bow and violin to his sides.

He handed them both to a child. Then he nodded to the warriors who had been assigned to carry the coffin to the Ottawa's Pawbame Cemetery a short distance from the village on a knoll overlooking a creek. Tombstones made in various ways, some of stone, some of wood, marked the resting places of many of those who had passed on to the other side.

Today Red Hawk would be buried beside his mother and father and infant baby sister. Wolf would be making a special stone for Red Hawk's final resting place.

With Wolf holding the front right side of the coffin, the procession began. But even before they reached the cemetery, blinding sheets of rain began falling from the heavens. Lightning bounced from treetop to treetop.

His jaw tight, his hair hanging in wet streamers down his back, Wolf kept walking onward, with everyone dutifully following.

Because of the dangerous lightning all around them, the ceremony was brief and the dirt, which was quickly becoming mud, was soon shoveled onto the coffin.

Everyone then ran toward their homes.

Wolf took the handles of the wheelchair from his mother, who was struggling to push it through the deepening mud of the path.

Jo pushed Judith Lynn in her wheelchair through the rain, afraid that one of the two chairs might be struck by lightning.

She was relieved to finally get safely inside her cabin and to know that Blue Moth and sleeping Bear were in the temporary cabin they were using.

Shivering, Jo collapsed on the floor before the fire, for with the rain had come the cold again.

"Jo, you've got to get out of those wet things," Wolf said, rushing to their bedroom. "I'm hurrying out of my wet clothes and then I'll see to Judith Lynn. You take care of yourself."

Remembering the little treasure inside her womb, Jo nodded and hurried to the bedroom behind him. He changed quickly and was gone again to see to Judith Lynn.

Her teeth chattering, Jo yanked off her wet clothes and shoes and soon was comfortably warm in her chenille robe and house shoes.

After brushing the wet tangles from her hair, Jo went back to the living room.

She stopped short and stared, her heart growing warm at the sight of Wolf and Judith Lynn sitting before the fire. He had wrapped the child in warm blankets and was holding her on his lap.

Jo listened, touched deeply by how Wolf sang to Judith Lynn, who was resting her cheek against his chest, her eyes already closed as she fell into an easy, contented sleep.

"I will put her in our bed for now," he said just loud enough for Jo to hear. "She will be much warmer there. Later, when we go to bed, we will place her on her pallet."

He rose from the blankets on the floor. "Soon, when the weather allows it, I will build Judith Lynn that bedroom I promised," he said, smiling at Jo as he walked past her into the bedroom.

"Yes, my darling," Jo whispered to herself, placing a hand over her abdomen. "But one day soon we will have more than one bed in that room." She giggled. "Our child will want her own, too, don't you think?"

"Did you say something?"

Wolf's voice brought Jo quickly around. She smiled mischievously at him as he came to her and swept her into his arms.

"Yes, I believe I did," Jo murmured, her eyes twinkling as she gazed up at him.

"Was it about me?" Wolf asked. His wife's eyes and nearness warmed that part of him that had been left cold by the death of his friend.

"It was about *us*," Jo said, snuggling against him as he swept her into his arms and carried her to the blankets before the fire.

"Tell me about us," Wolf said, gently placing her on the blanket and sitting down beside her.

"I will tell you about our *family*," Jo said, smiling softly at him. "How big it will soon be, my love."

She reached for his hand and brought it to her tummy. "Touch me there and you will be telling our child your first hello," she said, tears filling her eyes when she saw the wonder and happiness that filled his midnight dark eyes.

Wolf gingerly placed his hand across her abdomen, then drew Jo into his embrace. "No time could be better than now for news of a child," he said thickly. "Thank you, my wife. Thank you."

She was now glad that she had waited. It did seem the perfect time to fill his heart with the wonderful news.

When he placed his hands on her cheeks and drew her lips to his, he kissed her with a gentleness she never knew could exist between a man and a woman. Now she knew what to expect during her pregnancy. Her husband would treat her like a delicate flower getting ready to blossom on one of those warm, wonderful days of spring!

She was so happy she could burst, yet as always, her fear of Max persisted. She knew that he had sent Roy Bates to set the fire. But no matter how long Judge Harper and the posse had searched for Max after the fire, there had been no sign of him.

He *had* to be somewhere.

And *any*where was too close, as far as Jo was concerned!

She would never be able to relax until she knew that he was behind bars and no longer able to wreak havoc on her or Wolf's people.

"Darling, you never told me you played the violin," Jo whispered against his lips. "What else about you do I not know?"

"In time, you will know it all," he whispered, clasping his hands at her buttocks and pulling her even closer to his aroused body. "As I hope to know everything about you."

Having no skeletons in her closet, Jo relaxed, sighed, and moved with him down onto the blanket as he pressed against her body with his. Since Red Hawk's death, she had lost her husband to mourning.

Now she had him back, to love . . . to adore . . .

To comfort.

Chapter Thirty-nine

The winter had been a mild one, but Jo was still glad that spring was making its presence known across the countryside. It was the middle of April. The wildflowers in the forest were pushing through the decayed leaves beneath the trees. Some robins had already arrived with their musical, sweet morning and evening warblings. The last snowfall had fallen two weeks ago and had melted quickly beneath the caress of the warm sunshine.

Jo was so happy with her new life she almost burst at the seams with the bliss of it. She smiled as she swept flour dust from her kitchen table with a damp dishcloth. The apple pandowdy that she had made from the last of her father's stored apples was in the oven, baking and spreading its delicious smell throughout the cabin.

A pot roast also gave off a tantalizing aroma from the carrots, potatoes, and onions crowding the pot.

Green beans that Jo had canned last summer from her father's small backyard garden were simmering in bacon drippings in another pot on the stove, and coffee boiled in its pot in the hot coals of the fireplace.

Stopping to wipe her hands on her apron, Jo gazed around at the changes she had made in Wolf's cabin. She smiled at the wood-burning cook stove with its attached oven. Every other day she made fresh loaves of bread.

And she enjoyed using some of her mother's recipes, which her father had brought to her from where they had been stored in the attic with so many of her mother's things.

She looked past the kitchen area and admired again her new oak dining table which sat at the end of the parlor closest to the kitchen. Since she loved having company, she had made sure to purchase a dining set that had eight chairs.

Even today her father was coming with Judge Harper and Eileen, the judge's wife, who had traveled with the judge this time from Springfield while he tended to his latest jury trial in Detroit.

Jo smiled when she thought of who else would be there for the evening meal. Eileen was bringing her sister Kate who had been widowed a year ago. Eileen had played Cupid and it had seemed to work. Addison and Kate were a pair now, and Jo truly believed a wedding date would be set soon.

"Perhaps it can be discussed tonight at the dinner table," she whispered, cleaning up her baking mess in the kitchen.

Fast Horse had also been invited to dinner.

Jo was going to find a way to sneak a mention of the wedding into the conversation while Fast Horse was there.

"Yes, tonight will be the night," she whispered, giggling.

She slipped off her apron and went into the parlor. She stood at the window and gazed at the children at play outside in the sunshine.

It made her heart fill with joy to see how the Ottawa children always managed to pull Little Judith Lynn into their games; the wheelchair was no obstacle as far as they were concerned. They took turns wheeling Judith Lynn around. At heart, they had all become her brothers and sisters.

"But this summer she will have a true brother or sister," Jo whispered, sliding her hand over the swell of her stomach.

Although she was five months pregnant now, she still did not show her pregnancy very much.

But she knew that the baby was alright. It kicked up a storm inside her womb!

Sighing contentedly, she turned in a swirl of skirt and went to the room that the Ottawa warriors had helped Wolf build once the weather was mild enough to fell trees.

She stopped just inside Judith Lynn's room, which would also be the baby's.

Tears of joy came to her eyes as she gazed around at what she had done to make the room special for the children. She and Wolf had gone to Detroit and bought a pretty oak bed and a matching chest of drawers for Judith Lynn, and a cradle and a rocking chair for the baby.

She had bought bolts of cloth that had colorful clowns on a backdrop of white and had made curtains from them.

A thick, braided rug, which she had made during the cold winter days and nights, lay in the middle of the sparkling clean oak floor.

And she had made many baby clothes, which were stacked neatly on a table against the far wall and arranged in the drawers of the chest.

It just didn't seem real sometimes that she was married to such a wonderful, caring man, and that she already had a family with Judith Lynn, who felt so much like her true daughter.

Jo hadn't even considered returning to work. What she wanted in her life was right there in her home.

And when she wasn't busy with her own chores, she lent a hand to those who needed it in the Ottawa community. The hours spent with those she loved were far more important than those she might spend in her law office.

Hearing voices as someone came into the cabin, Jo came back to the present. Her visitors seemed to have arrived. She even heard Judith Lynn, which meant Wolf had brought her home to be with everyone before dinner.

Jo ran her fingers through her hair and pushed it back over her shoulders. She brushed at her cheeks with her hands to get off whatever smudges of flour might have gotten there while cooking.

She glanced down at her pretty doeskin dress which lay softly against her skin. It was loose-fitting and comfortable, as were the knee-high moccasins on her feet.

She had never guessed how comfortable Indian attire was until she wore her first dress and slid her feet into her first wonderfully soft moccasins.

She took the time to admire the beadwork on both the dress and moccasins. Blue Moth had enjoyed sewing them on the garments. But Jo was beading her own dress now. Blue Moth had shared her knowledge of beading with her.

Hearing Sleeping Bear's voice above the others, Jo sighed and smiled. She and Wolf's father had grown close. His father came and went with ease now in his wheelchair. Blue Moth no longer pushed him around in it. Sleeping Bear was proud to be able to get where he wished, anytime he wished, without asking someone to help him. The wheelchair had become his legs. He was glad to have it.

Lifting the hem of her dress, Jo rushed from the bedroom and on past her own room, which was across the hall from the children's. Adjoining it was another room that had been built just for Jo. Her law books lined the shelves in the room, as did her many books of fiction.

"My library," she proudly called it.

When Jo reached the parlor, she went from person to person, hugging and kissing them until everyone had been greeted and all were sitting around the room, eagerly chatting.

Wolf came and swept an arm around Jo's waist, drawing her next to him and brushing a soft kiss across her lips. "You have not done too much, have you?" he asked as he moved away from her and stared into the kitchen area. He frowned down at Jo. "I smell many different smells, which means you cooked many things. I did not want you tiring yourself. You know that no one comes specifically to eat. They come to be with us."

"I know," Jo said, taking his hand and squeezing it affectionately. "But we all need to eat, don't we? You know how I love to feed people."

"*Ae*, just like my *gee-mah-mah*," Wolf said, chuckling. He took her by the hand and sat down beside her on the sofa.

"I'm so glad you all could come for dinner," Jo said. She gave her father a mischievous glint. "Father, do you smell something familiar cooking in the oven?"

"Apple pandowdy," Addison said, his eyes dancing as he smiled over at Kate. "My daughter's specialty. She makes it from the red delicious apples I grow . . . grew . . . in my orchard."

Jo and Addison exchanged quick glances. She knew that her father hadn't told Kate about the incidents that had destroyed not only his prized roses and apples, but also a portion of their house. She knew that he would eventually tell Kate. It was just not something one could blurt out . . . that someone had tried to murder you.

Jo gazed admiringly at Kate. She was the same age as Addison and somewhat resembled Jo's beloved mother. She had grass-green eyes, red hair that had only a few threads of white running through it, and a petite shape even though Kate had borne five children. They were all boys and were grown now. They were college graduates who had prestigious jobs . . . doctors, attorneys, and one of them was a college professor.

The pride Kate felt for her children showed in her sparkling eyes when she spoke of them. Jo hoped to meet them all one day.

"Jo, your house is very cozy and pretty," Judge Harper said as he looked around at the plush chairs, the lacy doilies draped over tables, the fancy kerosene lamps with flower designs on the bases, and the large braided rug that her father had brought for her and Wolf as one of their wedding presents.

"Thank you, Judge Harper," Jo said, proudly smiling.

Judge Harper leaned forward. "Jo, don't you

369

think it's time you quit calling me 'Judge Harper'?" he said, his eyes warm and friendly. "Call me *Jack*. I've asked you so often to call me Jack."

"Sir—" she began, but was interrupted by Judge Harper.

"Jo, *please*," he said, sighing. "It's not 'sir,' nor is it 'Judge Harper' anymore when we're together. Please call me Jack."

"But it somehow seems disrespectful," Jo said, squirming uneasily in her chair. "And you know why I couldn't before. I was always afraid I might slip up in the courtroom and call you Jack instead of Judge. Now, that wouldn't do, would it? People would know we are friends and would believe I got favors in the courtroom because of it."

"Yes, I can see that, but, Jo, you've decided not to practice law again, at least not any time soon," Judge Harper said, resting against the back of his chair again. "So let's please drop the formalities. I'm Jack to you, Jo. Jack."

"Alright, Jack," Jo said, laughing softly.

Then he turned to Wolf. "Before we eat I'd like to tell you something that I feel is too important to keep from you any longer," he said. "Wolf, you have been chosen to represent your people at the Colombian Exposition in Chicago. It's the anniversary of the founding of America by Columbus. All tribes will have one special representative. Because of your leadership and education, you have been chosen to represent the Ottawa people. You will even be asked to give a speech in behalf of your people." He glanced over at Fast Horse and smiled and nodded, then looked at Wolf again. "Your friend Fast Horse will be representing his Chippewa people. You could all go together."

Thrilled at this honor for her husband, Jo smiled at Wolf. She was ready to encourage him, but her smile faded and she remained quiet when she saw how he received this news from Judge Harper. There was a silent anger in the depths of her husband's eyes and she could not understand why. She felt that he should see this as a wonderful opportunity to speak in behalf of his people.

Instead, he seemed angry at the mere suggestion of it.

Wolf had absorbed everything that Judge Harper had said about the Colombian Exposition, especially why it was being held: to celebrate the coming of someone who had, in a sense, begun the downfall of all red men?

No, he could never celebrate this white man called Columbus. But he *could* go and speak of things that needed to be said about his people . . . things that the white people would not want to hear.

Fast Horse leaned toward Wolf. "Wolf, we will go there as brothers," he said. "It is the best of opportunities to speak in behalf of both our peoples. Do you not see this as so?"

A slow smile quivered on Wolf's lips. "*Ae*, I see it, and I believe through the same eyes that you see it," he said. He nodded toward Judge Harper. "I will go."

Then he looked over at Jo. He took her hand. "My wife must be at my side at all times," he said hoarsely. "Is she included? If not, I cannot go."

"Jo, are you able to make the journey to Chicago?" Judge Harper asked. He glanced down at the slight swell of her stomach, then looked into her eyes. "Is it all right to travel at this stage of your pregnancy?" His wife had never had children. Her body had been too frail to chance it. So he knew not what was right or wrong for a woman who was this far along in her pregnancy.

"I'm fit as a fiddle and would love to accompany my husband to Chicago," Jo said, beaming now that she knew he was going to go.

They could have such great fun seeing the big city.

Detroit was a big city and had much to offer, but she had heard that Chicago surpassed Detroit.

Judith Lynn wheeled her chair over to Jo. "Can I go?" she asked, her eyes pleading with Jo.

Jo smiled and reached out and hugged the child. "You most certainly can," she said softly. "Wolf and I will take you to a place where you will see things you never knew existed."

"I've heard about the museums," Judith Lynn said. "I'm so anxious to go, Mommie. Thank you for agreeing to take me."

The smell of the apple pandowdy drew Jo quickly to her feet. "Excuse me," she said, rushing into the kitchen, her feet scarcely touching the floor in her excitement at what lay ahead for her family.

Chicago!

She had wanted to go there since she was a child.

Kate and Eileen came into the kitchen. "Please let us help," Kate said, grabbing an apron from a peg on the wall. She watched Jo take the oblong pan from the oven. She inhaled the wonderful fragrance of it. "And I want your recipe for the apple pandowdy."

Jo set the pan on a table, then turned smiling eyes to Kate. "Only if you'll share some of yours with me," she said. She was so happy for her father, for she could tell already that Kate was a pure treasure!

Chapter Forty

"It *is* an amazing city, isn't it?" Jo asked as she stood with Wolf, staring down from their fourth-story hotel window at the traffic moving below on the cobblestone street. "It seems people have come from all over for the convention."

She stretched her neck to see a fancy automobile chugging among other automobiles, horse-drawn carriages and buggies, and men on horseback. "I know that one should welcome progress in America, but I doubt that wheezing, coughing machine will last. I'd take my horse any time over the newest mode of transportation."

When Wolf didn't respond, Jo turned to him. She saw how tight his jaw was and could even see the moodiness in his eyes. She reached out and took his hands.

"What's wrong?" she murmured, searching his face. "You haven't said a word since we bade Fast Horse and Judith Lynn goodbye so they could explore more museums." She laughed. "Lordie, I didn't think my legs would hold me up another second. Judith Lynn couldn't get enough of seeing things. Poor thing, all she has known are the four walls of the orphanage. It's like . . . like . . . she's been reborn. Isn't it wonderful, Wolf, how she is seeing things for the first time and enjoying them so immensely?"

"Jo, tomorrow I make my speech," Wolf said as though he had not heard anything she had said. "You know in which direction I will take it. You also know the danger it might put us all in. These people don't want to hear the truth, to face the fact that they were a part of the ugliness."

"Are you saying you've changed your mind?" Jo murmured, understanding why Wolf would be concerned.

He was going to say several things that would inflame those who were prejudiced against everyone whose skin color differed from theirs.

Although greedy whites had taken so much from the Indians, they would never be satisfied until they had everything. Wolf was going to remind everyone in the huge convention hall of what had been taken.

She knew that her life could be in danger when she stepped up to the podium at her husband's side, for she was a white woman married to a "savage."

"Perhaps we should go home," she blurted out, more afraid for the baby than herself.

"I have made a promise to speak in behalf of my people and I never break promises," Wolf said. He eased his hands away from hers. He wove his long, lean fingers through her golden hair as he swept it back from her face. "But I *have* been thinking about necessary changes."

"What . . . sort . . . of changes?" Jo asked warily.

"You and Judith Lynn will stay in the hotel while I go to give my speech," Wolf said solemnly. "If my speech arouses anger, then you will not be a part of it."

Jo thought again of their unborn child, yet she knew that there was no way she would not back her husband one hundred percent to prove her loyalty to him.

"Judith Lynn can stay here, but I shan't," she said, lifting her chin stubbornly. "I want to be with you. I am so proud of you. I want everyone to see my pride as I stand at your side."

Wolf slid his hands down to her tummy. He caressed it through the doeskin fabric of her dress.

She had worried about wearing Indian attire, afraid it might call unnecessary attention to her choice to live as an Indian. But she had decided that she would never turn her back on

377

any part of her husband's heritage. She was proud to be Wolf's wife and she wanted everyone to know it.

"The baby?" Wolf said, his black eyes quietly questioning Jo. "Is this what is best for our baby?"

"Darling Wolf," Jo said, reaching a gentle hand up to his cheek. "The moment our child is born, he or she will be born into controversy, because our child will have an Indian father and a white mother. Our child is going to be raised among those who will always call him or her a 'breed.' So I'd rather stand up to that prejudice now."

Wolf swept his arms around Jo's waist and drew her close to him. "You are a woman of much spirit, hope, and determination," he said, his eyes now dancing. "Our child will be the same."

"Yes, *Netage-Winini*, lady unafraid," Jo murmured, then melted inside when Wolf placed a hand at the nape of her neck and drew her lips to his.

She twined her arms around his neck and returned his long, deep kiss as he slowly pushed her backward toward the bed with his body.

She smiled when she thought of his first reaction to the soft, thick mattress when they had first entered the hotel room. It had been the look of a child discovering candy for the first time.

And then there was the real candy that had been left on the bed by the hotel maid. A block of chocolate wrapped in red tissue paper and a single red rose had greeted them upon their arrival.

Jo had enjoyed seeing Wolf's reaction to everything. The carpet was so thick, his feet sank into it after he removed his moccasins to feel its softness against his bare toes.

Judith Lynn was equally awestruck by everything in the room, especially the full-length mirror on one wall. She had never before seen herself in the wheelchair.

Tears had come to Jo's eyes as Judith Lynn watched herself in the mirror. She turned the wheelchair in all directions, studying the wheelchair and how she looked in it. Jo had been afraid that the mirror might turn the child against the chair, for it wasn't a pretty sight.

But spinning herself one way and then another, seeing her golden curls bounce on her shoulders, had made Judith Lynn giggle.

Relieved, Jo had bent low and gathered the child into her arms and lifted her from the chair.

Judith Lynn was slight in build; Jo had been able to dance around the room with her while she clung around her neck, laughing and giggling.

The whole day had been one of discoveries as Jo, Wolf, and Fast Horse took turns wheeling Judith Lynn from place to place.

Fast Horse loved children and had claimed a "share" of Wolf and Jo's children since he would never have any of his own. A look of sheer joy appeared on his face when Jo and

Wolf handed Judith Lynn over to him for the rest of the afternoon while Jo rested her poor legs and feet in the hotel room.

Jo was filled with bliss as Wolf slowly undressed her. His hands touched her everywhere as she lay naked on the bed, awaiting the wondrous moment he would enter her. She smiled up at him as he hurried to undress himself, then moved onto the bed again, to straddle her.

His thumb lightly caressed her flushed cheeks as he drank in her nakedness with dark, hungry eyes.

Oh, there was such happiness within Jo. For the moment she had forgotten the dangers of tomorrow.

As Wolf's hands ran slowly up and down her flesh, all she could think about was Wolf and how he was slowly arousing her, causing the curl of heat to grow between her thighs.

And when he splayed his fingers over the mound of her womanhood, one of his fingers slowly entering her soft, warm valley, she closed her eyes and sucked in a breath of wild pleasure as her world began to melt away into something magical and wonderful.

Wolf's lips went to hers in a trembling, hot kiss as his fingers rubbed and stroked her almost to mindlessness.

And when he shoved his manhood deep into her throbbing slit, Jo whimpered with ecstasy against his lips, her senses now reeling with drunken pleasure.

Wolf smothered her with kisses, from her lips down across the long column of her throat, and then from breast to breast, as he moved rhythmically within her. He could feel their passion nearing the cresting point as everything within him became fluid with fire.

Still thrusting, Wolf slid his hands beneath Jo's hips and lifted her closer, yet always remembering the baby and being careful not to shove too deeply.

The way her inner walls clung so warmly to his manhood, as though there were fingers there, pulsating against him, made Wolf's breath quicken.

He drove in swiftly and surely as he laid his cheek against her bosom. He was trembling with readiness, yet waited and continued to move within her so that he could be sure that she was also ready.

"Now, Wolf," Jo moaned, feverish with blissful joy. "Oh, Wolf, I . . . am . . . ready!"

His lips went to hers in a crushing kiss as he made one last thrust into her that brought them both over the brink into ecstasy.

Their bodies quaked, spasmed, and then went quiet.

Wolf rolled to her side and drew her against him. He held her.

They both lay there silently thinking about tomorrow . . . his speech that would rock the very core of the convention and what the convention was supposed to stand for!

Chapter Forty-one

Too many people had arrived for the exposition to be held inside the auditorium that had been chosen for the celebration. Although the auditorium was huge, it was not large enough to seat the thousands upon thousands of people in attendance.

A large stage had been erected outside the entrance of the auditorium. As many seats as possible had been placed around the stage, but more people were standing, or sitting on blankets on the lawn, sidewalks, and streets than in the seats.

The breeze was cool as it swept in from the river. The sun was hidden behind puffy white clouds.

Jo was standing with Wolf at the podium as Chicago's mayor stepped up to him, smiling.

"Chief Wolf of the Ottawa tribe, I give you the honor of ringing the Liberty Bell that will officially open our celebration of Columbus," he said, gesturing toward a large bell.

"With this bell, Chief Wolf, we celebrate the arrival of Christopher Columbus on our shores, and liberty itself," said the mayor.

Jo scarcely breathed as she listened to what the mayor was saying. She looked down at the crowd and flinched when she saw the looks of hate in so many eyes.

Her insides turned cold when Wolf added to their hate by refusing to ring the bell.

"The bell stands for liberty?" Wolf said, his voice carrying to the throng of people. "Whose? It certainly does not stand for the liberty of my people. No. I will not ring the bell. No Indian should ever celebrate the coming of Christopher Columbus. Because of Columbus, the land is no longer in the hands of the red man . . . the true first people of this land . . . the true owners of this very land upon which you have built your tall buildings!"

Jo went pale at the gasps of horror that went through the crowd. She had known that Wolf was going to openly defy everything this exposition stood for, but never would she have guessed that he would go about it with such vehemence.

She sucked in a nervous breath and stood her ground beside Wolf as the mayor stepped closer to Wolf and whispered to him.

"Damn it, savage, why did you accept our kind invitation to be a part of this celebration when all you can do is degrade it?" the mayor hissed, his face beet red with anger. "I thought you were going to praise Columbus, not verbally assassinate him."

"Savage?" Wolf said, his eyes gleaming angrily as he gazed into the mayor's snapping gray eyes. "You call me a savage when I speak only the truth?"

"The truth as *you* see it," the mayor retorted, his hands tight fists at his sides. "I suggest you leave now."

"I have come to speak to your people," Wolf said stubbornly. "I shall speak, *then* leave."

"It's not wise to continue the way you began," the mayor said, nervously looking over his shoulder at the restless crowd. He leaned closer to Wolf and glared up at him. "Damn it all to hell, you could start a riot. You . . . might . . . even get shot on the spot."

"I have been threatened before and I still live," Wolf said, then looked over at Jo. "It is best that you go to the hotel. I see now that it was wrong for you to accompany me here."

"I'm afraid to leave by myself," Jo said, pleading with her eyes.

And she *was* afraid, more than ever before in her life. She didn't believe she or Wolf would make it back to the hotel in one piece if he continued his speech.

She looked over her shoulder at the other chiefs on the podium who had come to be a part of the exposition. She could tell by their smiles that Wolf had somehow prepared them ahead of time for what he was going to say today. They all were in agreement, it seemed. They were all ready to die, if required, to say what needed to be said today. Fast Horse, who was staying with Judith Lynn, would make his speech in support of Wolf later in the day.

"You are right, my wife," Wolf said, glancing out at the crowd. "You are only safe while with me."

"Please go on with your speech," Jo encouraged. "I know that it means a lot to you to be able to reach so many people with your words today."

Wolf smiled at her, nodded, then gazed again into the crowd.

The mayor stepped shakily away from Wolf. His face was drained of color. His eyes were wary as he kept watch on the crowd while Wolf began his speech.

"Let me tell you about the demise of the red man and our mistake in opening this land to a new culture that continues to threaten the Ottawa people and all other tribes," Wolf began, using articulate words that proved to everyone he was a man of education. "If your people and my people were put together in one place, and each group was called to answer for the crimes it had committed, which do you think would have the most crimes? And let me ask you this . . . can you charge the red man with murdering innocent women and children to get this land? Can you charge the red man with robbing whites of their culture, of their reason for being on this earth? Can you charge the red man with taking food from your children's mouths, denying you the right to hunt, to fish, the gifts of nature? No. You cannot make any of these claims against the red man, because they are the sins of the white man against my people."

He continued until he had said everything that was inside his heart, leaving everyone speechless.

Jo noticed how the expressions on most people's faces had changed from hate to shame.

And never had she been as proud to be a part of the Ottawa's lives as she was when she took Wolf's hand and left the stage, leaving the other chiefs behind to speak of their own people's plight.

Space was made for Jo and Wolf to walk through as people moved aside.

And when the crowd was left behind and Jo and Wolf walked in the shadows of the tall buildings toward their hotel, Jo hoped that no one would ever forget what Wolf had said.

The streets and sidewalks were all but deserted because the whole city seemed to be in attendance at the exposition. As she and Wolf walked past the dark shadows between some of the buildings, she looked uneasily into them, relieved when she didn't see anyone lurking there.

The farther they walked, the easier Jo felt. Just one more night and they would be leaving the city. She had never been as anxious to be anywhere as she was to get back to their home.

Although the people of Chicago had not re-
acted in a hostile way to Wolf's message, there
were always some who remained full of prejudice. They were the ones who said, "The only
good Indian is a dead Indian."

Lost in thought, Jo was wrenched back to
the present when the muffled sound of gunfire
rang out.

She grabbed at Wolf as a bullet just missed
his head.

She spun around at the same moment Wolf
turned and saw Max Schmidt standing in the
shadows of two buildings. Just as Max smiled
wickedly at Jo and began aiming again at
Wolf, Wolf lunged for Max and knocked him
to the ground.

Out of the struggle came a blast of gunfire.

Jo felt faint when she saw Wolf fall to one
side.

She felt frozen to the spot, expecting to see
blood all over his chest. Then she looked at
Max. He lay on the sidewalk, a pool of blood
spilling around him from a wound in *his*
chest.

"Thank God," Jo whispered, covering her
mouth as a sob lodged in her throat. She hurried to Wolf as he scrambled to his feet.

"I thought you were shot," Jo cried as she
flung herself into his arms. "Oh, Wolf, what
are we to do? You know that if someone saw
this happen, you will be blamed and . . . and
. . . locked behind bars."

Wolf held her close and looked around him.

He saw no one, nor did he hear anyone approaching. It was apparent that the sound of the gunfire had not carried much farther than the alley between the buildings. "No one saw, nor does it seem as though anyone heard, or they would be upon us by now," he said thickly.

"Let's hurry back to the hotel and get our belongings and return home," Jo sobbed as she crept from Wolf's arms to again gaze down at the dead man, someone who at one time had been so precious to her.

Wolf gazed at Max for a moment longer also, then took Jo's hand. Silently they fled back to the hotel. When they got there, Jo took Judith Lynn from the room as Wolf told Fast Horse about what had happened to Max.

"We must leave as originally planned, tomorrow," Fast Horse argued. "Fleeing would cast guilt your way if anyone realizes the connection between you, Jo, and the man who died."

"You are right," Wolf said.

"I will go and tell Jo it's alright to bring Judith Lynn back into the room," Fast Horse said, patting Wolf comfortingly on the back. "Do not think about what you did. It was not your fault. Feel blessed that you are alive. It was the hand of God that guided the bullet away from you."

Wolf remembered another time and place when bullets had been guided by an unseen force . . . when Jo had been placed on the cross to die!

He smiled, for he knew how they had been protected.

Gitchi Manitou.

When Jo came into the room she flung herself into Wolf's arms.

Max would never terrorize her or her husband again. Yes, it was finally finished!

Chapter Forty-two

Although it was a relief to know she would never have to worry about Max again, the manner of his death preyed on Jo's mind the whole night through. She expected someone to come pounding on their hotel door at any moment to take Wolf away.

When morning came, she was overjoyed to leave the hotel and board the train for Michigan.

Jo sat beside Judith Lynn while Wolf sat opposite her with Fast Horse, pointing things out to Judith Lynn through the window as the train sped on.

Both Wolf and Fast Horse were reading one of Chicago's morning papers, the *Sun*. When Wolf turned to the second page he flinched, for staring back at him was a picture of Max.

He read the article to himself about the authorities having found Max's body and their assumptions about who might have killed him. Max's death was blamed on his Chicago associates, who were known to have connections with criminal activity in Chicago. The article hinted at Max having double-crossed somebody.

Satisfying himself that there would be no serious investigation of Max's death, Wolf started to fold the paper to keep even the mention of Max from his wife.

But Jo had glanced over and had seen the picture as Wolf was reading the article. She leaned over and gently took the paper to read it.

Afterward she sighed and laid the paper aside. She smiled adoringly at Wolf, relieved that she would never have to worry again that her husband might be blamed for the tyrant's death!

"Tell me more about wolves," Judith Lynn said, grabbing Jo's hand to get her attention.

Wolf leaned around Jo and smiled at Judith Lynn. "One day I will tell you about *white* wolves," he said, then turned his eyes to Jo, who smiled.

Chapter Forty-three

It was *zee-gwun*, spring again. The air was filled with the sweet fragrance of wildflowers and apple blossoms on the trees Jo's father had planted behind Jo and Wolf's cabin.

The moon was high in the sky.

Small fires outside the Ottawa cabins reflected gold onto the dark heavens.

The white wolves were lying peacefully around Jo and Wolf's outdoor fire as Wolf told his three-year-old son Waking Horse and daughter Judith Lynn tales of his ancestors, and myths about wolves and bears.

The white wolves no longer had to stay in hiding since there were no more hunters after their pelts; the law now protected them as a rare species.

Heavy with child again, Jo sat quietly by on a

blanket, knitting booties for the newborn. She glanced up time and again at her husband and son. She was so proud that their son was the exact mirror image of his father and that he had his father's same kinship with forest creatures. An owl's eyes reflected in the darkness only a short distance away in a tree. It hooted and flew away as clouds slid over the moon.

Judith Lynn's giggles brought Jo's eyes to her again. Miracle of miracles, or perhaps due to the power of love itself, Judith Lynn was taking steps now on her own. Tears came to Jo's eyes as she recalled the very first time Judith Lynn discovered she could take a few steps from her wheelchair.

It was after Wolf had been patiently working with the child every day, holding her in his arms as she tried to put her full weight on her legs. When she said she was tired, he would immediately place her back in the chair.

And now everyone had hopes of her walking on her own soon. She would see a different side of the world on her two feet. Nothing would hold her back. The world would be hers!

Yes, everything in Jo's world seemed to have come together like pieces in a jigsaw puzzle. Her father had married Kate. He was so content he hardly ever limped anymore, as though a magic wand had swept his leg injury away.

Fast Horse had gotten past the idea that it was not meant for him to get married just because he had chosen the ministry. He had begun spending time with Rose Sunshine and her children. They had fallen in love and a marriage date had been set.

She and the children were going to move into Fast Horse's rectory in Lone Branch. She had already been introduced to his parishioners and had been accepted with open arms.

"Jo, lay your knitting aside and sit closer to your husband and children," Wolf said, reaching a hand out for her. "I believe you have some stories to tell about *your* family, do you not? About your mother? She will be kept alive inside the hearts and minds of our children in that way."

Touched by his thoughtfulness, and seeing that talking about her mother would not only keep her alive inside their children's hearts, but also Jo's own, she smiled and laid her knitting aside.

Groaning from the effort it took to move, she started to scoot over to the children, but seeing her struggles, Wolf swept them into his arms and set them down beside Jo.

Laughing softly at his thoughtfulness, Jo reached up and framed his face between her hands. "My husband, *gee-zah-gi-ee-nah*, do you love me?" she said teasingly.

"*Ae, ah-pah-nay*," he replied. Then forgetting their audience of children, he swept Jo into his arms. "My wife, you are so beautiful beneath the moonlight and very, very pregnant."

Her soft, sweet laughter wafted into the heavens and mingled with the stars, to twinkle forever and ever as one of them.

Dear Reader,

I hope you enjoyed reading *Savage Fires*. *Savage Grace*, the next book in my *Savage* series, is a special Indian romance. Shaylee, my heroine, is an angel at the very beginning of the book. How she becomes human again, to be with Standing Wolf, my Cherokee hero, is heartwarming and sweet . . . and was a joy to write.

Savage Grace will be in the stores in January, 2000. It will be filled with much emotion, adventure, and passion. I hope you will read it and enjoy it.

For those of you who are collecting all of the books in my *Savage* Indian series, and want to read about the backlist and my future books, please send a legal-sized, self-addressed, stamped envelope to the following address for my latest newsletter, autographed photograph, and my newest bookmark to:

> Cassie Edwards
> 6709 North Country Club Road
> Mattoon, IL 61938

Thank you for your support of my books. I truly appreciate all of you!

> Warmly,
> Cassie Edwards

THE **SAVAGE** SERIES

SAVAGE PRIDE

CASSIE EDWARDS

**Winner Of The *Romantic Times*
Reviewers' Choice Award
For Best Indian Series**

She is a fiery hellcat who can shoot like a man, a ravishing temptress with the courage to search the wilderness for her missing brother. But Malvina is only a woman with a woman's needs and desires. And from the moment Red Wing sweeps her up on his charging stallion, she is torn between family duty and heavenly pleasure.

A mighty Choctaw warrior, Red Wing is tantalized by the blistering sensuality of the sultry, flame-haired vixen. But it will take more than his heated caresses to make Malvina his own. Only with a love as pure as her radiant beauty can he hope to claim her heart, to win her trust, to tame her savage pride.

_3732-7 $5.99 US/$6.99 CAN

Dorchester Publishing Co., Inc.
P.O. Box 6640
Wayne, PA 19087-8640

Please add $1.75 for shipping and handling for the first book and $.50 for each book thereafter. NY, NYC, and PA residents, please add appropriate sales tax. No cash, stamps, or C.O.D.s. All orders shipped within 6 weeks via postal service book rate. Canadian orders require $2.00 extra postage and must be paid in U.S. dollars through a U.S. banking facility.

Name_____
Address_____
City_____ State_____ Zip_____
I have enclosed $_____ in payment for the checked book(s).
Payment <u>must</u> accompany all orders. ❑ Please send a free catalog.

THE **SAVAGE** SERIES

SAVAGE SECRETS   CASSIE EDWARDS

Winner Of The *Romantic Times* Reviewers' Choice Award For Best Indian Series

Searching the wilds of the Wyoming Territory for her outlaw brother, Rebecca Veach is captured by the one man who fulfills her heart's desire. But can she give herself to the virile warrior without telling him about her shameful quest?

Blazing Eagle is as strong as the winter wind, yet as gentle as a summer day. And although he wants Becky from the moment he takes her captive, hidden memories of a long-ago tragedy tear him away from the golden-haired vixen.

Strong-willed virgin and Cheyenne chieftain, Becky and Blazing Eagle share a passion that burns hotter than the prairie sun—until savage secrets from their past threaten to destroy them and the love they share.

_3823-4 $5.99 US/$7.99 CAN

Dorchester Publishing Co., Inc.
P.O. Box 6640
Wayne, PA 19087-8640

Please add $1.75 for shipping and handling for the first book and $.50 for each book thereafter. NY, NYC, and PA residents, please add appropriate sales tax. No cash, stamps, or C.O.D.s. All orders shipped within 6 weeks via postal service book rate. Canadian orders require $2.00 extra postage and must be paid in U.S. dollars through a U.S. banking facility.

Name_____
Address_____
City_____ State_____ Zip_____
I have enclosed $_____ in payment for the checked book(s).
Payment <u>must</u> accompany all orders. ☐ Please send a free catalog.

ATTENTION ROMANCE CUSTOMERS!

SPECIAL TOLL-FREE NUMBER
1-800-481-9191

Call Monday through Friday
10 a.m. to 9 p.m.
Eastern Time
Get a free catalogue,
join the Romance Book Club,
and order books using your
Visa, MasterCard,
or Discover®

Leisure
Books

GO ONLINE WITH US AT DORCHESTERPUB.COM